Other Books by Terah Edun

COURTLIGHT SERIES

SWORN TO RAISE (Book One)

SWORN TO TRANSFER (Book Two)

SWORN TO CONFLICT (Book Three)

SWORN TO SECRECY (Book Four)

SWORN TO DEFIANCE (Book Five)

SWORN TO ASCENSION (Book Six)*

CROWN SERVICE SERIES

BLADES OF MAGIC (Book One)

BLADES OF ILLUSION (Book Two)

BLADES OF SORCERY (Book Three)*

*Forthcoming

Want to get an email when my next book is released?

Sign up here: bit.ly/SubscribetoTerahsNewsletter

THE COURTLIGHT SERIES

BOOK TWO

TERAH EDUN

Published by Terah Edun

All characters in this book have no existence outside the imagination of the author and have no relation whatsoever to anyone bearing the same name or names.

Individuals known to the author inspire neither individuals nor incidents mentioned in this novel. All incidents are inventions of the author's imagination.

CHAPTER ONE

A storm was rolling in off the coast of Sandrin. Heavy rains buffeted the docks and high winds whipped the ends of coiled loops of thick sailor's rope up into the air across the deck of the large ship. Ciardis Weathervane huddled miserably as she felt the ice-cold wind and rain buffeting her every few minutes in steady waves. First the cold rain would slice into her face, and then a heavy stream of frosty air would strike, pushing her cloak back and soaking her front. Still, she stayed where she was, and she fought not to shiver under the thick blue cloak that she wore.

Prince Sebastian wasn't far from her side. If you could call across the ship with dozens of soldiers between them "not far." It was the closest he'd been to her in weeks, though. Ciardis felt her heart clench just a little when she thought about that. The distance that seemed to have grown between the two of them wasn't only physical. Shaking off her nerves and turning from the railing where she gazed pensively down into the gray, churning water of the ocean, she took in the gathering around her.

To her left stood a living hedge with hair, eyes, chattering teeth, and she was sure, frozen fingers. The guards stood at attention in neat rows with upright pikes in their right hands, their left hands gripping sheathed swords at their waists, and their golden armor dripping wet in the downpour. Staring stoically ahead to a man—and woman—the Prince Heir's guard didn't flinch at the monstrous sound of thunder and lightning cracking down over the ocean to the east of the ship.

Until ten minutes ago, Ciardis had been standing under the shelter provided by the Weather Mage traveling in the Prince Heir's retinue. She'd left to get some air, frustrated with her own self-doubt. It had been three months since she and Prince Sebastian had killed the Princess Heir. Three months since they'd danced on the beach in the glowing afternoon. She was trying hard to focus on her life now as a Companion trainee. But it was kind of hard to focus when you didn't know where you stood.

The Patron Hunt had been put on indefinite hold. Partially because having a Prince Heir as an interested party took precedence above all other candidates. Not that there hadn't been some grumbling among her other candidates, but Ciardis had not objected to the Prince Heir's monopoly. After politely sending notifications to all of her suiters, she had waited with growing impatience to hear from the Imperial Courts. Becoming a Companion to a Prince wasn't just *his* decision, a lot of protocol was involved and many other people held sway. She had tried to talk to Sebastian about it. But other than acknowledging his prominance as her premier candidate, nothing had been said.

And now she was stuck right back where she'd started. They hadn't formalized their contract as Patron and Companion. Hell, they hadn't even had discussions on what it meant. Oh she knew in theory from history what being a Companion to a powerful member of the imperial family would mean. But Sebastian hadn't *asked* her. He hadn't asked her if she wanted to stand by his side, rule in his stead in far-flung places, or act as his advisor in tempestuous times.

Instead he just seemed to prefer avoiding her like the plague and attending to whatever duties his father handed out. They had a relationship she would agree, but she couldn't say what kind. By the seven gods, in the past three months she'd spent less than three weeks in the Prince Heir's presence. His duties had kept him busy at his father's side in court functions and hers had kept her attending gala after gala. In coming out into the cold sea air and rain, she'd hoped to clear her mind of her worry over that bowl of worms as well as a long list of enemies that saw fit to make her life miserable. Her life in the Imperial Courts was turning out to be a never-ending series of crises. Mostly because of Sebastian – even if he wasn't currently talking to her.

A moment later a horn blast came from the front of ship.

That horn was the sound that called for all people aboard to take their proper places. She went forward while wishing that the ambassador flying in by delegation had elected to hold their meeting anywhere else. Preferably a place that was warm.

I wonder if they're coming in by winged horse? The pegasi steeds would have to be very strong to withstand the fierce winds of this storm. Another ship would be more likely. Aside from that, she wondered where the ambassador would be flying in from. No one had said a word about which country this mysterious delegation was representing.

As she reached the edge of the square block that made up the bulk of the Prince Heir's guard, she saw the wind shield—the large dome that took up the front half of the ship. It was only visible due to the harsh rain bouncing off and pouring down its sides. In the meantime, as Ciardis stood there taking in the retinue surrounding the Prince Heir, her hair was getting soaked and the cloak over the rest of her was starting to stick to her skin. It had a water repellant spell on it, but that only worked in lighter rains. This was turning into a downpour.

It was nothing compared to the turmoil in her heart.

Peering ahead she had an unobstructed view of the Prince. Across Sebastian's armor, runes glimmered with an iridescent light briefly, like a firefly in the night air, before the luminance would disappear in one spot and reappear in another on the metalwork. She stood still, staring at it, mesmerized for a second. She'd never lost the ability to see another's magic and had even gained a better grasp of sight into another mage's core—a Weathervane ability, according to Artis. A beautiful red cloak hung from Sebastian's shoulders, and he'd pushed it back from his left shoulder so that it hung at an angle. He wore a white, long-sleeved shirt between his skin and the chest plate and loose brown leather pants encased his legs.

As Ciardis stepped through the shield put up by the Weather Mage, she smiled and nodded over to him with that smile. As she turned to look around, from her right a woman stepped forward. She had previously stayed in the shadows and Ciardis had yet to get a good look at her. Ciardis paused what she was doing, her mind aflurry with disbelief. Even in the middle of the ocean on the deck of a ship, this woman was stunning. But that wasn't why Ciardis's pulse pounded in her ears and her eyes stayed glued to the woman coming forward. Power was radiating from her in the same way heat radiated from a roaring fire.

The woman wore a red dress with white stitching down the front and her hair flowed in waves of amber down her back. The dress, the color of the dark red heat of a coal fire, was more than just elegant; it was the garment of a Fire Mage. Impervious to heat and fire, the weave was one that she knew well from her days as a laundress. Smith and metalwork clans heading north to supply the war had bought the fabric for their sons and daughters. It had to be meticulously handstitched and was so resistant to heat that if its owners walked into a blazing potter's kiln, not a mark would appear on them. She'd seen it happen once.

Ciardis felt the press of the wet cloak on her cold, bare arms. She began to shiver and in doing so broke the magnetic hold of the woman before her. She felt like a drowned rat in front of the woman, who chose that moment to speak.

"Ciardis Weathervane?" said the woman as she placed her hands over Ciardis's left hand, stilling it from its quest to increase circulation and warmth in the opposite arm. Ciardis felt unease drip down her spin. She still couldn't get used to people she'd never met before recognizing her.

Mirth lit up in the woman's eyes for a moment as she said, "It's your eyes. Even from a distance there aren't so many around here with that color – golden like a finch's wings." Ciardis nodded as surprise began to overtake her unease. The woman's warm touch on her hand was nice. Heat had begun to rise off in stronger waves from the woman's skin; it was as if Ciardis stood next to the open door of a stove with fire-lit coals inside.

Respect began to build in her. She knew that for a mage to call this much heat in the middle of a storm-tossed ocean would take lots of power. The clash of the elements alone should have prevented the woman from doing all but the most basic tasks with her fire element.

Ciardis looked down at her hands, curious to see if the waves of heat were visible in the cold, miserable, gray morning. She couldn't quite contain a gasp of astonishment, which she quickly turned into a cough into her fisted right hand.

Ciardis watched in fascination as the heat emanated off the woman's skin and flowed with perfect control into her own body which welcomed it. Looking closely at the woman's magic, Ciardis traced the magic to the core. It was as bright as a sun, even on such a dreary and rainy day.

Snapping out of her reverie, Ciardis remembered that the woman had come over to question who she was. Although it felt more like an issue of confirmation than a query.

"Yes, and you are?"

"Linda Firelancer," the woman said in a low voice that barely echoed over the crash of waves on the ship.

There was nothing in the woman's tone that said she bore Ciardis any ill will or why she'd walked over. But that name was enough to still Ciardis and bring back flashing memories of the night Damias had died at the hands of the Princess Heir – hell bent on killing Ciardis and those with her for interfering in the inheritance rights.

As she stared at the woman before her, chestnut hair falling in waves and gentle hands still capturing Ciardis's own, she didn't quite know what to think of the sparks that blazed in Linda's eyes. Was it the spark of retribution or the sign of a fiery soul? In her mind's eye Ciardis could still see the woman's magic rippling across her hands in an intricate dance. The same heat could turn into a fiery inferno and incinerate Ciardis into a pile of ash, if she had been so inclined.

She hadn't, although Ciardis wasn't so sure she would have made the same decision, had she been in the woman's place. The silence stretched with a grim tension that could not be overlooked.

Ciardis bit her lip anxiously as she searched the eyes of the woman whose husband she had watched die.

Finally she said, "I'm sorry for your loss. I sent flowers… Damias was a wonderful man and instructor."

"Thank you, I loved him with all my heart." Careful and considerate.

"I hope you know that I did everything in my power to help him. We were ambushed and neither of us could have anticipated how the night would unfold."

"I wish I had been there. Princess Heir Marissa would not have survived the night," Linda said with a coldness that made Ciardis think that she might have ice rather than fire running through her veins.

"Yes," said Ciardis, "I…would have wished that, too. I wanted to greet you at the funeral, but…"

"I wasn't there," said Linda with a small shake of her head. "I was still on the emperor's assignment when I heard the news. I have made my peace in my own way—honoring his life at the shrines along the road."

Ciardis nodded in understanding as Linda stepped away.

"It was good to meet you, Ciardis. I wanted to give you my greetings personally and extend an invitation to converse further about what we had and still have in common, but for now you should join the Prince Heir," Linda said as she turned to take her place with the honor guard.

Ciardis nodded as another streak of lightning cracked overhead and the ship swayed in the ocean. As she turned toward Sebastian, she caught a glimpse of the Weather Mage frantically whispering to himself and pouring magic from his hands out into the surrounding ocean. The ship soon stopped swaying and the man visibly wiped his brow in relief.

Walking toward Sebastian, Ciardis noted with gratitude that not only was she warm, but her clothes were also perfectly dry. Tucking an errant strand of hair behind her ear, she glanced over at the Fire Mage in appreciation.

Then she took her place near Sebastian's side: to his right and two steps behind, as protocol demanded.

The honor guard, generals, and other courtiers arrayed themselves around them, and behind all of those on the dry deck the Imperial soldiers stood at attention in the rain. Ciardis frowned in dismay. She might not be as close to Sebastian as she once had been, but at least she could get him to listen to her.

Keeping her voice low, but loud enough to reach Sebastian's ear, she said, "Why can't the Weather Mage extend the bubble just a little? It's pouring rain and the lightning is worsening. The soldiers are getting soaked and must be freezing."

Sebastian stared straight ahead at the turbulent sea, the deck only moving slightly under their feet. *Another effect from the Weather Mage no doubt*, she mused.

"And their armor will rust!" she added in an attempt to show a practical reason for her concern.

"Their armor is weather and heat resistant. They'll be fine; as new officers, they need to prove themselves to their leaders," Sebastian said. He didn't turn his green eyes on her but she imagined they were hard and distant as they watched the water churn in the dark storm outside.

"Oh, yeah, standing in the pouring rain is a *great* way to prove your worth."

"It shows discipline and fortitude."

"It shows mindless sheep and a leader who doesn't care for the comfort of his troops," Ciardis retorted.

"Enough," came a baritone voice from the Prince Heir's left. Ciardis cringed but continued to stare straight ahead. She wasn't yet ready to give up on this topic, but neither was she willing to argue with the second-in-command of the Imperial forces.

From the corner of her eye she saw a small tic in Sebastian's right eye. *Good, he's irritated*, she thought. *He should be!*

For the moment she watched the harsh play of wind and rain as it struck the wind barrier encasing their little group. She smoothed her pursed mouth into a more acceptable smile and awaited their guest with composure.

It wouldn't be long now.

CHAPTER TWO

Out of the distant sky a roar sounded. It was the kind of roar that heralded trouble and made Ciardis itch for a decent crossbow. Over the last two months she had been expanding her Defense tutorials to include archery, practice with a staff as well as a glaive, and the all-important fan. She'd been taking archery lessons with the Weapons Initiates of the Imperial Guard. She knew the guard as a whole regarded her fumbling attempts to load the arrows into the crossbow with amusement. Most of the men there had been knocking arrows and hunting game since they were children. The fact that her arrow wobbled and struck dirt more often than it hit a target didn't help, either. But her aim was getting better every day.

But regardless of her clumsiness, knocking the arrow, and getting off a shot, even she couldn't possibly miss a target this large. With a roar like that, it had to be as big as the ship. A sea monster, maybe? But no, the sound had come from up above. And of course if she so much as twitched out of step, she'd never hear the end of it from Sebastian and the Companions' Guild leadership. Protocol was everything to them.

Her heart beat fast as she strained her eyes to pierce the clouds in the sky. It was an overcast day, and it was hard to see anything farther than ten feet in front of the ship with such a heavy rain. Out of the corner of her eye she saw something, a glint or glimmer on the eastern starboard. She kept looking out of the corner of her right eye. She really wanted to just stuff the protocol and turn to the right, but damned if she did it before anyone else did.

Then an excited murmur came from the man just behind her. The members of his row began to angle themselves so that they could see the right side of the ship, and Ciardis turned obediently with eagerness. They watched as the gossamer layers of cloud began to push outward and part before the massive form that flew through them. Scales, wings, and a flaming mouth peeked through in small glimpses that had Ciardis aching for a strong wind to push the dense clouds out of the way. She couldn't stop a gasp of delight from escaping her mouth when she saw the massive form begin to descend out of the cloud layer. First a claw appeared, then an arm, and finally the full body came into view.

As a dragon emerged out of the harsh fall sky, Ciardis could see that it was resplendent. Even from a distance, its scales—a brilliant emerald green—shone as if a thousand suns were above the dragon's mighty form instead of this dull and gray day overcast with rolling thunder, clouds, and rain. As it drew closer, Ciardis felt the flesh on her skin rise in alarm. Goosebumps arose on her upper arms under the cloak and at the nape of her neck. Her magic was reacting to the presence of not only the mages surrounding her, but also the oncoming dragon—a being that could best be described as living magic.

The dragon's mighty roar sounded again as it swiftly banked its wings to glide in and land…on nothing? Sahalia's dragons were *kith*, magical beings of non-human form that could wield some sort of power over the elements around them. Of course, that was what the humans called anything they didn't understand and couldn't beat with a stick.

The dragons of Sahalia were just as fond of referring to their human allies as *snacks*. Sahalian dragons were immortal, powerful, and vain creatures. Their pride was said to be their weakness. In Ciardis's awestruck mind it could only be their strength. The dragon in front of her was gorgeous.

And heading straight into the open water. What could it be thinking? It would fall directly into the water. If the envoy drowned, relations between the Algardis Empire and Sahalia would be ruined.

In the back of her mind she noted that her hand was gripping another with the strength of death. Glancing down, she saw it was Sebastian's. She didn't remember grasping his. Reluctantly she started to pull away. She felt his hand flex in what suspiciously felt like a squeeze. "Relax," he said while squeezing her hand again. She wondered absentmindedly if his hand was spasming…apparently not quietly enough. His amusement rolled through their mind link as he said, "The Sahalian dragons know what they're doing."

"I don't think he does. The Sahalian envoy is heading directly for the open water. With his size and the wings as an encumbrance, he'll drown. Are you willing to risk the fragile peace between our two empires if that happens?"

Frowning, Ciardis continued to peer doubtfully at the approaching dragon. It was coming in quite fast, although it was still a long distance off.

He chuckled while unlocking her fingers.

"No one will drown; just watch."

The closer it flew, the more of its wingspan she could admire. Mighty horns arrayed the top of its head like a crown. From wingtip to wingtip, the dragon was easily the size of the three-masted ship she stood on. Each wing had a fine bone structure, like the bats that dwelled deep in the mountain caves of Vaneis and only emerged at night to hunt the bugs in the countryside. Between the bones of the wings was webbed skin on the underside and layered scales on the other. The scales on its belly and neck were a luminescent pearl color while the scales on its back, wings, legs, and head were the same shade of green she'd admired earlier.

It was a beautiful sight to see.

Sebastian called out to the Weather Mage, "Extend the shield by another twenty feet into the ocean and steady the ship."

Nervously the man nodded, perspiration dripping down his forehead in the dry confines of the wind shield he'd erected. The other people beneath the shield, even Ciardis, were dry and warm.

Perhaps the momentousness of the occasion was making the man nervous?

It wasn't often that a Sahalian dragon made an appearance anywhere near the Algardis Empire. They didn't view humans as equals, and given the history between Sahalia and Algardis after the empire's founding, preferred to stay away. Ciardis eyed the Weather Mage more closely. Her mouth set in a thin line as she glanced back and forth between the oncoming dragon and the man set to smooth its way. She was loath to take her eyes from the magnificent dragon but the Weather Mage looked almost…ill.

He stood, swaying slightly, as if the spell he'd made to steady the ship had no effect on him. Pulling a looped chain from under his robes, he picked up the talisman at the end. The Weather Mage stepped forward through the edge of the wind shield and into the downpour on the deck. Once he reached the ship's rails, he lifted his hands from the talisman and pushed outward. As his hands pushed outward, the sleeting rain surrounding him arced backward as if pushed by an invisible wall. Quickly the wind shield grew larger, encompassing first the entire ship and then the ocean immediately surrounding it in a circle.

With a short nod to himself, the Weather Mage licked his finger and held it up to the sky. Was he testing the wind? Or changing the current with such a simple gesture? It didn't look like anything significant was happening. He licked his lips nervously and Ciardis knew something was wrong.

No, thought Ciardis. *He's stalling.*

And yet he'd completed one task successfully. She slipped into her mage sight to get a gauge on his core. Even from a distance she could see the power in his mage core dwindling rapidly. The Weather Mage couldn't possibly be able to stabilize such a turbulent natural force as the ocean in the midst of a gale. She wasn't an expert on weather magic but even she could see that he couldn't do another task as momumental as the one asked of him with his depleted core.

The next minute, the Weather Mage stepped back from the rail and looked over his shoulder at the gathered retinue. He gave a short bow to the assembled group, specifically looking at Prince Heir Sebastian for acknowledgement.

Sebastian gave a short nod in return and turned aside to speak with the waiting general of the Imperial forces. The Weather Mage turned back to his task, and just for a moment, fear swept over his face. He picked up the talisman again. Even though he was still facing her, Ciardis couldn't see the markings on the disc he held at the end of a length of a gold chain. She wasn't close enough to figure out if it was the relic she thought it was, and, more importantly, if it stored magic.

Glancing sideways, Ciardis noted that Sebastian was still speaking quietly with his compatriot. She decided to see if she could escape notice and leave. Unfortunately for her, while she and Sebastian had been apart for weeks, he was just as aware of her every movement now as he had been when they'd been miles underground in the vale near the White Mountains while trying to reach the cavern of the Land Wight.

He didn't move an inch but she felt his presence reach out. They couldn't talk mind-to-mind now that he'd released her hand. But she could still sense his concern. Oddly enough, that momentary feeling of worry was enough to soothe her anxiety about them. It showed that underneath that cold, princely exterior he hadn't changed. He was still the same boy she'd walked through fire for. Although he managed to surprise her this time. Months of no contact and it was almost like they hadn't been apart at all. With a wicked grin that he couldn't see, as he was still turned aside to face his compatriot, she opened her thoughts and send him a mixture of emotions—happiness and a wicked sense of amusement.

Don't worry. I won't get into too much trouble, she thought fondly at him. She knew he wouldn't be able to hear her thought, but still, the emotions would flow through the link.

Firmly, she elected to focus on the present and pushed the swirl of feelings from Sebastian away. As they faded, the dread that pooled in her stomach began to take precedence. Taking in the Weather Mage's shaken form, she realized she had a bad feeling about this…a very bad feeling. Edging sideways with a whispered, "Excuse me, pardon me," she eased around the gathered officials and towards the Weather Mage's side.

He didn't look any better close up. Practically shaking in his unsteady stance. Reaching out a hand instinctively, she sought to steady him as she asked, "Sir, are you unwell?"

"Back away," snapped the perspiring mage. "How dare you interrupt a solemn ceremony?"

"I came to see if you were able to finish. You don't look well."

"This is none of your concern, child."

"I beg your pardon? I am offering to *help* you."

He gripped the talisman in his hand so hard that his knuckles turned white. "Perhaps I wasn't clear. The aid of the Companions' Guild is not necessary here. Dismissed."

Back stiff at the censure Ciardis returned to her place at the Prince Heir's side. She smoothed her face over as she passed Linda Firelancer's position among the group. Before she could pass her completely, Linda swiftly grabbed Ciardis's hand and said, "What did you see?"

"Nothing, I thought the Weather Master was unwell. I must have been mistaken."

Turning to look at the man, the Fire Mage said quietly, "And perhaps not. Some people don't know how to ask for help. And some people are forever too proud to accept it."

"Stand here. Wait for my signal," the Fire Mage said.

Linda walked over with a no-nonsense look on her face to the Weather Mage's side. He had yet to follow the Prince Heir's second command to steady the ship, which was swaying side-to-side erratically. And the wind shield was beginning to falter, as well. To make matters worse, holes were forming in the shield and gusts of sharp wind and rain would come through the holes and rip across the deck in a fury. As people started to stumble back and forth, they began to murmur disparagingly about the talents of the hired Weather Mage.

Ciardis was more worried about his health than talent. Any mage under this much stress, battling Mother Nature herself to force calm when the weather was anything but still, would need to be an excellent practitioner, powerful and prepared. And this man seemed to be anything but ready for the task. As Ciardis watched the planks across the decks tremble, she noted that the Weather Mage seemed to be losing his grip. Whatever Linda was going to do, Ciardis hoped she was able to do it fast.

Meanwhile, a second roar shattered Ciardis's focus on the Weather Mage and brought it back abruptly to their oncoming guest. Staring at the dragon Ciardis saw the most curious thing. It was *hovering*. Its wings weren't moving and neither were its legs. How the massive beast was staying in the air was a mystery to her. But she decided to file that away for another time. It was still vocalizing its displeasure. Ciardis wasn't exactly sure what the dragon was roaring about. She spoke Sahalian, thanks to a certain Companion, but this roar wasn't in the dragon tongue of the Sahalian courts with the fluid language and subtle hisses of its consonants. No, this was primal. The roar was the natural language of one dragon to another, and something that no other being could translate. That didn't mean she didn't understand anger when she heard it.

And then suddenly it was moving again. The dragon banked its wings and prepared to land on the water. Incoming with its wings spread like that, it looked like it planned to grab onto the ship with the claws and rend it to pieces or to sink it, whichever came first. No one on the deck looked anything but calm. Ciardis tried to emulate their serene, well-practiced looks, but she wasn't a convincing liar on her best days. In fact, she'd been told quite a few times that the only reason she hadn't been outright assassinated was because her enemies were convinced she couldn't manipulate herself, let alone someone else. She'd like to keep it that way. She had enough problems as it was with people trying to kill Sebastian without adding her own assassination to the list.

Then the dragon began to glow.

Ciardis went pale. He was about to cast a spell. Secret glances at the honor guard around her, including three battle mages, told her that they weren't worried. Their visages were calm and steady, each stood with hands folded in front of them, and all courteous attention was being paid to the dragon envoy. That didn't mean *she* wasn't worried. Then suddenly a small ball of blue flame winked into existence at her feet and winked out again just as quickly. Ciardis was certain she was the only one who had seen the flame appear and disappear.

She glanced over at Linda's direction and saw her pointedly staring at her. *I guess that was my signal to get over there.*

CHAPTER THREE

As she joined Linda's side, she heard her speaking in a low voice to the Weather Mage.

It was in Sahalian, but she caught most of it.

"This Weathervane might be the only thing standing between you and the next world, Marcus," Linda said while nodding to Ciardis, "We can't afford to loose another mage. Not if we want our numbers to stay strong. Strong enough to defeat the hordes in the North."

The man looked over at her with bloodshot eyes. He sucked in a breath and broke once more into a chanting trance. When he awakened, *if* he awakened, his choice would be clear. Taking Ciardis's hand, Linda Firelancer shared her mage vision. His aura was fading and his core was depleting.

It was the first time she'd seen a mage dying.

The man's breath was shallow, his magic erratic, his pulse fading, and still he hesitated. Ciardis reached forward hesitantly to grasp his hand. To give him what he couldn't ask for because of his damn pride. And then Linda caught her wrist in a bruising grip. She hadn't moved. Her face was still turned to the Weather Mage's as she sought to tell him a story of sacrifice and pride with just her eyes.

But the grip she held Ciardis's hand in was iron tight. In her mind, Ciardis heard the Fire Mage speaking.

Never, Ciardis, Linda said, *never interrupt a dying mage, not unless you want to die alongside them. If he rises from the trance, he will make his choice.*

Ciardis couldn't pull her hands from Linda's grip and couldn't take her eyes off of the Weather Mage. Occasional drifts of wind blew her hair in her face and she didn't move. She was silent as raindrops began to pelt their skin. She didn't answer as the retinue began to question their stillness. Her eyes and Linda's stayed firmly fixed upon the man before them. The man who had a choice to live or die. To accept help or to put his pride before his downfall.

She felt her breath become slower. Minutes passed that felt like hours.

And then he was conscious, opening his eyes and emerging from the trance. With a slow breath he reached a shaky hand forward and grasped Ciardis's. Linda's shoulders relaxed and she looked as if the world had been lifted from her shoulders. She nodded to Ciardis.

With a rush of power, Ciardis replenished the mage's lagging store. Together they fixed the wind shield, pushing it outward and making it stronger. With a squeeze of her hand, he said, "I'm going to dive into the sea with my power and still the waters. The currents are swift and they are strong. Magically and physically. You shall act as my anchor, but if anything goes wrong, you are to let me go. Do you understand?"

"Yes." Ciardis nodded.

He looked out over the ocean with a fond and tired smile, "Weather is a particularly difficult power to master and manipulate. I don't know what you've been told. But mages do not forsake that oath. In every instance the younger mage is to take all precautions to protect their lives. I expect you to do the same."

"She will," Linda said with strength in her voice. "I will be here to assure that she does."

And then it began. Ciardis felt the pull from his magic to hers. He began drawing immense amounts as he shot down in a spiral—no, a maelstrom—of power into the element of water. She watched as he wove her enhancement power into his spool of power. He began to weave the two cords together in a simple stitch that fell into the wild and chaotic swirl of power that was the water element. No matter how much power he had, she instinctively knew that it wouldn't be able to harness water. Not this fierce and wild beauty that moved with the freeness of a spirit in the ocean.

She felt him change tactics. Instead of trying to harness the water element, the Weather Mage began to coax it into playing a game. With flashes of lightning emitting from his fingertips and a calm soothing voice he called it closer. And closer it came until it was near enough that he could entrap it a complex web. The elemental didn't even notice when the web began to close around it. It was too entranced in playing as it bounced from point to point on the web and gave the Weather Mage the time he needed to still the waters surrounding the ship.

He began to tie off the ends of the magic neatly to form a self-sustaining cradle that would feed the elemental's desire for the quest until the web dissipated. Back in her body, Ciardis blinked and stared into the concerned eyes of the Weather Mage and the Fire Mage. They stood in a tight circle.

In a low voice Linda said "Everything all right?"

"Fine," said Ciardis faintly.

"Good," the Weather Mage said with a curtness that Ciardis tried not to take offense at.

With a push, Linda sent Ciardis back to Prince Heir Sebastian's side.

Turning back to their guest, she put her thoughts on the Weather Mage's illness aside before Sebastian could pick up on it. In front of her she took in the dragon envoy. This dragon, *all* dragons, were from Sahalia. They nested nowhere else. No one knew why. Sahalia was an empire far off in the Western Sea, ruled by a loose amalgamation of a dozen families united only in the belief in the supremacy of dragons above all other species and a firm desire to wrest more power and wealth for themselves. For thousands of years, dragons had not left their empire's shores. They'd seen no reason to leave the comfort of their homes for distant lands and certainly wouldn't cross an ocean to do it. Even now they tended to avoid the lands of Algardis because of the Initiate Wars centuries earlier.

Their primary reason for being homebound?

Laziness.

The ocean trek would require a large amount of magical power and three days of constant flight to reach land. In fact, it hadn't been until five centuries ago, almost two hundred years after the founding of the Empire and the Great War and three years before the start of the Initiate Wars, that many dragons began making the journey across the waters from Sahalia to Algardis. The merchants on both sides of the sea were ecstatic; trade was the best it had been since the founding of the empire.

It wasn't until an intrepid dragon explorer, known as the Wanderer, had left Sahalia and returned to its shores with human followers that the journey across the ocean began to hold any interest for the ruling Sahalian families. To put it bluntly, the Wanderer came back with an oddity: humans. All the dragons soon wanted their own. First, the humans brought back on the long cross-ocean voyage started out as pampered pets, and then rapidly became servants to dragons who wanted their every whim catered to from trimming their nails to buffing their scales.

But there was also something weird in the rapid change of direction from ignoring Algardis to a sudden desire for a flurry of travel across the large ocean. Greed was one thing; ability quite another. Why was the voyage so easy for the dragons now? Even the less powerful dragons were able to make the journey. Ciardis had this question on her mind as she watched the dragon flap its wings and dispel the hovering state it was in. It was too large to land on the ship's deck—that had been established. And then she felt its power rise again. First it was like pinpricks on her skin. Feeling the uncomfortable sensation, she tried to rub it away like an itch, but it only spread. She could tell Sebastian felt it, too.

And then the dragon spoke. When it spoke, letters illuminated the sky. The letters formed words, the words became sentences, and the sentences combined into a thought. When the thought was complete, the action began. And they watched as water rose from the sea, foaming. The water grew five feet, ten feet, and then stopped at fifteen feet, a giant wall of water. With another breath, the dragon formed a second sentence and the water flattened. In a shape of a disc, the water stilled fifteen feet above the ocean's surface and the dragon landed on the platform with a satisfied huff.

She had heard Sahalian magic was different. A literal interpretation of words and spells. Until now, she hadn't seen it for herself. As the Sahalian dragon stood waiting, Prince Heir Sebastian walked forward until he was five feet from the ship's railing. In the calm of the Weather Mage's shield, man and dragon stared at each other. Sebastian wore his light armor with a sword at his waist. The dragon's scales gleamed like armor of its own.

With his head tilted back, the Prince Heir called out, "Welcome, Ambassador Sedaris, it is a pleasure to have you visit the Empire of Algardis."

*****

The dragon chuffed and stared down at the gathering of humans arrayed below it on the ship's deck. For a few moments it let silence descend over the humans, broken only by the exhale of its smoky breath. It wondered with amusement if the soldiers formed in single file behind the Prince Heir's party were meant as a warning. If so, the humans had much to learn and much to remember. Dragons feared no one and nothing.

The pleasure is mine Prince Heir Sebastian, said a decidedly female voice echoing in their heads. Dragons generally chose to mind-speak, having way too many problems with accidental spells when speaking in the human tongue through their large jaws.

Ciardis felt surprise ripple through the gathered retinue. She was surprised, having expected the envoy with grandiose horns to be a male. But her surprise was nothing compared to the horrified shock that she felt permeating through the surrounding group.

Glancing around her she took in the stiff, almost petrified forms of the retinue. Several hands had dropped inconspicuously to blades at their sides. *Now they want to get worried? What were these battle mages thinking minutes ago when a half ton dragon was looking like it would either fall onto the ship or into the sea?*

Ciardis felt Sebastian's fear radiating outward before she even recognized what the emotion was. He was too well-trained to grip the pommel of his sword but the frantic swirl of emotions in his head told Ciardis he wanted to. So it was female. Big to-do. Right?

Irritated, Ciardis would have given her right arm at that moment to know *why* everyone was so upset about the dragon's gender. She couldn't step forward to touch Sebastian and demand an answer. The protocol officer present would throw a fit.

To her surprise it was that same officer that stepped up to her side. His piercing gray eyes and blond hair were striking alongside the svelte form that could have him mistaken for a member of Sebastian's personal guard as well.

Keeping his voice low and pitched for her ears he said, "We would ask that you don't venture out of your place *again* Lady Weathervane."

"How did you know I was going to move?"

"Training has made me apt at capturing movements of the body. Besides you were fidgeting."

Ciardis said nothing.

"In any case it is important that the envoy is not angered."

He hesitated and then admitted honestly, "This was unexpected....unexpected and unwelcome. The females are the ones that fought on the battlefield, the warriors of the dragon race. They are known far and wide as bloodthirsty and insatiable."

"Well, this sucks," she whispered back.

He didn't bother commenting. There was nothing to say. They were faced with a high-ranking Ambassador of the most fearsome gender of the dragon race. If she decided to kill them – they were dead.

As he stepped back to his place she reached out to latch on his sleeve, "Thank you. For the explanation I mean."

He bowed slightly, "You are welcome."

Ciardis inhaled deeply and sought to calm herself. She couldn't imagine how Sebastian felt, standing right beneath her jaws. It probably didn't help that he was also staring up into a closed mouth that was larger than his whole body. When the Ambassador opened her mouth and she saw the serrated teeth as long as her whole body, the sensation of being a rabbit staring in fear into the mouth of a ravenous wolf was hard to ignore.

Turning its head away from the humans, it chuffed once more. This time a big black ball of gook shot out, straight into the ocean. It looked digusting as it passed over their heads and smelled even worse.

Ciardis had the urge to run her fingers through her hair just to be sure that none of the liquid had lodged in her curls. It would be her rotten luck if it did.

Is it sick? she wondered.

"I am not sick," proclaimed a booming voice in her head.

The rest of the sailing party hadn't heard Ciardis's query, but they had certainly heard the directed response. And they knew it was directed at her. If censure could be palpable, the vibe she was getting from the surrounding retinue was like a heavy blanket of displeasure weighing down on her.

So I'm not supposed to think now? Delightful.

"Ambassador Sedaris," said Sebastian smoothly, "You flew three hundred miles to our empire. Let us pay our respects and welcome you properly."

The female's head titled to the side until a bright amber eye stared directly at Sebastian.

"Yessss," its mind spoke, a hint of a slither in its voice.

"I confess, Ambassador, we have wondered at your reasons for asking for a meeting to be held on the ocean."

"Neutral territory."

"Come again?"

The dragon lowered its head until it was level with the ship, "I did not misspeak."

"Indeed," Sebastian said with a cautious glance at the commander to his left. What was this dragon up to? The ship was much too small to maneuver. The honor guard of pike men and soldiers he'd brought along were just that: an *honor* guard. They were tightly packed in for a display; they weren't meant to fight. And they certainly weren't meant to battle a dragon with the advantage of unlimited skies at a push of its wings and the ability to breathe fire down upon their ship.

"My sisters have sent me here for one reason and one reason alone," she proclaimed. "We have received grievances against your empire."

"Grievances?"

"*Kith*," she hissed, "*Kith* who have come to us with tales of death and magic devoid of life."

"Ambassador, I—*we*—have heard no such tales. The Algardis Empire has maintained peace with the *kith* peoples for centuries."

"Our grievance is not about peace. It is about the dead—the living dead. Souls trapped in this life while their bodies have gone to the next."

She raised her wings and lifted her forelegs in the air. "I will rest in the guest quarters for my kind in your capitol city, Prince Heir. I will stay as long as needed to ensure this is addressed. But be warned: Our patience is limited."

Without any warning she lifted off and flew into the skies. She was heading east toward Sandrin.

Ciardis was sure she wasn't the only person left behind wondering what the hell had just happened. As she stared at Sebastian and he looked back at her, her confusion mirrored in his eyes, she got the feeling that life in the courts had just gotten a lot more interesting.

As the ship returned to port Sebastian pulled her aside. It was but a moment—to whisper a message in her ear. And then he left her standing still.

CHAPTER FOUR

As the ship docked back in the bay, the Weather Mage said proper goodbyes to his Imperial retinue and walked down the gangplank. Seeing that all of the carriages available at the dock were reserved for the Prince Heir, he decided to walk towards the wharf and see if he could find a tuk-tuk. Wiping his brow of the perspiration that had accumulated there, he lugged his heavy bag in one hand, breathing a sigh of relief that it was over.

Marcus hadn't been feeling well all week and today was no exception. As he walked farther up the dock, a sharp pain in his head nearly drove him to his knees and he cried out.

None of the sailors surrounding him paid the least bit of attention. Most made sure they were looking in the opposite direction. A group of men off to the side coiling ropes near a docked ship began mumbling amongst themselves. These sailors were careful not to speak loudly enough for the stumbling mage to overhear them though.

"Just another drunk mage on the docks with one too many shots of whiskey in his belly", said one.

"When they get drunk like that leave them be," another replied, "The magic folk are nothing but trouble. Drunk ones are worse."

One sailor with an oiled and pointed black beard grinned and bared a mouth full of rotten teeth as he brandished a long, curved blade, "This will show em what's what."

The first sailor to speak turned and spit over his shoulder – wishing away the foolish words of the man before him, "You couldn't rob them because they'd set you on fire with their minds, but if you tried to help, they'd stiff you the minute they were well, their noses up in the air. Who needs that kind of grief?"

Their muttering continued as the Weather Mage staggered up the dock. He only paused once – a momentary lapse as another wave of pain hit him.

As he crouched in pain, the Weather Mage took deep breaths and looked around for a quiet place. He needed to take his medication and he didn't want any onlookers interfering. Standing up, he raced toward the open doors of a large storage house. None of the workers were going near it as dusk fell, and it looked as if it had been recently emptied, straw everywhere and some smashed crates near the entrance.

As he hobbled into the building, the pain was getting worse—much worse than it had ever been before. He fell against a wall and slid down onto the dirty floor. Ignoring the state of his robes, he desperately fiddled with the clasps on his baggage. It was one of those confounded mechanical ones that kept thieves from getting into his prized possessions, but at the moment with his pain-clouded mind, it was only prolonging his misery. Finally getting the combination lock to unsnap using the symbols he'd set, the bag popped open with a distinct *click*.

Wasting no time, he dug into the depths until he found the vial he was looking for. Pulling it up out of the bag, he held it to his lips. In the darkness of the huge storage building, he couldn't see the dark liquid that moved around inside the vial, but he knew it was there. As he pulled out the stopper, he reflected on how he'd gotten to where he was.

Months ago, after a debilitating headache had left him incapacitated for the fifth time in a week, he'd gone to the imperial healers for a sixth time. He was losing far too many shifts to stay in the emperor's service much longer. The healers had muttered and chanted and probed, but finally had to explain that they couldn't find any source for the headaches. He'd nearly cried when they'd pushed seeds of poppy into his hands again. The seeds weren't working. They just made him drowsy.

Seeing the state he was in, the healer he'd come to see on his sixth visit - an old friend from the school for mages, had looked around and then leaned over to whisper, "This isn't sanctioned, but I've heard stories."

He'd hesitated.

The Weather Mage had grabbed the lapels of the healer's coat and dragged him closer with bloodshot eyes. "What? A cure? For this malady?"

"Calm down, man," the healer had said soothingly while unlatching the Weather Mage's fingers from his coat. "Yes, in the markets. Healers, natural ones that get their training from the clans."

"Hedge witches?" the Weather Mage had said, shrinking back in distaste.

"You may have no other choice."

Taking the man's written directions in trembling hands, the Weather Mage had gone to see the hedge witch in the local market. Down side streets and behind an alley, he finally found the rundown shack the man was supposed to be in. When he had entered, he was met by a foul smell and a shrouded figure in black. Stammering his apologies, he'd stumbled back and prepared to leave.

The voice had called him back, saying, "You have an illness—a throbbing, striking pain that leaves you half mad."

Raising his hand, the hedge witch held out a vial of indeterminate substance. "I have the answer."

"How? How did you know?" stammered the mage while eyeing the vial. It was filled with a black liquid that shone with a metallic gleam even in the darkness of these quarters.

The Weather Mage couldn't see the hedge witch, but he could hear the smile in his voice as he'd said, "Call it a gift."

The Weather Mage was usually a cautious man, but every passing day the headaches grew worse. Soon he feared he wouldn't be able to perform his duties at all, not to mention the fact that he was slowly losing his mind from all of the pain.

"How much?"

"Fifty shillings for three. After three you will need no more."

Frazzled, tired and desperate for a cure the Weather Mage was willing to try anything. Especially for such a small price. The Weather Mage had held out the paltry amount and snapped, "Here. Take it."

Rushing out of the shack, he'd pretended that he didn't see the shadows moving or smell the overwhelming stench of the dead. Anything to end the cursed headaches.

He hurried out so fast that he stepped around the body of the true hedge witch, bloated and lying under a discarded burlap sack. Behind him the charlatan smiled in the dark and vanished without a trace, his task completed.

Back in the storage house, the Weather Mage prepared to drink the last of his treatment vials that he had acquired. Over the last few days the headaches had lessened until they were almost gone. Sometimes he'd gotten sharp pangs that distracted him or hit him by surprise, but nothing compared to the monstrous headaches that had left him an invalid in his bed for days when they'd struck before. Preparing to drink the disgusting substance, he held his nostrils pinched closed and tilted back his head.

It was the only way he could get it down. The liquid smelled like tar and oozed down his throat like a slug. Drinking it down, he shook his head rapidly to clear the smell. As he gulped the tonic a sharp headache surfaced. He winced, waiting for the pain to rise in a crest like it always did. In utter surprise he felt it die down almost immediately – dwindling until he felt nothing more. He began smiling with joy, thinking the cure was working, and *it was.*

His joy was short-lived. Out of the shadows emerged a cloaked figure.

Stumbling up and leaving his bags on the floor, the Weather Mage demanded, "Who are you? What do you want?"

"Why, what I've always wanted, Weather Mage. *You.*"

The Weather Mage vaguely recognized the man's voice but couldn't place it. Deciding that he'd teach this idiot a lesson, he called lightning to his fingertips. A costly magical measure, but one that always sent thieves and vagabonds running away as fast as they could. The cloaked man didn't move.

Smiling, the Weather Mage thought just before he threw the ball of lightning, *He can't say I didn't warn him.*

He watched as the ball of lightning—enough to destroy a man, and usually in spectacular fashion—arced toward his victim. He had to give the man praise; he didn't run, he didn't scream or cower. Instead he stood still in the face of certain death. And when the lightning ball his him directly in the chest, the man *absorbed* it. The Weather Mage watched in astonishment as the lightning hit a writhing dark, shadowy thing on the person's chest and was gone, like it was never there. And then the Weather Mage knew dread. He was in trouble.

The cloaked man laughed and strode forward, unafraid. When the Weather Mage tried to run, he felt the wall behind him grab him. Screaming in fear, he saw dark shadows come down over his shoulders and slither up his thighs to bind him to the wall. As the cloaked man stopped in front of him and pulled back his hood to reveal his face, the Weather Mage still didn't recognize him. But he recognized that *smell*—the smell of death.

Shaking as the man traced a finger down his trembling face, the Weather Mage licked his lips and said, "Please. I'm a wealthy man. Anything. *Anything* I have can be yours."

"You see, Weather Mage," said the man with surprising gentleness, "I already have what I want."

And then he clutched the Weather Mage's face in one hand, and shadows began to pour down the mage's throat. Before he lost consciousness, the Weather Mage thought, *They feel just like slugs.*

CHAPTER FIVE

A few hours later, Ciardis was rushing across the outer courtyard of the Companions' Guild. As she reached the courtyard's center where the cobblestones started radiating out in ever-growing rings, she stopped and stuck out her hand in confusion. Frowning, she took in the falling precipation in dismay. It was *snowing*…in fall. It was far too early for this sort of nonsense. It shouldn't be snowing for at least another four months. Maybe five. And even then the snow was only likely to fall in the early morning hours when night had yet to release its hold and the sun still slept.

Snow never lasted long in Sandrin. The capitol city was too close to the sea and too warm year-round for it to have a regular annual snowfall. She lifted her hand hesitantly and watched as snowflakes dropped from the sky and dissolved in the heat of her palm.

So why I am looking up in the sky and seeing flurries come down?

Shaking her head at the bizarre weather, Ciardis hurried forward to get access to the Archives. She hadn't wanted to go her normal route through the colonnade and into the main entrance. Too many prying eyes. So instead she went outside, across the courtyard, and cut through a side garden to a small entrance adjacent to the side garden's entrance.

It allowed direct access to the older portion of the Archives where the large, detailed maps of the Algardis Empire were on display. Moving around the long tables and framed panels quickly, she found a quiet reading nook to curl up in. Sighing heavily, she fingered the ankle bracelet on her leg and hoped this worked.

Five minutes passed, then ten minutes, as Ciardis anxiously waited. What if he had forgotten or deemed a court function more important than their rendezvous?

And then she felt the familiar tug of power radiating from the bracelet and she reappeared in the Aether Realm, seated in a flowering garden bower. She stared in surprise at the blissful spring surroundings. She sat on a stone bench in a bower filled with honeysuckle - the small, delicate flower that had a trumpet shape and a sweet smell. As she broke a handful off at the stem their smell wafted into her nose and she felt the slight stickiness of resin on her hands.

This was much more pleasant than the winter weather in Sandrin. The Aether Realm was a dangerous place, which could drain your magic if a mage wasn't careful, but it had it's upsides as well – beautiful spring weather in the dead of fall being one of them. She heard a twig snap behind her and quickly turned toward the only way in or out of the bower: an entrance with a rounded trellis surrounding it. It, too, was adorned with honeysuckle. Underneath the blooming arc of white flowers stood Sebastian, an awkward smile on his face. Ciardis quickly stood and moved around the fountain that took up the bower center.

Grasping his hands before he could speak, she laid a chaste kiss on each of his cheeks.

"It's good to see you, Prince Sebastian."

He grinned and returned the cheek kisses. "What—you're not still mad at me for ignoring you on the ship?"

She snorted. "Was I supposed to be?"

Narrowing her eyes and stepping back, she regarded him carefully.

Sighing, he walked around her and towards the water fountain in the center of the garden.

"I don't want to have an argument, Ciardis."

"Good, neither do I."

"I don't want to be nagged, either."

All of this was said with his back turned to her, so he didn't see it when her hand came flying out and slapped him on the back of the head.

"I don't nag," she snapped. "And, quite frankly, I'm not your wife, your lover, or your court flunkie. I'm your *friend.* So I suggest you treat me with some respect."

He turned around chagrined and sat down on the fountain's edge as he looked up at her towering over him with her hands placed angrily on her hips and a stormy expression on her face.

Continuing, she said, "You asked me to come here as I recall." She was staring down at him, her stomach knotted with anxiety, trying to hide the sickened dismay and the feeling of her heart in her throat.

He rolled his shoulder at an uncomfortable angle – nervous in the face of her ire.

"So I did."

He swallowed as he said, "When did this happen?"

She raised an eyebrow.

"This…weird conflict between us?"

"Oh, I don't know. When you walked in five minutes ago?"

"No," he protested. "You've been weird for *months…*"

"Wrong, Sebastian," she said fiercely. "It's *you* that's been avoiding me. Every time I requested an audience over the summer it was denied. Not a letter or a word for months."

He wilted. It was true. "You don't understand."

"Make me understand!"

For a long moment his dark green eyes and her golden ones held each other's gaze. Turmoil in one gaze. Fierce pride in the other.

And then she collapsed to her knees in nervous laughter so that he, seated, looked down upon her. Reaching forward with trembling hands, she gathered his in her own.

"You've been busy doing the emperor's work, Sebastian," she said quietly. "I know this. But I also know about the rumored attempts on your life. I've been busy with functions of my own, but I never stopped worrying about you. And wondering why…why we aren't still friends."

Squeezing her hands with slight pressure, he licked his lips. "We still are. But I don't know whom to trust. The Imperial Guard, my father…hell, even the nobles are acting oddly."

She gave him a wry grin. "Aren't they always?"

"More oddly than usual." With a pause he continued on with a tenseness in his voice.

"The dragon was right, Ciardis. There have been deaths," he said.

"Where?" she questioned, alarmed.

"Murders, we think. In the Ameles Forest." He amended, "So far they've been scattered occurences. Infrequent attacks, really. But they're adding up. If it's not taken care of we could have a revolt from the local populace. And what's more the envoy that the residents of the Ameles Forest trust most is dead."

"You don't mean…"

He nodded.

He was referring to the dead Princess Heir, Marissa Algardis. Prince Sebastian's aunt, who had been trying to have him removed from the inheritance rights of the Algardis throne by draining his mage core since he was five. When that tactic was thwarted by Ciardis last spring she had tried to kill Ciardis in retribution while vowing to do the same to Sebastian. Sebastian and Ciardis, together with his loyal guard, had managed to kill her instead. But only at the expense of quite a few lives, including that of Damias Lancer, Ciardis's tutorials instructor and a man she had considered a friend.

Ciardis swore enough to make a sailor proud. "I knew that bitch would come back to haunt us."

He laughed wryly. "In more ways than one."

"But surely there's not someone out there deliberately attacking the *kith*?"

"My father thinks there is," Sebastian said slowly.

The *kith* were the magical races of creatures who were the original inhabitants of the Algardis Empire. Over the centuries they had grown to cohabit with humans peacefully. But the Ameles Forest held a special significance for many of the *kith*. As a consequence, a large portion including the mythical griffins and the *cardiara* called it home. If they were being attacked and murdered, it was a concern for all of the Ameles Forest *kith* and the surrounding communities.

"Something must be done," she said.

He nodded. "And something will. My father has ordered me to travel with an official presence to the forest in the coming weeks. Lord Meres Kinsight will be going ahead in the next week with others as an advance party."

"Well, that's good."

"But the forest deaths are just *one* concern among many," he said bitterly.

"And the other concerns are?"

"Well, my uncle the Duke of Cinnis wants me dead, and the Western Isles are demanding a new treaty enforced by the Lord of the Windswept Isles."

"The first I can see as a problem. But the second?"

"The treaty between the Western Isles and the Algardis Empire has always been negotiated by the heir to the throne directly with the representive of the Western isles. The fact that they've asked for the Lord of the Windswept Isles as an intermediary is an insult."

"Hmm, yeah, that could be a problem. What has the emperor said?"

"My father stands by my side. He assures me that I will be present for the negotiations."

Ciardis took that in stride. But she knew that having a presence in the room wasn't the same thing as being a negotiator at the table.

But first things first. "So tell me more about this duke."

They spoke long into the afternoon about his uncle, Duke of Cinnis. A distant relative of Prince Sebastian's, he seemed out for his nephew's blood. Before Prince Sebastian had to leave, they agreed to meet at a local tavern later in the week, as traveling to the Aether Realm was magically taxing. The bracelet she wore on her ankle had limitations and, as far as Prince Sebatian could tell, could only be used once a week before it went inactive.

When Ciardis returned to the Companions' Archive, she decided she needed to do some snooping of her own. This Duke of Cinnis was trouble. Regardless of the fact that he was Sebastian's family, he was clearly not feeling familial enough to avoid trying to kill him. Deciding to take matters into her own hands, she slipped on a cloak and strode out into the rainy mist. Slipping through the outer gates which barred entrance to the Companions' Guild in the mid-afternoon wasn't hard.

The flurries of snow had given way to a light, icy rain that made the guards less likely to venture outside of their gatehouse to interrogate individuals who were seeking to leave the Companions' Guild. They'd reserve their treks in the bitterly cold rain for those who wanted to obtain entrance to the castle grounds.

This worked in Ciardis's favor as she headed for the nearest available conveyance that would take her to the Imperial Courts. She had some friends she needed to talk to. As she descended from the carrier she'd taken, she made sure to walk to one of the palace side gates instead of the main one. She didn't want to attract attention. She just wanted to get inside.

She flashed a sunny grin at the guard on duty, whom she knew from weapons training, she said, "Hello, Morris. Cold afternoon, isn't it?"

"Aye, it is. Bloody cold weather."

She nodded, "I'm here to see Varis Turnfeather." No sign of recognition crossed his face.

"Lord Varis?" she clarified.

"Have an invitation?"

"No," she said slowly, trying to think of a way to get entrance, "but it's just a quick visit."

"Lass, you know I can't let you on palace grounds without a palace invitation. Not with all the deaths and whatnot within the past three months."

"Oh, I know," she said quickly. "But perhaps you could summon him for me?"

"That I could do." He turned aside quickly and put two fingers in his mouth, whistling sharply. The earsplitting screech was directed at the gate barracks just around the corner. Ciardis couldn't see it from her vantage point, but she certainly heard the crash of metal upon metal that rang out.

Morris cursed and shook his head in disgust. "Boy was probably napping on the job. Was supposed to be hammering nails."

That last bit was said loudly enough for the spindly boy rushing around the corner to hear. His red hair stuck up every which way as he hurried over, and a red flush spread from his neck to the tips of his ears.

"Sorry, Morris," he said hurriedly. "I just knocked some pails over. Nothing big."

The glare Morris leveled at the bony boy said it was a problem if he said it was problem. The boy hunched his shoulders like a whipped dog and ducked his head.

"You'll be cleaning that up," Morris advised. The boy immediately turned to rush back to the barracks and pick up the scattered nails.

"Not *now*, numbskull."

"Right."

Morris sighed in irritation. "Go and get Lord Varis. Tell him Mistress Weathervane is waiting at the gate."

As the name emerged from Morris's lips, the boy turned toward Ciardis in awe.

"*The* Weathervane?" he said.

"Get GOING!"

Ciardis giggled into her hand as she watched the boy scramble away.

Within minutes, Varis Turnfeather was escorted to the gate. Smiling as he wiped his hands on a handkerchief, he said to Ciardis, "Well, what an unexpected pleasure it is to see you today, Mistress Weathervane."

Ciardis looped a companionable hand into the crook of his elbow as they proceeded to walk across the main street in front of the Imperial palace.

"I know, but I'm glad it's a pleasant one," she said as they reached the other side of the street and walked into the city's public gardens. It was the only green area maintained by the Imperial household, a gift from the emperor to the city's inhabitants.

"Well?" he said, tapping an occasional rock in their path with his long cane.

"Haven't you ever heard that patience is a virtue, Milord?"

"Yes, but it's not one of the virtues that I've known you to be even passable at."

"That's true," said Ciardis as a rueful smile graced her lips. Looking up towards the sky she couldn't help but admire the wits of the tall, but gangly man who towered above her with long gray hair falling to his shoulders.

"I need your help, Lord Varis," she admitted. "Just with information."

"There's nothing just about seeking information, Ciardis Weathervane. Particularly in the Imperial Courts. What is it that you wish to know?"

"Why is the Duke of Cinnis trying to kill Prince Sebastian?"

"He's not."

"But…"

"He's trying to kill *you.*"

"That's impossible. There have not been any attacks on me…not recently, anyway."

"That you know of," he pointed out.

Varis looked down at her thoughtfully and then said, "That information was free, Ciardis. Ask me another question."

She stood flummoxed for a moment, but decided there was only one question that was pertinent now. "What can I do about it?"

"Not why? Very good. You can run…"

Her stiff expression told him what she thought of that idea.

"Or you can fight," he said.

Ciardis nodded. "The latter will be more to my style."

"And the most likely to get you in trouble," he said dryly. "Well, my dear, according to the ears I have on the ground, no one has made direct moves against you yet."

"And indirectly?"

"Rumors circling around. Some courtiers of the Duke have been whispering unpleasant things about you to receptive Imperial ears. Not the Prince Heir's mind you, but the ears of those he must pay attention to if you catch my meaning."

She did. If the Duke had enough clout to poison the Emperor's thoughts against her it was no wonder that Prince Sebastian had been avoiding her for months.

"But it doesn't seem to have the desired effect. Prince Sebastian has closed his ranks, has begun relying only on trusted advisors," Varis said in a lower voice. "And he hasn't renounced his intention to make you his Companion. Despite significant pressure."

Ciardis nodded, trying to keep her face impassive. To be honest, she hadn't been aware that was even a consideration.

"The duke is not appreciative of your influence on Prince Sebastian."

"Well, I'm not appreciative of his butting into my personal affairs."

Vardis sighed and cautioned her, "Be careful. You aren't protected by Imperial forces. And the duke is quite sure the Prince Heir's bold endeavors in the matters of the Imperial Courts are a direct result of your whispers in his ear."

"Impossible."

"Why? One would think the rumors are true. You are practically his unofficial Companion and it's said that he invites you to the Aether Realm for private consultations."

Ciardis frowned, while partly true she didn't feel like opening up about her relationship with Sebastian. They'd just gotten back on friendly terms. "It's not relevant."

As they headed back to the palace, Varis left her with whispered warnings.

"Most of all, Ciardis, keep your head down. The duke shouldn't attack if you don't strike first. And stay out of trouble. Your court escapades over the summer have angered quite a few, the Duke not least among them."

CHAPTER SIX

The next morning Ciardis rose bright and early. A light fog had drifted in on the coast and she watched it silently from the balcony of her apartment. Staring out at the sea, she quietly gathered her thoughts. She knew, deep down, that many things were about to change.

For better or for worse, she couldn't tell.

The door to her bedroom banged open with a loud crack.

Starting now.

Turning swiftly in her gown and robe, Ciardis confronted the person who'd barged into her room. She stared in shock at Stephanie, a transfer Companion with the talent to copy and deliver a specific talent from one person to another. Ciardis hadn't seen the girl in almost half a year—not since they'd made the transfer deal for the Sahalian language at the very beginning of her arrival at the Companions' Guild.

"What in a demon's ass do you think you're doing?" Ciardis demanded in outrage. She swiftly strode forward, intent on pushing the woman out of her room. But then Stephanie stepped around the bed and Ciardis stopped in her tracks. She held a loaded crossbow in her hands.

Hastily backing up a step, she said, "I mean…Stephanie, it's been so long."

She saw the second weapon she'd been training with out of the corner of her eye: her glaive. It stood in the corner, a wooden staff built of the finest hardwood with a wicked sharp curved blade on the end. She was as good at wielding the staff as she was at firing a bow and arrow. But it was something to defend herself with. Ciardis lunged for it and brought the weapon up so that the sharp end was pointed at her opponent. Standing with the glaive in her hands, her feet spread for traction and swift movement and her nightgown fluttering in the morning air, she didn't look like the greatest warrior. But it didn't matter so long as she came out of this alive.

"I'm not here to hurt you," Stephanie said with exasperation.

"Oh, well, then I guess I should put the glaive down." She wasn't stupid; the weapon didn't move an inch.

Sighing, Stephanie tossed the loaded crossbow on the bed and held her hands out by her sides.

"Better?"

"I'll ask you again: What in a demon's ass do you think you're doing?"

"Saving your neck."

Stephanie lunged towards Ciardis's bed and grabbed her loaded crossbow in a smooth movement. Turning toward Ciardis, she fired a bolt. Ciardis dropped to the floor, evading the shot but unfortunately putting herself at a disadvantage. The glaive had fallen. And the way her body lay facedown made it hard to use the staff for any sort of defense. As she pushed herself off of the floor, keeping an angry eye on Stephanie, she frowned at sudden wetness on her hand. Bringing her hand up to her face, she stared in horror at the red blood dripping down her fingers.

She wasn't wounded. But someone was.

Turning around, Ciardis saw a man lying on the floor. Face up, with a crossbolt sticking out of his chest.

Standing up and moving off the bed, Stephanie said with sarcasm, "You're welcome."

"What? Who?"

"One of the Duke of Cinnis's men," answered Stephanie as she came over and yanked her crossbolt out of his chest. "I don't think I have to tell you why."

Pale and shaky, Ciardis moved away from the body, laid the glaive down on the bed, and sat down.

"I've been doing this all wrong, haven't I?"

"If by 'all wrong' you mean making enemies, pushing away allies, and generally making a nuisance of yourself, then I'd say yes."

Ciardis grimaced. "I did what I had to do to save Sebastian's life."

"And endangered your own. Did you think that you were the only one who cared?"

"I was the only one who did anything when his powers were failing," countered Ciardis.

"We were working on that behind the scenes. You managed to turn a two-year investigation into the loss of the Prince's powers on its head in less than a week."

"I solved it in less than a week."

Stephanie put an impatient hand on her hip and glared.

"Who's 'we,' by the way?" asked Ciardis innocently.

The look Stephanie returned said she wasn't fooled. "That's not important right now."

"Really? I think it is."

"You know what is important?"

Ciardis stood. She was tired of being talked down to.

"Getting some straight answers out of you."

"No, getting this body out of here before someone sees him."

They both looked down at the dead man lying on the floor. Ciardis couldn't say she disagreed. A dead man would be one more thing she would have to answer for and with the way things were going she didn't have much faith in the Companions' Guild backing her against charges of murder from a Duke. All of this made her wonder why Stephanie was here though…surely the Guild hadn't sent her?

Stephanie sighed, "Look we don't have much time and I can't explain to the council that I'm here so we *have* to get rid of the body."

An hour later, they had him wrapped in a blanket and were busy hauling him through a tunnel that existed behind a secret door in Ciardis's room. The man was big, and carrying him was putting a strain on both women.

"Some stairs are coming up," said Stephanie as they wedged around a corner.

Ciardis gritted her teeth as she lifted his feet while Stephanie angled his upper body, taking most of the weight, as they went up the stairs. Luckily it was just a few steps, and then they were in a different tunnel.

"About five feet to the right there's a hole," Stephanie said.

"A hole large enough to drop a body?" Ciardis questioned.

"It's the trash chute that goes direct to the underground sewer, so yes."

As they knelt down and awkwardly shifted the body around to drop him in head first, Ciardis had to wonder what her life had come to. From laundress to Companions' Guild trainee to accomplice in a murder who couldn't talk about the murder in case the assassin's master wanted to take another shot at her. Meanwhile, Stephanie searched the dead man's vest. She was methodical, looking for anything that would link him to the duke. In his inner pocket she found just what she needed: a bronze crow pin. The duke's symbol, and worth its weight in gold.

"I have what I need to prove the duke ordered the man to kill you," Stephanie said.

"Why would he be carrying that?" said Ciardis.

"I suspect because he never thought you'd catch him."

"And the Duke? Once his man fails to return he'll find a way to pin this on me or send another assassin." Bitterly Ciardis spoke, "I'm not sure which would be preferable. Accussations of murder or another attempt."

"With this pin I can make sure the Duke knows that we know about him. He won't try again," Stephanie said cryptically.

"Fair enough, as long as I'm not indicted for this crime."

Stephanie nodded. She didn't want to be accused of a crime, either.

Together they pushed the man over the side.

As they walked back in silence through the tunnels, Ciardis thought of the past. For a long time the only life she had known was the vale—the day-to-day drudgery of being a laundress and the hope of marrying well. She almost felt as if she'd left that life too soon. She had come into the courts eager to succeed, eager to show that she belonged. Now she was dumping bodies in holes, ducking arrows and breaking up assassination plots. In many ways she was worse than those at the courts she had initially sought to emulate.

"Wake up, airhead," said Stephanie, "We're back."

And so they were. Opening the door into Ciardis's room, they walked in to silence. The room looked normal except for the glaive and crossbow resting on the bed. And the pool of blood on the marble floor.

"We need to clean up the blood," said Stephanie, looking around for cloth.

Ciardis was already on her way to the bathroom. "I've got it." She returned with a bucket filled with lemon water and sanitizer as well as some rags. Stooping down, she started wiping to get every drop of red.

*****

Sitting down on the bed, Stephanie watched as the young woman bent over the floor. Ciardis wasn't saying a word. Stephanie was wondering if she was in shock or perhaps planning. Either way, she hoped the pretty hair and the soft nightgown hid a young woman who could do more than speak and dance well.

The Shadow Council needed people who could do more, people with talents, people with the strength to make a difference, and those willing to sacrifice for the common good. Ciardis had shown that she had two of those three qualities. But her performance needed a lot more polishing.

"Where have you been?" said Ciardis, not looking up. The blood had already turned the bucket water red, though there were still spots to clean up. She didn't see Stephanie watching her as she finished cleaning off the crossbolt that Stephanie had removed from the dead man's chest with a handkerchief from Ciardis's nightstand.

"Away," the woman said. "Training."

"With whom?"

"You ask a lot of questions."

"And you evade all of my answers," said Ciardis pointedly.

She put the clean crossbolt back into the bow and primed it to fire. "Not unintentionally."

Ciardis dropped the last rag in the bucket and raised an irritated eyebrow."Look, you come in here criticizing the way I handle things—"

"And saved your life."

"And want me to do things your way," Ciardis continued without pause. "But you won't tell me what the way is or how you knew about the duke's man."

Standing up, Stephanie tossed her an irritated look. "The duke's man was obvious—the Duke of Cinnis hasn't been subtle in his loathing of you ever since you revealed that he cheated on his wife."

"Why does *everyone* focus on that?" Ciardis said, her temper rising, "He was trying to assassinate Sebastian, but does anyone mention that? No! It's always, 'Oh, that evil Ciardis, she exposed him in bed with another woman.'"

Stephanie snorted. "You've got a lot to learn. Scandal always trumps murder. The only thing better is if it's a scandalous murder."

Heading over to the door, Stephanie said, "Let's go; I've got something to show you."

Biting her tongue, Ciardis put away the cleaning supplies, changed her clothes, and put the glaive back in its corner. On her way past the nightstand, she grabbed a small dagger and a wrist sheath to hold it. With one last look at her bedroom, she followed Stephanie out. They left the palace through a side entrance and went across the bridge to the nobility's quarters.

It was the quarter that Stephanie had moved to after being inducted as a full Companion and receiving a Patron. As they walked through the tree-lined streets, Ciardis expected them to go into one of the beautiful mansions. But as they ducked in and out of side rows, cut across lawns, and finally ended up in the artisan's district, she had more concerns about where they were going than why.

"Where are you taking—"

Stephanie held up a silencing hand. She ducked behind another building into an alley filthier than the last. Ciardis had no choice but to follow. Not if she wanted answers. As they raced up the back stairs of a derelict building Ciardis caught glimpses of soldiers spreading out through a crowd in the market square. A man was giving them directions and groups were peeling off to go down different streets. They were looking for someone.

For me? she thought in a panic. *Do they know about the dead assassin? How could they know?*

Stephanie opened the door to a room. Well, "opened" was a nice way to put it; she had to kick in the door after the latch caught on something. "Damn piece of junk," she murmured as they went inside. Ciardis took in the dust, the cobwebs, and the mothballed sheets covering everything with distaste. It was an artist's studio long abandoned. Wood easels leaned on the walls and half-finished paintings covered in cobwebs stood in testament to an artist long gone. Ciardis hiked up her new sleeves to ensure none of the dirt got on the long, trailing fabric. There was nothing she could do about the bottom of her skirt except pray.

Closing the door and facing Ciardis, Stephanie asked, "What do you want to be, Ciardis?"

This sounded familiar. "A great Companion—"

Stephanie waved her hand. "No bullshit."

"I wish you'd stop interrupting me," Ciardis snapped.

"Look—"

"No," Ciardis said, standing up straight. Her eyes turned steely as she propped her hands firmly on her waist, trailing fabric forgotten in the heat of the moment. "I've had just about enough of this. I was nearly murdered this morning. I'm being targeted and I want to know how to fix it."

Stephanie waited a moment to see if her tirade had finished. "Fix it?" she said dryly while trailing a finger through dust that had been gathering on a cabinet top for at least a year.

"You can't fix it," Stephanie continued, "What you can do is *control* it…with help. The problem is your powers. You try to help Prince Sebastian and somehow your magical interference ends up spilling over to enhance more than you intended."

A knock interrupted their conversation, echoing in the room. It sounded like it was coming from behind the wall. Stephanie walked over and opened up a panel in the back of the room.

Out walked a young man with blue eyes, black hair, and a radiant smile.

"Took you long enough," he said jovially while dusting off his pants.

Stephanie rolled her eyes and examined her fingernails for dirt. She was studiously avoiding his gaze. There was something going there. Ciardis could feel it. The man cleared his throat, looked over at Ciardis, and introduced himself as Christian Somner.

"Well, Christian, are you in on this, too?" Ciardis said.

"In on what?" he said with a polite grin.

"This shadow organization that wants to make me not me."

Before Stephanie could interrupt, Christian said, "The Shadow Council doesn't want to *change* you; we want to mold you."

Ciardis grinned, triumphant; she had just gotten him to reveal the group. Stephanie slapped him on the back of the head. "You idiot! She wasn't supposed to know the name."

He looked over, miffed. "But she said…"

"I was fishing," Ciardis admitted smugly.

He rolled his eyes. "Well, now that you know the name. What do you truly know about what we are?"

"Nothing," she admitted.

"Exactly," he said with his own triumphant eye roll at Stephanie.

She didn't let go of the glare plastered on her face. "You started this. Why don't you go right on ahead and finish it?" Let him stick his foot in the stink. She wasn't going to be in trouble when the Shadow Council heard about it.

Ciardis eyed them both warily. She'd never heard of the Shadow Council. Who were they? What were their goals? Were they a threat to Sebastian or an ally? She knew that today she would find out something about them but the lingering question remained: would it be enough to trust them? To trust Stephanie? The woman had been an excellent fighter during her years as a Companion trainee, but the Companions' Guild didn't prepare you to kill someone or dispose of the body. And yet she'd done both without blinking an eye. Not to mention this weird and stealthy way she had about going through the city streets. What did she have to hide?

Besides Companions were skilled, but they weren't *that* skilled.

"The Shadow Council is an elite organization of mages created to protect the realm. We recruit the most talented individuals across the land for missions and assignments to ensure that the stability and peace of as well as the security of the empire is always assured," Christian explained.

Ciardis raised her eyebrows at the rather lofty goals of his Shadow Council.

"Isn't it the *gardis* and military's role to protect the realm? To ensure peace?"

"It is," he said. "But the *gardis*'s primary role as the guardians of the realm are to police the city and countryside to ensure general peace. And the military is fighting the battle in the North and has been for quite a while. In the end they cannot do so alone. We have the power and the strength to assure that things are dealt with quickly and secretly."

Secretly? Ciardis was uneasy about this. They sounded more like an assassin's league than a council.

"How would you go about that?"

He wagged his finger in rebuke. "I think that's enough about the Shadow Council for now. Just know that we are on your side."

"Don't lie to her," interjected Stephanie.

He corrected, "Or, rather, Stephanie and I are on your side."

With a frown, he continued, "There are some in the organization who would prefer you dead."

"I only just heard about the duke's plans to kill you this morning," said Stephanie. "The Council has known about it for days."

"Is that why you came?" questioned Ciardis. "You went against them to save me?"

Stephanie said softly, "No, sweetheart, we're here because they decided to give you a second chance. Change your ways, or next time the Shadow Council will be the one to put a contract out on you."

CHAPTER SEVEN

Stephanie was kind enough to escort Ciardis back to the gates of the Companions' Guild. As they parted ways and Stephanie began to walk away, she turned back and quickly reached into her pocket for something. Pushing it into Ciardis's hand, she said, "Flick this open if you need me in an emergency. And you *will* need me. Until then, see you around." And then she was gone.

Unfortunately, just because Ciardis had a death sentence hanging over her head didn't mean she could shirk her duties. Lady Vana and Lady Serena were waiting in the outer solar room for her. When she arrived, more bedraggled than usual, it raised eyebrows. But thankfully no one aside from Terris, Lady Vana's Companion trainee and Ciardis's best friend, was concerned enough to question her about it.

"What happened to you? Did you fall into a ditch again?" asked Terris with frank appraisal while their sponsors set up the afternoon's activities on the other side of the garden.

"No," said Ciardis, pouting. "That only happened *once*."

"And it's a day that no one will ever forget," Terris said with a giggle as she swung a friendly arm about her friend's shoulders. "The Incident," as Ciardis liked to refer to it in private, would have been hilarious and something they could have whispered over into the night—if it had happened to someone else.

She had been riding with the Imperial hunting party on a chilly day as they scouted for boar. The meat from the animal was a nice delicacy that would be on the dinner table that cold night. Riding with the party she'd been ambitious and hoped to be noticed for talents beyond her magical abilities – like her graceful riding skills. Which was why she'd chosen to ride sidesaddle. But even a slow pace turned out to be more difficult than she imagined.

Unfortunately that day she'd gotten excited, kneed her mare into a canter, and gone tumbling into the bushes in full view of the Imperial party. She had been humiliated and, what was worse, she'd spooked the mare so badly that it had refused to let her mount back up. She'd ridden double with a kind knight the whole way back to the palace, her face flaming.

Ciardis waved her hand impatiently to dispel the embarrassing memories.

"What are we in for today?" she said in exasperation.

The darker skinned girl shrugged. "I'm not sure, but Vana and Serena are excited about it."

Lady Vana called out, "Girls, girls, come over here!"

As they walked toward her, they saw that servants had set out a tall object with a cloth hanging over it. As they walked Ciardis noted with admiration that Terris had woven beautiful beads into her thick black hair which clanked together with her every step. Ciardis tried to ask her how her Patron Hunt was going, she knew that Terris had narrowed her choice down to two candidates, but didn't have enough time. When they reached the two sponsors, Vana pulled off the cloth to reveal a full-length mirror.

"Today we're going to work on presentation and illusion," said Serena. "You both will soon be presented to court and before the Companions Council as the Companion of an esteemed Patron. Terris, I've been told that you've yet to decide on your Patron. Is that correct?"

Terris nodded. "Yes, ma'am. I believe it's an important decision and I'd like to take some more time to get to know my suitors."

"Which is a perfectly acceptable choice for such a large commitment," Lady Serena said smoothly. In the meantime, Ciardis watched the conversation with boredom and dismay. She loved the pretty dresses and the pageantry of being a Companion, but surely there was more to it than this. And on top of that, she was being targeted for murder. Did Lady Serena even know? What was more, did she care?

No wonder my mother ran away, she thought bitterly, *I wonder what she thought of this? What was it like for her?* And then it was if a light clicked on in Ciardis's head – she was surprised that she hadn't thought of it sooner. She had had very few memories of her mother from before she became an orphan but that didn't mean others didn't. At the first ball of the Patron Hunt she had met someone who *had* known her mother. In fact that someone was still at court: the duke of Carne!

Ciardis tuned out of Lady Serena's instructions, which mostly pertained to how to use refracted light to subtlety enhance yourself. Perhaps knowing more about her mother and the history of the Weathervanes could help her control those powers.

"Lady Serena," said Ciardis politely once Serena had stopped speaking, "I was asked to call upon the duke of Carne's event this afternoon. If you would be so kind as to allow me use of the carriage for the evening?"

"Really?" said Lady Vana, "Terris was invited for afternoon salon, as well."

Ciardis had a moment of panic. Looking over at her protégé, Vana said, "My dear, you didn't tell me that Ciardis would be coming along."

Terris glanced over at Ciardis out of the corner of her eye, just in time to catch a look of panic cross her face. She knew that Ciardis hadn't been invited to come along. They would have been in their rooms planning their dresses for hours if she had. But she wasn't going to leave her friend hanging in the wind either.

"Oh yes, Milady," she quickly said, "An invitation was sent; it just arrived later than usual." She squeezed Ciardis's hand in reassurance. "We are both meant to attend."

"Very well," said Serena, oblivious.

Lady Vana pursed her mouth dissatisfied. She knew the two trainees were hiding something, she just had to hope that whatever it was couldn't be too bad. After all Terris was an excellent protégé and role model for other trainees. She'd never get into the sort of displays that Ciardis did.

"I expect a full report from you in the morning," Vana instructed.

"Yes, ma'am," they said together to their respective sponsors.

As they headed off to the outdoor salon, Ciardis took a moment to change. Certain times called for presentable clothes, and certain times called for drop-dead gorgeous attire. This was the latter. She was going to meet not only the duke of Carne and his family, but he also held court with the oldest noble families of Sandrin. They were sure to be in attendance. None would miss an afternoon soirée in the duke of Carne's salon if they could help it. He was known for his intellectual gatherings once a month, and they were always the talk of the city for weeks afterward.

He had been known to invite authors, artists, military officials, and even diplomats to speak on the various topics and host discussions surrounding their chosen fields. That being said, many of the attendees came to the soirée to see and be seen. Intellect was a fashionable accessory in the high courts, education being highly favored by the emperor, but you didn't have to be smart to be able to repeat intelligent phrases. As they swept down the long colonnade to the outdoor gazebo where the event was being held, Ciardis fought the distinct urge to tug on her dress—a bad habit she'd been trying to break since she arrived as a trainee at the Companions' Guild. It wasn't that the dress itched or was uncomfortable; merely that she was nervous and needed something to do with her hands.

As they approached, Ciardis could see that they were using the Swan Lake gazebo. Located near to the empress's rose garden, it was actually built on a mage-made island in the center of Swan Lake. A thankfully short line of people waited before the single crossing onto the island—a charmingly carved bridge that arced over the water. As Ciardis walked forward in her fine gossamer dress the color of struck silver, she took in the richly attired guests. The woman two people ahead of her wore a small tiara with inset rubies that matched her mage robes. In contrast to Ciardis's hair, which was pulled up into a messy ponytail with curls scattered haphazardly around her face and down her neck, most of the women wore elegant hairstyles including buns and elaborate twisted curls with hats. Ciardis had tried to improve her last minute hairdo, but there was only so much she could do with the bouncing curls in so little time.

As she eyed the full gazebo that she drifted ever closer to while in the line, Ciardis saw two distinct clusters of people alongside several smaller groups of individuals chatting. The first cluster surrounded the older Duke of Carne as he raised a wine glass and exuberantly talked about some topic. Another cluster surrounded another figure that Ciardis couldn't quite see, but the conversation looked just as animated.

When they reached the gazebo, Ciardis wanted to head straight to the corner where the duke held court. Terris convinced her otherwise, that she must mingle before approaching the host and his guest of honor. So talk she did. She tried polite chatter and was managing it for some time. Until the second cluster parted and she finally got a view of the central figure. It was none other than Sebastian. With surprise, Ciardis noted that she hadn't felt him when she'd entered the gazebo. It was large, but not *that* large, and she should have been able to sense his emotions from across the bridge in an area this small. Weird. Taking a glass of wine, she walked forward. Sebastian turned just slightly and caught her eye. She couldn't read his expression and couldn't feel his emotions. Did he want her there?

Halting with uncertainty, Ciardis prepared to quickly melt back into the surrounding crowd before the courtiers around the prince could see that she was approaching. And then he turned fully and held out a hand, palm up, with a welcoming smile. Gingerly, Ciardis walked forward and took his hand in hers. He tugged on her hand gently so she moved to his side, and he turned his smile back on the man in front of him.

"Lord Admiral Kanter, may I present Ciardis Weathervane, Companion Trainee."

As Sebastian spoke, she felt him in her mind, as well. Relief and worry colored his thoughts.

"*Ciardis, I've heard some disturbing news. My uncle, Duke of Cinnis, is not pleased with you.*"

"*Yes, I know*," she replied.

"*This isn't the time to be flippant. It could mean your life.*"

Before she could explain further, Lord Admiral Kanter smiled and spoke. "Miss Weathervane. It's a pleasure. I've heard that you were in our courts but am delighted to finally meet you in person."

He reached out a hand to take Ciardis's and she had no choice but to release Sebastian's and hold out her left hand as protocol demanded. Lord Admiral Kanter smoothly bent over and laid a chaste kiss on the back.

Smiling, he said, "Are you enjoying your time in the courts of Sandrin?"

"Very much so," she said politely, dipping into a curtsy.

They exchanged further courtesies, and she turned to see Prince Sebastian was now engaged in a heated conversation with a man who looked nothing like the surrounding nobility. Curious, she turned to move forward into that conversational sphere. But then she halted in surprise. She'd just caught a glimpse of the duke's guest of honor. In a floor-length silk gown the color of the forest, with bronzed hair and dazzling green eyes, she enchanted all of those who stood around her. Now that Ciardis was focused on her she could pick out the woman's laughter ringing out over the low conversations in the crowd.

Who is this beautiful woman?

When a gap opened in the crowd Ciardis decided that now was an appropriate time to approach the host and his guest of honor. Nervously, she appeared before the duke and curtsied.

His Grace stared at her surprise. "Ah, little Weathervane. I didn't realize you were coming."

Ciardis blushed crimson, but before she could say anything, his wife intervened. "Ciardis Weathervane?"

Peering over her ornamental glasses, she looked at the girl curtseying before her. As Ciardis nodded hesitantly in confirmation, the Duchess clasped her hands together in excitement.

"I've been quite interested in meeting you," she said, her blue eyes twinkling in delight under a halo of white hair. "It's been so long since a person with your esteemed talents has graced our courts."

"That is true," the duke said thoughtfully. "How are you adjusting to your new position, Mademoiselle Weathervane?"

"Fairly well," Ciardis said, lying through her teeth.

He snorted. "Yes, of course. Your mother was the same way. She wouldn't ask for any help until she was neck deep into whatever adventure she'd thrown herself into."

"She was adventurous, then?"

"Oh, so adventurous," exclaimed the duke's wife. "I was older than her by a few years, but the stories she told of her nights out, and the *escapades*. Oh my word."

Her voice dipped into a theatrical whisper. "You know your mother was very fond of…well, dare I say…*commoners.*"

Does this woman know where I come from? Probably just doesn't care.

"Now, Leah, there's nothing wrong with a dip on the other side now and then," said the duke.

"Oh?" said his wife, her tone noticeably cooler. From the look they exchanged, Ciardis got the feeling there might be some history between the duke and the 'other side.'

A short while later, Duchess Leah excused herself to grab a glass of wine, leaving Ciardis with the duke and his guest. The woman had been noticeably silent during their conversation, merely listening in.

Turning to her courteously, Ciardis asked, "It's a pleasure to meet you, Madame. From where do you hail?"

The woman raised a curious eyebrow and flicked an amused glance at the duke of Carne.

He chuckled.

"You do not recognize me?" the woman purred with a noticeably foreign accent. Ciardis glanced between the two of them, waiting to be let in on the joke. She noticed the woman's eyes then. They weren't a normal green – neither the color of a new spring meadow nor the dark of a deep forest. What's more – Ciardis could swear she had flecks of brown or maybe gold in them. A brilliant and captivating mixture.

"My dear," the duke said gently to his guest of honor, "Your people are so rarely guests in Sandrin. Many of the young have forgotten."

And then the woman's eyes flashed, and Ciardis could see the flecks of gold floating in the green. She sucked in a breath as the memory came back. The memory of speaking to the dragon on the storm-tossed ship deck just a few days ago. The woman's voice had the same accent that had echoed in Ciardis's head when she first met the Sahalian Ambassador.

Feeling foolish but having to know if she was right, Ciardis tentatively said, "Ambassador Sedaris?"

"Who else would I be?"

"Your mother had very much the same look of stupefied surprise on her face when she met her first dragon," said the duke of Carne.

"So Lady Weathervane, how are you enjoying the festivities?" the dragon ambassador questioned with a hint of a hiss on the tip of her tongue.

"It's very well received," said Ciardis politely as she brought her drink up to her mouth and hastily took a gulp. Very well received indeed, if you counted a dragon in human form. When had that happened? Could they all do that?

Ciardis felt a wave of vertigo sweep over her as the dragon standing before her spoke into her mind again. "*You are an interesting child. And yes, all of my race can transform.*"

Speaking aloud, the woman smiled and said, "I admire a curious mind. Particularly by one who flatters me," she said.

Ciardis could hear a tone of affection in the dragon's voice. No, affection wasn't it...it was more of a possessive overtone? The ambassador had only been here for a few days, really, but she had already turned the palace on its head. Ciardis had heard of the shouting matches between the ambassador and the emperor. She had heard that the ambassador had emerged victorious in them all. Drowning out the human courtiers in her anger and contempt with her voice alone. Until now, Ciardis had assumed it had been the dragon roaring that had cowed the courtiers.

Now, as she looked into the golden-flecked green eyes of the woman standing before her, she had to wonder if it was dragon in human form that had cowed the courtiers.

"Of course it was," said the woman smugly. "I am Sedaris. I don't need my birth form to cow you mere mortals."

She felt the weirdest sensations when speaking with the woman. It was like being connected to Sebastian but more intense. It was if she was *falling* into the dragon's feelings. She could feel the vast depths of her pride in being a dragon, her disgust with the overpowering smell of the human perfumes around her, and a small core inside of her that was filled with worry.

"What?" said Ciardis, feeling for that core, trying to navigate through the thick layers of memories slowly consuming her vision. If she could just see what made the dragon so upset, perhaps she could help Prince Heir Sebastian and get the people in the forest some help.

The dragon gave her gentle push out of her mind. Gentle for a dragon. Harsh for a human. Ciardis was pushed back into her body so abruptly that she stumbled and would have fallen if it weren't for the duke's quick arm out to catch her.

"My dear, are you well?" he questioned solicitously.

As he leaned over her he tightened his grip on her arm as he looked into her eyes. His eyes sharpened, and just for a moment, she saw a flash of surprise, perhaps even fear. "Of course I am." His lips tightened into a thin line. He visibly got a hold of himself and made sure to steady her with a solicitous hand on her back.

The brittle smile on his face didn't escape Ciardis's notice. She flashed back to the dragon's overwhelming mental presence – it had been as if she had been drowning in the mind and magic of Ambassador Sedaris. Perhaps the Duke had felt that?

"*We will speak later,* sarin," was the last thing Ciardis heard from the dragon.

As the duke watched the dragon glide away, he slowly walked Ciardis over to a nearby bench to rest. His eyes opened wide in surprise and worry as he heard the Ambassador call Ciardis "*Sarin*" while she walked away.

"I'm too old for this nonsense," whispered the duke as he helped Ciardis settle down on the couch. He put a sight and sound shield up around them just in case.

He looked straight in her eyes. The serious expression on his face told Ciardis she wasn't going to like what he was going to say.

"What nonsense?" she questioned groggily as she took a sip of wine, hoping to shock herself out of whatever this was.

The duke grabbed his own glass and knocked back a shot of whiskey before he answered her question.

"A *sarin*. She called you her *sarin*," he said, "Being a *sarin*, in essence a representative and companion to the dragon, would turn the Imperial courts on its head. This would be a problem if any human became a *sarin* – they were generally troublesome figures even if powerless. But a Weathervane? It would be catastrophic."

"And?"

"Do you know what a *sarin* is? It's Sahalian for 'companion,' but not just any companion. A bond mate and representative of the dragon."

"I'm sure you're mistaken," Ciardis said politely. "We just met. Why would she pick me for such an important position?"

"It's not a position so much as a lifestyle," he said as he took a second shot of whiskey.

He looked over his shoulder and back down to her, "There's a chance the dragon will forget. It's best that you do as well. Nothing good can come of this."

Ciardis lifted a chin and glared, "I don't even know what *this* is. But as long as it's not going to bite me in the ass I will happily forget about it."

Staring into his empty glass miserably, the Duke looked like he wanted to get drunk at his own party.

"You know your mother—Lily—was always getting into trouble. Just like you. But when she met a dragon and he tried to claim her even she knew to run," the duke said in a mumble.

"Wait, sir," Ciardis said while grasping his forearm urgently. "You said my *mother* was running from a dragon? When?"

He looked at her and said with a barely concealed bitterness. "Why child…right before she disappeared."

Ciardis stared at him, uncomprehending, for a moment. It upset her that her mother had been running from something. Running from a dragon even more so.

"Well?" said the slightly drunk duke. Ciardis didn't reply. She was weighing his words. He might have been a tad drunk, but she heard truth in them. The question was what to do about it. The dragon calling her a *sarin* could be pushed off as a mistake, but her mother's disappearance was different. She needed to know more. Why had she truly left the courts?

"I want to know more," said Ciardis quietly. "I want to know everything about why my mother left court and I want to know now."

"Then you're talking with the wrong person," said the Duchess of Carne. She had quietly entered her husband's protective shield and stood looking down at Ciardis with a sad smile on her face.

"Come with me, Ciardis Weathervane," she said. "It's time someone told you the truth."

With a backwards glance as she followed the duchess, Ciardis caught sight of Prince Sebastian as he was preparing to leave. She'd have to catch him up on the events pertaining to the Duke of Cinnis another day.

CHAPTER EIGHT

Miles away on the road to the home of the *kith*, the Weather Mage was riding at a breakneck pace on a stallion built for long distances. Beside him, astride a horse of similar merit, rode the person the Weather Mage internally referred to as "the Shadow Mage." Externally whenever he addressed the mage, he called him "Master." He did it reluctantly. But he had learned swiftly in the few days they'd been together that the man would tolerate nothing less than absolute subservience.

The Weather Mage was a man of pride as most mages were. The Shadow Mage had entrapped his mind with his magic and could control his actions with just a surge of his magic. It was humiliating and frustrating - rankling his pride like a dog with too many fleas. He constantly itched to throw off the yoke that hobbled him and had finally sought to revolt against the Shadow Mage one night. It had not gone well. As punishment the Shadow Mage had his dark, ink-like creatures carve into the skin of the Weather Mage's back with claws made of shadows. They left his flesh torn and in bloody ruins, causing rivulets of blood to run down and his poor back to feel like it was on fire. After that he'd never talked back—not aloud. He couldn't help his thoughts, and he suspected the Shadow Mage could hear them. But he never responded to them.

They rode at a hard pace toward the only destination that this road led directly to: the Forest of Ameles. With a shudder the Weather Mage thought of what lay there: inhuman creatures with the powers of mages, creatures that could talk and were sentient. It made him ill to think about it. He had no hope of escaping once there. The creatures would eat him alive if he left the Shadow Mage's side; after all, every mage knew the number one rule when entering the Forest of Ameles. Safety in numbers.

Sighing, he bit his lip and hoped he could escape before the shadows inside of him erupted again. They were always there. A dark presence that invaded his magic and his mind. Occasionally the Shadow Mage would call upon the shadows to overtake his mind. Once he'd even ordered him asleep when he'd been preparing a spell. He had begged the man not to. When he slept, he was surrounded by the darkness of the shadows in his dreams. He did his best to stay awake at all times now, which was why his eyes still looked bloodshot and his appearance unkempt. Aside from the ungodly hours the Shadow Mage kept, the Weather Mage was afraid—he was afraid to fall asleep, fearing his dreams and fearing what he'd wake up to.

When they were twenty miles from the forest, the Shadow Mage pulled their horses to a stop at a fork in the road. The straight path would get them to the forest in less than a day. The branch off the road led somewhere else. Practically trembling with exhaustion, the Weather Mage lifted his head, pushing back dank hair from his forehead to read the sign on the road ahead. Carved into wood with an arrow pointing east were the words, "*Borden Village – ten miles.*"

The Shadow Mage threw back the hood that shrouded his face from view. He turned to the Weather Mage with cold glee in his eyes. "It's time to go home, Marcus." Those whispered words sent dread down the Weather Mage's spine.

The Weather Mage licked his dried and cracked lips while apprehension filled him.

"To the Ameles Forest?" he choked out from a parched throat. They'd been riding for hours, and before that the Shadow Mage had kept him locked in a cellar with little substanance.

The Shadow Mage looked to the forest with an odd smile on this face.

"Things have already been set in motion there. Tonight we go to Borden."

*****

Hours later they reached the village of Borden and dusk had already fallen. The village looked like an ordinary one, with fewer than five hundred souls judging by the number of homes he could see. As children scampered under their horses and mothers shooed them home with admonishments, the Weather Mage felt like shouting, "Go! Run, save your families!" But he knew if he did anything of the sort, he would be worse off in the end. He wouldn't have minded so much if the Shadow Mage killed him in retribution. But in the time spent with the silent, shrouded figure, he had realized that this wasn't that type of man. A person who would make it a clean death. The Shadow Mage would torture the Weather Mage first and do it without a shred of regret.

And then the big butcher, his homespun apron of patches and canvas splotched with blood, spotted them. Heaving a big cleaver back to rest on his shoulder, he came out of his small, fly-covered shop.

"Well, I'll be," shouted the big butcher. "It's you. Timmoris! You little scamp. Where ya been?"

Confused, the Weather Mage looked around. If he didn't know any better, he'd think the butcher was referring to the Shadow Mage in such a congenial manner. As he stared, the Weather Mage noted with apprehension that the shadows on the underside of the buildings, in the shade of trees, and even behind people were moving independently. But none of the villagers seem to notice. Or if they did, they were attributing it to the clouds moving swiftly overhead.

The Weather Mage got down from his horse with a brittle smile.

The butcher let out a robust laugh as he slapped the Shadow Mage on the shoulder, "I knew you'd be back. Couldn't stray too far from home. Not like your brother, the adventurer. No, not you."

The man was practically crowing. The Weather Mage realized, in disbelief, that he was *mocking* the Shadow Mage.

"It's certainly a pleasure to be back," said the Shadow Mage quietly.

The only sign that he was upset was the moving shadows that had yet to distance themselves too far from their normal habitats and his glittering eyes.

"Well," said the butcher, perhaps realizing he'd gone too far, "your home is gone. We razed it to plant land for the cattlefeed."

Or perhaps not. The Shadow Mage's hand gripped into a tight fist that was noticeable to all passing. A woman stepped forward. "Now, now, Glendon. You know this was neither the time nor the place to say all that."

"He was bound to find out, trying to find a place to lay his head," protested the butcher.

She rolled her eyes and snapped her rag at him. "Off with you."

Putting a motherly hand on Timmoris's shoulder, she said, "Timmoris, you and your friend can sleep at my inn tonight. We can talk about the land in the morning."

"Of course," said the Shadow Mage in an even tone.

Soon enough, two boys ran up to take their horses and they were installed in a small room with two cots, a basin with hot water, and a large tray filled with soup and bread. The Weather Mage watched the Shadow Mage carefully as he paced around the room. He was waiting for the explosion of darkness and wrath. Eventually he took the offered food and washed up after it was clear that the Shadow Mage wouldn't speak.

The Shadow Mage turned back to him from where he was contemplating the dirt on the floor with a distasteful expression. "You should see your face. The fear, the trepidation. It's there like lines written into your skin."

The Weather Mage said nothing. What was there to say?

"You know," the Shadow Mage said, considering, "they've always treated me this way. Even when my brother was here—*especially* when my brother was here. As something to pity."

Then he smiled in satisfaction. "Well, no more."

"What do you mean, Master?" he finally replied.

"Sleep," the Shadow Mage said soothingly, "I'll need you at peak strength for the morning."

It sounded like a request, but with the push of his shadow magic, the Shadow Mage commanded it and the Weather Mage fell screaming into the darkness of his dreams. In the meantime, the Shadow Mage got to work as night fell and the lights in the village winked on one by one. He ordered his shadows to prepare the pyre.

*****

The next morning, the Weather Mage woke to the sound of a young girl's scream. He scrambled up from where he lay on the floor. The Shadow Mage hadn't bothered to make sure he was lying on the cot when he'd commanded him to sleep. Groaning he tried to ignore the soreness that came from laying on a hard, wooden floor all night. Without pause he went for the door to get outside. It was locked from the other side. Frustrated he banged on the door, "Open this door! I'm a Mage of the Emperor."

Suddenly one of the people running by stopped in the hallway with a jangle of metal. "You're out of luck mate. No one can open the door but the person with the key and that would be the other man you're with." The Weather Mage cursed and backed away. The door was solid oak – there was no way he was going through it. Turning around he looked for another way out of the room and spotted the small, dirty window.

"That'll do," said the Weather Mage. He grabbed a stool, stood on it and proceeded to squeeze his way out of the small frame after pushing the window pane out in the open air. Luckily they weren't very far up from the ground. He called up his winds and dropped out of the window. The winds caught him in a soft landing on the ground behind the inn. For a moment he hesitated. He was free. No one knew he'd escaped. He could get away. But then the screaming started again and he couldn't run away.

Looking around he spotted an alley going back towards the front of the inn. Hustling between the leaning walls of the homes surrounding the alley, he ignored the shit on the ground and made his way to the main road. Once there he paused to get his bearings. He didn't see anything strange at first look.

Across the way a mother stood over a young girl while holding her firmly by the shoulders.

He could hear the mother saying, "Hush Beth! I told you not to listen to your brother's tales again."

The mother looked up at the Shadow Mage with the embarrassed look of a parent, "Forgive her, Sir. Her brother has been spinning long tales of the Necromancer again." Giving her little girl a little shake she said tightly, "Isn't that right Beth?"

The girl refused to look at the Shadow Mage. She turned to bury her head in her mother's skirts but then she spotted him. The Weather Mage gave her what he thought was a reassuring smile as he said, "Now lass. What could be amiss? You've seen the Necromancer now?"

He was joking. She wasn't. With a shaky finger and a tear tracked face she pointed at the Shadow Mage's shadow. It was moving and walking around while the man stood still. The Weather Mage gulped and looked at his riding companion and jailer. Her mother tried to hush Beth again but this time she saw what had made the little girl scream. She clasped her hand to her face to halt her own scream as she, too, saw the moving shadow.

The butcher, whom the Weather Mage was beginning to see was never idle, said, "What's going on here?" He had walked out of his shop with nothing but a pair of pants on. He looked like a battle-hardened warrior with skin gleaming in the morning as sweat and blood trickled down his muscled abdomen from a pig that he'd recently skinned. A man who could tear the Shadow Mage into pieces at the slightest provocation.

Grimacing when he saw who it was, the butcher said, "Timmoris, you and your weird childhood tricks. They've no place here. You're a *man* now, as much as anyone like you could be."

He looked over his shoulder at the gathered village men with a grin. They laughed in response. The Shadow Mage stood unmoving, still as a statue in the middle of the road.

"Now, get your dark creature away from the woman and apologize to the girl," the butcher said with authority in his voice. As the little girl backed into her mother's leg and the mother denied that an apology was needed, desperate just to go home, the butcher swaggered forward.

"Timmoris, don't go all silent on me. We can't have you scaring children, now," the butcher said as he stepped in front of the Shadow Mage. With a smirk on his face he continued to taunt the Shadow Mage openly. Baiting him.

"Do we need to go somewhere, Timmy?" the butcher said in a whisper for Timmoris's ears alone. "Are you going to wet yourself again?"

The Weather Mage watched in sick fascination. The Shadow Mage wasn't like other mages. As far as he could tell, his magic levels didn't spike when he was angry and his powers didn't get away from him when he was threatened. A possible reason why these villagers didn't know he was a mage.

The Shadow Mage lifted his head up from where he'd been staring at the ground with a deep intensity. Whatever was in his eyes had the mother pick up her daughter and hurry quickly from the village square. Fear does that. The stupid butcher didn't notice, and in the next second the shadows had converged. The first one went directly for the butcher. It was the Shadow Mage's own shadow, and it molded the hand of its human shape into a spear. The butcher never knew it was behind him. It thrust its dark spear into his back and through his heart, and the butcher arched back in surprise.

He was dead in an instant, but in the moment just before the light left his eyes, the true Timmoris was standing before him. As the villagers ran away screaming, many were attacked by the shadows and hacked to pieces. Those were the lucky ones. The Shadow Mage continued killing indiscriminately, ordering his shadow legion to kill and dispose of the bodies into the large funeral pyre of stacked logs in the village center.

The Weather Mage watched silently as raging men, defiant women, and crying children fell under the mage's advance until it stopped. Proudly, the Shadow Mage strode around in front of his new creation. On top of the stacked wood with the hacked limbs of victims blood dripped down in the harsh sunlight. The Weather Mage fought to keep his food in his stomach and turned away in the disgust.

"Now, now, my pet," said the Shadow Mage, seeing the Weather Mage turn away. "That was only the beginning."

The Weather Mage flinched, wondering what could possibly be worse. And then the shadows started converging. Each one pushing a human in front of them, all of the remaining villagers who had hidden wherever they could. There weren't many. The Weather Mage heard screams as they were dragged from their hiding places in lofts, cellars, behind buildings, and the surrounding fields. Finally they stood in a huddled mass before the dripping, unlit pyre.

The innkeeper from the night before was among them. Her face was streaked with blood, her hair disheveled, and she had two young children clinging to her skirts.

Fear must have consumed her, and yet she didn't hesitate to step forward with her chin proudly raised. She would not beg.

The Shadow Mage watched her walk toward him impassively.

"You've done something so horrible, child," she said, her voice dipping in pain. "How could you destroy your home? Your community?"

"This was never my home."

He turned away from her and began to count off how many villagers stood before him.

"Ninety-five," he said.

Looking back at the older woman, he continued, "Do you remember how many lashes I got for stealing that bread? How many days I was locked in that dank hole in the ground while the butcher boys stood over the grate at the top and pissed down on me?"

The carpenter stepped forward, dragging his leg. "I remember, Timmoris." If he hoped for leniency the Weather Mage knew he looked at the wrong person.

Before he could continue, the innkeeper inserted, "We were wrong for that. So harsh a punishment for a young boy, but we had to set an example. You understand? An example for all the boys left behind without parents or guardians during the war. We could not just let you run wild."

"How many?"

With a nervous and miserable glance at the innkeeper, the carpenter spoke, "Ten lashes and twenty-four days in the hole for what you stole."

"Yes, for *one* loaf of bread."

"An example had to be set."

"An example?" he said, laughing cruelly. "I was always the example for failure in this town. Never good enough to have a family take me in, never good enough for my brother, never good enough to go to war."

And then he stopped laughing. "Thirty-four. It looks like thirty-four is all I need."

"Fire Mage, come forward," commanded the Shadow Mage. And another man who the Weather Mage hadn't seen before appeared from the shadows as if transported there. With a sweep of his hand, the Shadow Man ordered his creatures to finish off those not needed.

The shadow creatures stepped forward and the people were culled until only twenty-four men and ten women and children still stood. The innkeeper had been the last to die—she did so with dignity. Silent to the end, with eyes that judged the Shadow Mage for his crimes even in death.

He turned to the Weather Mage with Fire Mage by his side "Now, my pets. It's your turn. Let's see what you can do."

"No, no!" shouted the Weather Mage. "I'll have no part in this."

The Fire Mage stood silently as if all life and resistance had been drained from his body.

"You'll do as I say," shouted the Shadow Mage. Reaching out with his power, he swamped the Weather Mage's mind in living darkness, taking over every ounce of his control and inserting his own will.

Cringing as he felt the torment of the villagers wash over him in their agony, the Weather Mage watched while locked within his own mind as he called forth thunder and lightning side by side with the fire-calling mage. There was nothing he could do to stop it. To stop the torture and the pain. So much torment that they were sure to pass to the afterlife with the pain locked in their soul.

No one deserves to die like this.

And when the Weather Mage finally gave up trying to resist and sought to retreat into his thoughts—to block out the sounds of screams throughout the air, the smell of burnt skin and the taste of charred flesh on his tongue—he found that he couldn't. He was forced into his experiences just as much as he was locked into his mind.

No wonder the Fire Mage had looked like the living dead if this is what he had experienced day after day under the Shadow Mage's control. It was enough to shatter a person's soul.

Before the day had ended, ten bodies lay on the ground in an orderly fashion with piles of ash just behind them. And the Weather Mage lay sobbing on the ground at the acts he had committed.

"Very good, my pets," said the Shadow Mage soothingly, "I have one more task for you though."

"We must build a signal. A signal to all of Algardis that they will never forget. But it must be special and it must be timed for effect," he said with a cruel smile while reaching down to tilt up the head of the crouched Weather Mage.

Marcus looked up into the face of his tormenter with fury bright in his eyes as he clenched an angry fist.

What could he possibly want now? I've already tortured for him.

"What I want is an ever-burning fire, an inferno that will not die," he said softly.

"I can't do that," the Weather Man said honestly, turning to look over at the convalescent Fire Mage.

"Oh, I know," the Shadow Mage said with glee, "but here is what you *can* do."

When he finished his instructions, the Weather Mage closed his eyes.

CHAPTER NINE

As they left the party and walked into the court gardens side-by-side, Ciardis couldn't let the peace of the moment slip into her consciousness. Oh, she wanted to, how she wanted to, but all she could think of was the woman named Lily and what could have possibly forced her to give up a life as magnificent as the one Ciardis had now—death threats aside.

"Why would she leave?" Ciardis questioned with fierceness. "My mother had to be forced to. She *had* to be."

The duchess chuckled. "My dear, your innocence—your *love*—of the Imperial courts is charming. The glamour, the politics, the history – it is all glamorous. You're too young to see it, but the life here is a monstrous beast that will consume you. You think you have troubles now? They've only just begun."

She paused and looked over at Ciardis. Brushing an errant curl back from the girl's face, she gave her a smile that a mother would give her daughter. It was a sad smile, the kind of smile that said hope for the best, but expect the worst.

"Your mother had been planning to leave for years," she said. "I should know—I was going to go with her."

Ciardis stared at her, disbelieving. Recognizing her disbelief, the duchess said, "Let me tell you a story. A story of life in the courts under Emperor Cymus. The late emperor was a large man. Robust in his taste for life and his taste for women. His courts were magical for a young noblewoman. Parties every night until dawn, extravagant dinners for every occasion, and salons for just about everything you could think of."

She sounded wistful. Ciardis couldn't blame her; it sounded wonderful.

"Court then was very different than it is now. Emperor Cymus ruled with a lax hand; nobles did as they pleased, mages knew no restrictions, and the court treasury was like the emperor's treasure chest. He would gift loyal friends with gold and jewels in the morning and hand them titles at night. It was because of this lax hand that Algardis is in so much debt now, and I think the reason for the current emperor's tight-fisted rule. But that is not of concern right now."

She cleared her throat and continued, "Your mother, Lily, was born into this world of extravagance. She was the last, at that time, of a long line of powerful Weathervanes with a talent that made others green with envy. Her beauty, her power, and her grace made her the first on the list for every invitation and soirée. When she officially debuted at the courts, she was requested and accepted a position as lady-in-waiting to the empress, the current emperor's mother. I, at the time, was Mistress of the Robes for her household and in charge of all of the ladies-in-waiting. Your mother was a vivacious young woman. We became inseparable.

Even with our fifteen-year age difference we understood each other in many ways."

Looking off toward Swan Lake, she said, "And in many ways, we didn't." The salon was still in full swing and laughter rang out over the lake.

"What do you mean?" prodded Ciardis in an attempt to get the Duchess of Carne back on track.

"Your mother wanted to leave the Imperial courts from the moment she got there. To put it simply, she detested it: the fakeness, the frivolity, the life of a spoiled noblewoman. She wanted adventure. At least, that's what she always said," the duchess continued with a chuckle. "Make no mistake, she was a consummate actress, charming all of those who met her and making them feel as if they were the only person in the world when she spoke to them. She made sure her feelings about her life here were well hidden, and only discussed them in private under the cover of darkness."

"Would it have been so bad?" Ciardis whispered. "If people had known? And she had left for a season or two?"

"Oh, my dear," said the woman beside her as she resumed walking. "You sound so young. You *are* young. But Lily was your age when she joined the courts, and she knew well what the dangers were. But growing up in the Courts of Sandrin, she had to."

Firmly, she continued, "You have to understand two things. The first is this: Your mother would have never done anything to disgrace her family name and leaving court, particularly the service of an empress, would have done that. And second: Emperor Cymus was a lax, generous, and bountiful ruler. But he was also spiteful, selfish, and ornery. He didn't like it when his courtiers strayed too far from his side—what he liked to call his 'orbit.' If all of the noblemen and mages were present in court, drunk and satiated, it was easier for him to keep an eye on them. To make sure they weren't plotting against him."

She pursed her mouth in distaste. "I can't say his plan didn't work. Throughout his rule, he never had any trouble with uprisings or conflict. Not from the wealthy, anyway."

"Soon, like everyone else, he began to fall in love with your mother," she said with a heavy sigh. "And that's when her troubles began."

"Your husband mentioned something about another dragon," Ciardis said.

The duchess gave her rueful smile. "I had not forgotten, child."

"But the dragon—the dragon I know less about. He came to court and set it a flurry with his surprise visit. He was beautiful, the kind of elegance you see only in stone statues. A living tribute to the gods. His eyes were different than the Ambassador's but brilliant in their own right. A vibrant golden with green specks."

Pausing, she asked thoughtfully, "Do you know what those specks mean? What their eyes say?"

She didn't wait for a response. "All male Sahalians have those eyes. When born, their eyes are a warm brown color. They slowly lighten as they grow into the golden hue. Sometime during childhood is when the green specks appear. *He* told me that."

No need to ask who "he" was. From the tone of her voice, Ciardis could assume it was the beautiful male dragon.

"But he also mentioned a lot of other things," said the duchess with a shudder. "Things I will not mention here. But know this: it is rare for a Sahalian dragon to consider humans as their equal. Then and now they are our allies. But you can hear it in their voice, see it in their stride; they consider us beneath them. Mere playthings for their entertainment, and that was what the dragon considered your mother: an entertaining diversion."

Her tone dipped into a coldness that Ciardis didn't think the duchess was capable of, "But your mother didn't want to play. Unlike the courtiers who constantly surrounded her, the dragon could read her emotions, and, she told me, hear her thoughts, as well. As much as she tried to avoid him, he still knew when he saw her that she was lying, and he didn't like it. Not one bit. He couldn't see why she wouldn't worship him as all the others did, and he poked at her, trying to push down the barriers she was erecting before him. That same season, she disappeared."

"Well, what happened?" Ciardis said.

"All I know is one night she came into my room in tears," the duchess said. "She wouldn't wait the three months until the ship we had planned to run away on was coming to port. She was leaving that very night and nothing could stop her. I couldn't leave so soon…I wouldn't leave so soon. She disappeared that night, and I never heard a word from her after that."

Ciardis sighed. Another dead end.

"But," said the duchess, "before she left, she gave me something to give to a minstrel who played in a local tavern frequented by the wealthy noblemen of the court."

"What was it?" said Ciardis breathlessly.

The duchess looked at the young girl standing before her. Eager and smart but naive. The Duchess had a look on her face as if she was seeing a vision – a vision of the past.

"You know you look very much like her and you're so much less cautious. You should be wary," she said while staring at Ciardis, "But this is what you seek." She raised her right hand and called in her magic. In her palm appeared an oval locket. It was simple and carved of wood.

Ciardis took it tentatively from the duchess's outstretched hand. The outside was glossy and she could see hinges on the side with a straight line running along the curve of the oval. She tried to open it, but it wouldn't budge.

"Who was this minstrel?"

"A friend—a friend of your mother's who still plays at The Blue Duck Inn on the east bank of the Sandrin River," the duchess replied. "Every night," she added significantly.

"Thank you," said Ciardis.

As the girl walked away cupping the locket in her hands, the duchess thought, *Don't thank me yet, child. I've given you more questions than answers. More mysteries than resolutions. If only you could see that.*

Ciardis quickly went to her room and changed into something more reasonable. Head rushing with hope she grabbed the first tuk-tuk she could find and instructed them to take her to The Blue Duck Inn. It was dusk now and night was falling. The minstrel who played there should be preparing for his performance.

As she walked in the door, the old dark wood creaked between her feet and rafters soaring above her head. What looked like a three-story building from the outside was actually just one large room. On the main floor were chairs and round tables strategically placed to face the large main stage. Along the wall was a huge bar that curved the length of the room, with three bartenders strategically placed to take orders.

The room was empty except for a few early drinkers. The bartenders knew most of the goings-on of the patrons and performers at any inn. Picking the one currently shining mugs and glasses, Ciardis walked over and ordered a cup of hot cider.

"Will the minstrel be playing tonight?" she asked as she handed over two shillings and took her mug.

"Aye, every night. He's up first on stage," said the man with the final wipe of a glass. "You should stick around for the jugglers, though," he continued, tossing the towel onto his shoulder. "Their fire act can't be beat. Not another one in town."

"I'll be sure to," said Ciardis while walking away.

She took a seat off to the side. Close enough to the stage to take in the details of the minstrel, but far enough into a dark corner to not catch his eye. She wanted to see him first, to know more about him before they met. And they would meet tonight; she had no doubt about that as she fingered the locket in her pouch.

Before an hour had passed, the inn and tables had filled with patrons. Ciardis hoped Terris wasn't too worried about her. She'd have to fill her in later on why she'd left the gathering earlier than planned.

And then he came on stage. With curly black hair and a small goatee, he looked like many of the minstrels who'd come to Vaneis in traveling caravans. They'd played in the village inns, accepting coins and a free meal for their performances. As many of them did, he carried a lute, a small string instrument with a melodious overtone. But as he began to sing, Ciardis saw why he performed every night, regardless of the fire-tossing jugglers. His voice enraptured the crowd and his ballads brought back memories of times of old.

As he bowed and came offstage, Ciardis maneuvered herself so that she could intercept him on his way to the bar. Coming up to him, she said, "Good sir, may we speak just for a minute?"

"Now for pretty young woman such as yourself, I have quite a few minutes," he said with a lecherous wink.

Ciardis decided to ignore the lecherous look and speak plainly.

"You knew my mother," she said simply.

"Your mother, aye?" he said, continuing on to the bar, "I've known a lot of women." Taking a glass of water from the bartender, he said, "And a lot of women have known me. What's it to you? You my daughter?"

Ciardis grimaced. "I hope not. But I was hoping you could help with some information on her."

He snorted. "Well, who was this mysterious woman?"

"Lily," Ciardis said quietly. "Lily Weathervane."

He turned as pale as a sheet. "You…you cannot be here." With urgency in his tone, he turned his full attention to her. "Be gone."

"I can't," Ciardis said. "I need to know what you know."

Ignoring her protests, he opened his instrument case and reached in for a cloak. "Take this and go. I'll be in my room, number five, in a half hour. Meet me there."

"I'm not meeting you there," she protested. "Tell me now."

"If you truly want to know about your mother," he said grimly, "you'll do it."

Then he walked back onstage without another word.

CHAPTER TEN

Ciardis had no choice. She was *not* going to miss a chance to get answers from him. But she wasn't foolish enough to meet him alone. She stepped outside The Blue Duck Inn and took out the mechanical lighter Stephanie had given her. Holding it down by her waist and shielding it from view, she flicked it open and closed it, hoping the girl would come.

Ten minutes passed, then twenty, and suddenly a cloaked figure emerged out of the evening fog. Walking toward Ciardis with a confident stride, the figure pulled the hood back and Ciardis could see her clearly. It was Stephanie in tight pants, a white shirt, and, oddly enough, with a sword at her waist.

"Thank you for coming," said Ciardis.

"Let's go inside," said Stephanie, looking around the street quickly.

Going in, the two grabbed the nearest table. A waitress came up immediately and asked for their order. As she was preparing to go back to the kitchens, the waitress snapped her fingers at

Stephanie to get her attention, "No hidden magical weapons. Tavern rule."

Stephanie didn't comment. She simply took out the dagger out of her sleeve and placed it on the table. The waitress didn't seem interested in making any further fuss and left to get their order ready.

Stephanie traced the edge of the blade with her fingertip. "Why'd you call me here?"

"There's a minstrel here. He knows my—"

"A minstrel? Is he trying to kill you?"

Ciardis lifted a brow. "Well, no, not precisely."

Stephanie sheathed her dagger and got up to leave.

Rising quickly, Ciardis latched a desperate hand on her sleeve. "Wait!"

Stephanie looked pointedly at her grip and Ciardis released her quickly—she might lose her hand otherwise.

"I said to only contact me in an emergency," she hissed, "What about 'emergency' don't you understand?"

"He knew the last Weathervane. Apparently pretty well," Ciardis said.

"You mean your mother?"

Ciardis nodded, "And the duchess of Carne said I should see him."

At the mention of Leah of Carne's name, Stephanie paused. The duchess was one of the most influential women of court and one of the most diabolical. She had her fingers in every pie and was crafty like a spider sitting in a web. Stephanie had yet to figure out if she had been behind Princess Heir Marissa's scheming, but she suspected so, and so did the Shadow Council. The Princess Heir and Leah were close friends as the Princess

Heir grew up and had bonded while the duchess was in the empress's service. Would that woman be after Ciardis Weathervane? Not unless she had something she wanted.

"All right," Stephanie said reluctantly. "What's his name?"

"I don't know," said Ciardis, blushing red in embarrassment.

Stephanie didn't bother commenting.

"But he's agreed to meet us in his room in five minutes," Ciardis rushed to add.

"Then let's go."

When they reached the ministrel's room he was already there, waiting with the door cracked. As Stephanie pushed open the door with a cautious hand he looked up from where he was re-stringing his lute on his bed. He stood up slowly and set the lute in his case.

"So you are the one they call the new Weathervane?" he said, "Or at least that is what you'd have me suspect. And who is your partner?"

He looked toward Stephanie, whose hand loitered dangerously close to the sword pommel at her waist.

"Doesn't matter. Just think of me as an interested party."

He raised his eyebrows and looked back at Ciardis.

"I could ask you the same question," she said.

"It's you who has sought me out."

"There is only one way to prove I am a Weathervane."

"A way that would not work on me. You can't enhance something that I don't have. I believe your mage kind call us 'mundane,'" he said, wiggling his fingers.

"My eyes aren't enough?"

He gave a sharp smile, "Can be faked."

"Would this convince you, then?" Ciardis said, opening her hand to display the locket.

He turned as pale as a ghost and shook his head. "That…that is a locket I haven't seen in over thirty years. Where did you get it?"

"From another interested party," she said.

He swallowed and sighed. "What do you want to know?"

"Why was she planning to run?"

"Why *wasn't* she, you mean? Your mother had enemies," he said. "Just like you."

Ciardis frowned. "The duchess said that she was loved by everyone."

"The duchess? *Which* duchess?" he said in a voice as cold as frost.

Ciardis exchanged a glance with Stephanie before saying at last, "The duchess of Carne."

"And she sent you here?"

Ciardis nodded.

He began muttering to himself.

"She knew where you were," Ciardis said. "She was only trying to help."

"If you think that woman was helping, you need your ears checked."

Stephanie interrupted, "What do you know about her?"

"I know the Duchess has been scheming for the throne since the last emperor's reign."

"Can you prove it?"

"Ha! You want proof?" he said. "There's your proof!" He was pointing at the locket in Ciardis's hand.

"What?" said both Stephanie and Ciardis in confusion.

"It holds records of conversations between the duchess and the first-born son of Emperor Cymus. The one who also disappeared under mysterious circumstances. Leah told me he had been scheming to take the throne from his father. He disappeared one night but there was no proof that the duchess had been involved. After he was gone she turned her attention and friendship to the Princess Heir."

"And my mother?" asked Ciardis softly. "How would the duchess have gotten this locket from her?"

He sighed heavily. "The night before your mother disappeared, she was supposed to bring the locket to a mage of wind magic and me. The key to opening it takes a mundane and a mage working together in concert. But she never showed."

"If this is what you say it is, the duchess wouldn't have just given the locket to Ciardis," Stephanie pointed out.

"She would if she thought she couldn't open it by any other means," he said. "After your mother was accused of crimes against the throne that same night, she disappeared..."

He never got to finish his sentence. A resounding *boom* echoed in the room. The walls of the room shattered and they were all thrown off of their feet.

CHAPTER ELEVEN

Minutes later Ciardis was struggling to remember where she was. Her ears were ringing, her head pounding, and her whole body felt like it had been run over by a horse at full gallop. Pushing herself up on her hands and knees, she felt wooden shards and glass under her hands. The minstrel, who'd been closest to the outer wall, was unconscious on the floor. She was shocked to see a piece of glass the size of her arm sticking out of his shoulder with blood quickly pooling beneath.

Before she could go to him, a voice stopped her. "If you want him to live, you'll leave him there." The duchess of Carne stood in the wreckage of the outer wall which had been blown apart. Her silver hair glinting in the moonlight as she smiled and said gently, "And you'll come with me, Ciardis Weathervane."

Her head still fuzzy, Ciardis tried to reason out in her head where the woman had come from. The wall was gone, shattered, and in its place stood the duchess. Frowning, Ciardis took in the two guards behind her. One with his hand on the duchess of

Carne's shoulders; an impropriety that usually would not be tolerated. Usually. Ciardis wondered if he had his hand on the duchess to pull her back to safety if necessary. But that couldn't be the case. There was nothing but open air behind them, where the hole in the wall was.

Blinking Ciardis opened her mage sight and saw that man was glowing. He had some kind of power. It wasn't the huge glow of a full mage, but it was sizeable enough to get what he needed done.

"I do not have all night," the duchess snapped. "Take my hand and we'll be transported back to the palace grounds by my guard. You have my word."

Ciardis eyed the duchess but couldn't see a hint of magic on her body. She wasn't planning on anything nefarious with magic anyway. At this point it didn't look like Ciardis had much of a choice.

Ciardis didn't see Stephanie. Where was she? Abruptly she noticed that half of the wall had come down where the girl had been standing. Was she alive or was she dead?

"Be a good girl and come along," the duchess said with impatience. "I don't know how long that minstrel will survive bleeding like that. The sooner we leave, the sooner the healers can arrive."

Ciardis had the knife up her sleeve. She was contemplating using it, stabbing the duchess and making a run for it. And then the lighter in her pocket lit up with heat against her thigh. Not enough to burn her, but enough to give her caution and hope. Perhaps Stephanie was alive.

Relying on Stephanie wasn't Ciardis's preferred option, but then again the duchess might know more about her mother's last night at court. Then again, she might just try to kill her.

Reluctantly, Ciardis took the duchess's offered hand. "Good girl."

And then they were gone.

*****

Kicking off the portion of fallen wall that covered her, Stephanie picked herself up off the floor. Quickly she went over to the minstrel and felt for a pulse. The duchess had been right: He was alive, but barely. The blood was beginning to pool beneath his body and the only thing stopping it from becoming a torrent was the very thing that caused the wound. The glass was preventing more than a trickle from escaping. Which meant Stephanie couldn't remove it and tend to the wound herself. She had medical training, but not enough to stop the blood flow and heal the wound at the same time.

Her hearing tuned for any movement, she heard what she assumed were tavern patrons beginning to clear the fallen debris from behind the door. When she looked up she saw structural damage to the roof, which would have caused the beams and walls to fall all around them. It would take the rescuers some time to get inside the room, but hopefully they were fast enough to save this man's life. There was nothing more she could do here. She had to go after that idiot girl.

Stopping quickly for a resupply of weapons in her apartment she left a note for Christian telling him were she'd gone and why. She hoped she'd be on time. Otherwise she feared Ciardis would disappear just like her mother did so many years ago, only this time she would be dead.

Ciardis, the duchess, and her guards reappeared in the court gardens not far from Swan Lake. She snatched the locket from Ciardis's hands immediately.

"Now," said the duchess leisurely while holding up the locket, "why don't we see about destroying this locket, shall we?"

Ciardis stared at her mouth agape.

"Why keep it all these years? Why didn't you destroy it before?"

The duchess almost snorted. Magic was a fickle thing and objects imbued with residual magic in particular were hard to handle. Walking around Ciardis in circle, she wondered not for the first time if the girl truly was as smart as her mother. And who was her father?

Perhaps I'll find out tonight. Before she dies.

"If you can keep something close to you, it's better than losing it forever, or having it fall into enemy hands; it might be useful one day ," she replied.

"By that logic, you should be keeping snakes."

The duchess was no longer amused. "You and I are going to destroy this locket together. You see, my dear, since you inherited it and your mother is dead, that means you can destroy it."

"And why would I do that?"

"Because you don't want to die."

"It sounds like you want to kill me anyway."

The duchess gave her a cold smile. "Perhaps I could use someone with your…talents."

*****

Uneasily Ciardis thought, *Over my dead body.*

Suddenly Ciardis felt a sharp slice in the palm of her hand. She held it up to see a deep cut in her palm with blood already welling up in the wound and flowing off of her hand into the grass. She looked around, but there was no one else near her. Just the duchess. Her guards stood five feet back, at attention. The duchess smiled cruelly, "Now you see."

Ciardis stared in confusion. She could see a dark hint of mage power radiating from the duchess now. But she'd checked her at The Blue Duck Inn. She couldn't suddenly just *have* magical talents.

The duchess laughed with mirth as she read the shocked look on Ciardis's face. "No one has shown you how to hide a magical signature, I suppose? Ah well, now you know."

Neither of the duchess's hands moved but just as suddenly there was a long cut on her cheek. Ciardis brought trembling fingers up to her face as she backed away swiftly. The duchess didn't move and the attacks kept coming. Along her back a long slice appeared, and then a shallow cut on her thigh, and another cut on her arms. And then they grew too numerous to count – cut after cut appearing without end. Ciardis fell to the ground, dizzy with blood loss. The duchess sauntered up and knelt down in front of the severely bleeding girl.

She traced a light finger over the wound on her cheek, smearing the blood. The delight on her face could have frozen Hell.

"I told you, Ciardis, you have to be wary at court," she cooed.

As the duchess moved her finger back across the wound, Ciardis felt her flesh knit back together and the pain from that one scar ebb away.

"Just as I can give pain, Ciardis, I can take it away," she said gently.

She sat on the ground beside the shuddering girl. "Now, why don't we see about destroying that locket?"

Ciardis watched as the woman lowered the locket in front of her and picked up her hand, placing it above her own so that their two palms cupped the object.

"Blood of the line? Check!" the duchess said with a girlish grin. "You know, it's nothing personal. But that locket could undo a lot of work. Work we've been doing to ensure this empire returns to its rightful place."

Ciardis drew in a pain-filled breath. "The Princess Heir is dead. There is no one else to inherit."

"This isn't about the throne. It's about filthy inhuman creatures with the same rights as humans; it's about mundane people living above their station; it's about righting wrongs done to the nobility decades ago."

"Now I need you to will the locket open," she said in a motherly tone. "Very simple, right?"

Teeth gritted in pain and almost unconscious from the blood loss, Ciardis prepared to do as the duchess asked. There was no alternative.

And then a roar split the skies. Out of the night air dropped a nightmarish form. The duchess lurched up and quickly looked to the sky. Shouting, she called for her guards.

The dragon kept coming.

Her vision going in and out, Ciardis couldn't help but wonder what the dragon was doing here. It couldn't be anyone else but Ambassador Sedaris. A rustle sounded off to the side. Stephanie and Christian crept out of the bushes to ease over to Ciardis's fallen form. The duchess didn't notice them; she was busy rushing towards her two guards. The dragon landed with swift wings, right between Leah of Carne and her two protectors. That didn't stop the men from assaulting the dragon.

As Stephanie watched the battle she had to admit those guards had guts. Who stood up to a dragon and thought they would live? A minute later, her answer came. Those guards weren't just ordinary men—they were mages. One was an Earthcaster and proved it when the ground underneath the dragon began to shake and rumble with a threatening earthquake. The dragon didn't care too much for his tactics and targeted him.

Crouching next to Stephanie Christian used his healer's abilities to patch up Ciardis.

Ambassador Sedaris could see magic like the entire Sahalian race. It was why she'd been attracted to the young Weathervane; not only did she have immense potential to enhance others' magic, but she was also a powerful mage, or least she would be. Seeing the waves of power coming off the the guard who was clearly an earth mage and surmising his intent, she ate him first and followed up with his partner quickly.

When she felt a slice along her underbelly, she roared in fury. Deciding that the duchess deserved worse, far worse than being eaten alive, she transformed into her human form. By this time Ciardis was sitting up with the help of Christian. She watched in wonder as the transformed Sahalian strode across the garden like an avenging angel. When she reached the duchess, she hit her so hard that the woman flew ten feet to land in a crumpled heap before Ciardis, Christian, and Stephanie.

Reaching them, the dragon eyed the duchess with distaste. She put her heeled foot on the duchess's midsection to keep her pinned and called up liquid fire into the palm of her hand. This wasn't just any fire – it was everlasting. The fire would burn a person from the inside out over a slow period of time. A nasty remnant of the Initiate Wars and one not many mages could call upon. With a smile, she said, "I think being burned alive will suffice, don't you?"

"Wait!" shouted Stephanie and Christian.

The dragon looked at all three of them with rage in her eyes.

"Please—we need her."

"For *what*? You have the testimony. It's enough to convict her in absentia."

"But not the people that are threatening the throne and the empire itself. We need her in order to find and convict them," said Stephanie.

"We want to use her to flush them out. To end the murders, the deaths and conflict," Christian said.

"'We?'" said the dragon coolly.

"The Shadow Council," Ciardis said from where she stood in between the two young people. She looked down at the duchess with anger in her eyes.

"They're still around?" said the dragon with narrowed eyes.

"Fuck," muttered Christian quietly.

From the woman curled up on the ground in pain came a startled laugh.

"You have no idea who you're dealing with," the duchess taunted. "With my death, more will take my place in the fight."

The dragon simply ground her heel into the duchess's bruised chest and waited for her screams to die down into whimpers.

"She tried to kill you, *sarin*," the dragon said, ignoring the squirming woman on the ground. "Is this what you want?"

"Yes," replied Ciardis, "and what's more, so should you. I think she's been working with the group behind the conflict in the Ameles Forest."

The dragon looked at the three of them with unreadable eyes. And then she doused the flame.

"Very well," she said. "Call your *gardis*."

When Stephanie and Christian tried to renegotiate and get her to release the duchess to the Shadow Council, she looked at them and said, "No. This is your only chance. Call in your emperor's men or she dies here and now."

They spent the next two hours explaining the history of the locket, Ciardis's mother, and the potential plot between the duchess and the emperor's son. When the *gardis* left—saying they would be interviewing all of the duchess's household, as well—they were exhausted. The dragon just looked irritated. The gardis hadn't even bothered trying to question the ambassador. The look she leveled at them plus the fact that she had diplomatic immunity said that she would be more trouble than she was worth without a direct order from the emperor.

Citations for Christian, Ciardis, and Stephanie were issued, instructing them to appear in the court of magistrates tomorrow to recount their story before a magistrate, as well. And then they were bid goodnight.

Ciardis thanked Stephanie and Christian for coming to her aid. With barely a goodbye, they disappeared, muttering something about the Shadow Council coming down on their heads before the night was over. That left Ciardis alone with the dragon that had saved her life.

The ambassador looked over the girl covered in blood with measured eyes. She was contemplating her; Ciardis was far too tired to care what for. Unfortunately, that tiredness led to an increased inclination to be rude. She was fed up with running in circles and finding out that people knew far more about her and her heritage than she did.

"Why?" she asked bluntly.

"Why did I save you?"

"No, why did you call me your *sarin*?"

The dragon turned away from her and looked up at the full moon lighting the night sky.

After a few minutes in silence had passed, Ciardis began contemplating making the trek back up the palace with the dread reserved for a walk through the desert at high noon.

"Because," said the dragon, turning back with a wicked smile, "you are the one I would choose to name my closest human companion—my *sarin*. And by surviving that attack tonight you have proved worthy of the name."

"Right," mumbled Ciardis. It made sense that the dragon would be as cryptic as everyone else tonight. Nothing else made sense; why would she?

"I'm just…going back to my room now," she said as she stumbled away like the walking dead.

"*Sarin*," said the dragon behind her with amusement, "You have much to learn. Luckily I'm in a teaching mood."

The last thing Ciardis wanted, needed, or desired was a lesson right now.

She was therefore surprised when the dragon came up behind her and with no further words swept her off of her tired feet. The sensation of being carried was disorientating for a minute, but she soon grew comfortable. The last thing she remembered as she rested her head on Sedaris's shoulder was that the dragon smelled surprisingly like roses.

CHAPTER TWELVE

The next morning Ciardis woke up in her bed when she heard a loud knock at her door. She sat up abruptly, remembering last night's events and barely recalling how she had arrived home in her apartment. Pushing the covers back, she looked down and saw she'd been cleaned up and redressed in a nightgown. Deciding to put that thought out of her head for now, she put on her robe and answered the door. And there was Terris's smiling face staring at her.

She took one look at Ciardis and pushed her way into the room. "What happened now?"

"What makes you think anything happened?" Ciardis asked guiltily.

Terris flashed her an amused grin. "Because it's *you.*"

Sighing, Ciardis closed the door and hobbled her way back over to the bed. Christian had healed her last night but there were still residual twinges underneath her skin. He'd basically brought her back from death and her body was still in a little bit of shock.

"It's…um…complicated."

"We don't have time for 'complicated,'" was the exasperated response, "We have to report to Lady Vana this morning, remember?"

"Oh yeah…"

"And the last time I saw you, you were speaking with the duke of Carne, his wife, and the Sahalian ambassador. What was she like?"

"The duchess?"

"No," said Terris with an irritated toss of her braids from in front of her shoulder to her back. "The ambassador."

"Interesting."

"That's it?"

"And powerful?"

Terris gave her a disbelieving look, "I can feel you holding back from over here you know. Kind of feels like a too tight corset right?"

"All of those secrets," she continued playfully.

Grimacing Ciardis said, "I have to appear before the court of Magistrates today. The duchess tried to kill me last night and might have tried to kill my mother eighteen years ago."

Terris whistled in awe. "Oh, Serena is *not* going to like this."

Flopping back on the bed, Ciardis groaned. "I know. For once, why can't my life be easy?"

"Yeah," said Terris. "I'll go to Vana's room and let her know. Serena's already there so I'll have her meet you at the court of Magistrates."

With a wince and a sigh, Terris continued, "Good luck—you're going to need it."

Ciardis threw a pillow at her on the way out with a growled, "Thanks a lot."

She made it on time to the court of the Magistrates and got in line with Stephanie and Christian. They looked no more happy to see her than they had the night before. In fact, Stephanie gave her a glare than made Ciardis feel like she should check to see if her boots were on fire.

Christian said affably, "Don't mind her. She's not a morning person."

"And the council is pissed," he added as he bit into an apple.

"Why?" Ciardis asked.

"Well, for one, they were hoping to personally torture the duchess themselves," he said lightheartedly. "But lucky for them, the emperor's best torturer is on leave now and his second is our man. So they'll still get the information they want."

"Torture?" echoed Ciardis in disbelief.

"What?" snapped Stephanie "Did you think they'd just put her in a room and say 'pretty please' until she divulged her network of contacts?"

"And," said Christian stepping in to diffuse the tension, "they also don't like that the dragon knows we're back, and that is a whole different kettle of fish."

"What about you?" asked Christian. "How'd your sponsors take it?"

Take what? The fact that I'm now a dragon's best friend, that I was almost murdered last night, or that I'm appearing before the court of the Magistrates this morning?

"Well," said Ciardis, "They don't exactly—"

"Ciardis Weathervane!" came a screech that echoed in the antechamber and had every man, woman, and child standing in line angling their head to view the door where Lady Serena stood staring straight at them. Spying Ciardis, Serena pushed through the crowd with uncustomarily angry shoves and elbows in soft stomachs. Looking over Christian and Stephanie as if they were filth beneath her boots, she hissed at Ciardis, "What is the meaning of this?"

"This?"

"This!" said Lady Serena, waving a letter about in front of her face.

"I don't know what that is."

"It's a summons to the court of the Magistrate for the trial of the Duchess of Carne, *as well* as a letter of complaint filed in the Imperial courts by the Duke of Carne."

Ciardis took the letter hesitantly.

Lady Serena blew up. "What did you *do*?"

Ciardis decided to give a full confession on the events of the previous afternoon. It didn't calm Lady Serena down. In fact, she had a fainting spell.

"That's some sponsor you got there," said Christian wryly.

For a moment, sympathy actually crossed Stephanie's face as she said, "No wonder you're as hopeless as you are. No one could learn with *that* as their teacher."

Ciardis decided that it was too early in the morning to be offended. Especially at someone who'd saved her life the night before.

"For the pre-trial hearing about Duchess Leah of Carne, all witnesses are called forward," said a man standing by the courtroom doors.

With a collective sigh, Ciardis, Stephanie and Christian went forward into the room. Ciardis, Stephanie, and Christian spent most of the morning recalling what they'd learned. A minstrel and wind mage were called in to open the locket and an unknown mage was present to have the contents sealed in a memory ball for records. The ministrel from the night at the Blue Duck Inn had hobbled into the court with a broken leg and a neck swathed in gauze to tell his experience. The locket was as he surmised - a conversation between a much younger duchess and the former heir to the Algardis Empire discussing ways to kill his father and take the throne.

The judge heard their thoughts, reviewed the matter, and announced that the closed trial of the Duchess of Carne would commence tomorrow before the emperor, a superior magistrate, and the head of the mages. No further efforts from the witnesses would be needed.

"Thank the gods," muttered Stephanie as they exited the building.

"Where's your dragon friend?" questioned Christian.

"No idea," muttered Ciardis as she looked around for Lady Serena.

She walked down the steps with heavy feet. Ciardis knew that she needed a break. Her head was rushing and not many things were making sense. When Christian and Stephanie tried to follow, she brushed them off, telling them she needed some air before disappearing into the crowd. She had no idea where she was going and had no set direction. She just wanted to get away. With hunched shoulders, she decided to go to the one place where there were no distractions, where she could sit for a few hours and no one would question her. Crossing three streets and a bridge brought her into the bookbinders's district and to the doorstep of her favorite shop.

As she walked into the dusty front portion of the shop, she sighed in happiness that nothing had changed. Books still covered every surface, including the sides of the stairs, and a smell of old paper wafted to her nostrils the minute she opened the door. She decided to browse for a minute before heading upstairs. Ignoring the one other patron who was there at this hour, she walked around, tracing her fingers along the spines of books and opening up pages to glance at their contents.

But she couldn't help but notice the quiet in the air. Not the comforting quiet of an absorbing read, but the silence of a fixed target before a kill. Her heart beat a little faster as she looked over her shoulder, cautiously trying to take a peek at the man on the far side of the room. She was disturbed to see that he was staring right at her.

More disturbing than that were his eyes. Ciardis turned to face him fully, so startled that she dropped the book she'd been browsing through on the floor. She stepped over the fallen book, unseeing, and tried to make sure her eyes weren't playing tricks on her.

I'm sure lots of people have golden eyes. It must be a common trait for a few families.

The man sat still, looking at her, until Ciardis couldn't take it anymore.

"What do you want?" she snapped.

"It's odd, isn't it? Seeing someone you'd never thought you'd see," he said softly.

"Who are you?" she said, her voice shaking.

"You know who I am. I shouldn't have come so soon. But I had to know you were alive. I had to see for myself."

"What?" said Ciardis.

Swallowing harshly and not quite believing her luck this week she said, "Are you a Weathervane?"

He smiled and tipped the end of his cap toward her in salutation. Just as quickly, he walked out of the front of the shop. She raced to follow him, sure of what she'd seen but not believing.

When she got outside, the streets were empty and there was no sign of the mysterious gentleman.

Ciardis unsteadily fell back onto the solid oak door and put a shaky hand up to her mouth.

Could there be another Weathervane?

She had to investigate this further. Ciardis rushed back to her quarters in the Imperial palace to look for the Weathervane journal in her room. Once she found it, she pored over the text until she came to the passage that described the characteristics of each Weathervane. It was clear that all of those with the powers in her family had golden eyes.

But why assume he's family? There could be other yellow-eyed people on the streets of Sandrin.

"Right," she said with a shaky laugh. "I'm sure there are green-eyed ducks in the street fountains, as well."

What could this mean? Did she have family that she wasn't aware of? Why hadn't he said so? What was his name?

A knock at her door interrupted her thoughts. As she got up from her writing desk to answer, she tried to compose herself.

"Lady Serena has returned to her quarters and requests your presence in the Companions' Guild hall," a messenger announced, when she opened her door.

CHAPTER THIRTEEN

In the old days, the Companions' Guild—sometimes called the Hall of Order by nitwits who lived and breathed by the rules of the guild—had invested the Companions' Council as the governing body of all trainees and companions. The council's rule was law, and had been since the investment. Times had changed since then.

Just not enough for Ciardis.

Maree Amber, Head of the Companions' Council, was in a foul mood. She stared gloomily ahead as she walked toward the moon room. In her hands she clutched a tightly rolled scroll. The scroll with embossed edges had the Imperial seal of a rampant lion on it – making it official. This sort of missive was generally a very fine letter for the guild to receive. It promised wealth, opportunity, and power. This letter, on the other hand, was the exact opposite. The desire to shred it into a thousand pieces with her sharp nails was overwhelming.

It was also the last straw that would break Ciardis. To think that the Companions' Guild had been reprimanded by the Imperial courts was mortifying. Over a trainee, no less, was intolerable. Ciardis was ignorant, impulsive, and snippy. The girl had no respect for her elders and certainly wasn't taking her responsibilities seriously. As she approached the moon room's wide double doors Maree saw Lady Serena waiting for her.

Maree Amber smiled at her and held out her hand for a kiss. The smile looked sweet. But it didn't reach her cold and calculating eyes. Maree Amber didn't like Ciardis or her cohort of friends, if you could call them that. In particular she was fed up with Lady Serena; the woman's ineffective attitude and unobservant demeanor was letting the girl run wild. In addition, in Maree's opinion, Lady Serena took the word "vapid" to a whole new level.

Serena was supposedly in charge of introducing Ciardis to the nobility across the city, ensuring that she met the right people and increased her magical and mundane talents, as well as instilling within her their code of ethics and loyalty. So far all she'd done was teach the girl to dance and how to shop for pretty dresses. From the reports that Maree Amber had received from Damias before his untimely death and from select observers she had placed in the court herself, the girl seemed to be more inclined to discover her talents by accident, or at least without adequate instruction. That just wouldn't do.

In her hands Maree Amber held the third warning from the Imperial Courts. The letter detailed a new transgression, apparently dealing with the Duke of Cinnis. As a result the letter said that the Companions' Guild was being threatened with restricted access to multiple court functions. This atrocious mess could and would be laid down squarely at the offending party's feet. It was time to get their house in order, and Maree Amber would be lying if she said she wasn't gleefully prepared to do so.

With a snap of her fingers, she ordered the large doors to be swung open. The loud clicking of her heels echoed as she walked on the marble pathway to her seat at the half-moon table. Serena followed closed behind and took a seat to Maree's right. Three other colleagues had already taken their place. None said a word as they waited.

Above them a round circle in the middle of the domed roof opened to the sky. A full moon lit the room and cleverly placed glass panes reflected the light so that it shone directly on the single, lonely stool that sat in front of the panel.

Maree Amber heard a firm knock echo in the moon room chamber from the doors at the opposite entranceway. She leaned forward with a predatory smile. The knock was followed by the door slowly opening and a calm, monotone voice announcing, "Companion Trainee Ciardis Weathervane appears before the council."

Maree eyed the girl, the source of all of their trouble in the past few weeks. Ciardis had on a light green coat, a tunic, breeches, and boots. Her brown hair curled haphazardly around her face and her bronze skin had tanned to a deeper brown in the hot sun. She looked glamorous...and tense. Her tread was heavy and plodding, as if she thought that if she delayed the meeting by even a second the outcome would be better.

"So good of you to join us," Maree said. "We have much to discuss. Please take a seat."

Ciardis swept forward to take the only place available: the stool in the center of the room. As Ciardis walked forward into the round hall, her steps echoed with every click of her boots, and she could feel the tension in the air. Raising her chin proudly, she looked over each of the five seated panel members carefully. Four out of the five members of the Companions' Council sat before her, with the addition of Lady Serena.

A bead of sweat formed at the back of Ciardis's neck and slipped down her back. Today's meeting was not going to be a good one. She could tell that already.

"Very good," said Maree Amber. "Let us begin."

Maree Amber's tone was polite, almost cordial, but her posture was the stiffest Ciardis had ever seen. Sitting with her back to the entranceway, Ciardis eyed the council's positions high above her. Their raised dais was only meant to make her feel insecure; the trouble was that it was working.

"You have been deficient in your role as a trainee, Ciardis Weathervane," said Maree without preamble. "I blame this partly on your lackluster sponsor and partly on your innate ability to foul up even the simplest social situations."

Ciardis opened her mouth, ready to object. She wasn't really upset about the slander against Serena. But she thought she'd been fairly good in the courts…so far. Aside from a few minor indiscretions all of which were done in the service of the Prince Heir. But she couldn't speak. As soon as she opened her mouth she'd felt it close just as fast. Her lips were sealed shut as if by magic. She lurched up from the stool or at least she tried. It was impossible to do.

Straining her body, she felt the shackles of air tighten around her waist and legs; the air was weighing against her body. It was as if an invisible force had been dropped on top of her. Her body began to tremble—not in fear, but in fury. She narrowed her eyes as she stared from face to face on the council trying to determine who it was that bound her to her seat. Unfortunately two of the panelists were unknown to her; she was sure they were council members, but the new rotation had just started and so she wasn't sure which ones they were.

She looked to Madame Maree's right, knowing that this wasn't her power. The magic that bound her was one of compulsion. It felt like air magic, but she'd studied enough to know that this wasn't natural.

Finally she caught the eye of the one male panelist whom she knew. The one they called the Rithmatist. Ciardis stayed silent. She knew confronting him about it would be futile. Ciardis was brave but not stupid.

The Rithmatist was known for his fondness for cruelty and his heartless approach to discipline. He was known throughout the streets of Sandrin for his exotic tastes and his fixation on street girls. One of the servant boys, a friend of hers who often gave her gossip in the halls, had told her to watch out for the man.

"At first glance you'll think you're with your grandpapa," the boy had told her while scrubbing a banister. He was slowly edging down the steps backwards, carefully cleaning and polishing the wood along the rail.

"But that man is a snake. A snake in fine clothing, so watch your step," he said. A woman had come up behind them at that moment. "What was that?"

"I said watch your step, ma'am," he quickly muttered. "Just polished the floors and they're a bit slippery."

The woman raised an eyebrow, nodded coolly, and hurried off. Ciardis left just as quickly.

Back in the moon room, the Rithmatist continued to stare, unblinking. He was the stern-looking man that was eyeing her through eyeglasses with his chin was perched on his folded hands.

"Miss Weathervane, I don't believe you were invited to speak," he intoned. "In fact, we would prefer you did not."

For the first time Maree Amber let a genuine smile grace her lips, one of cold delight. "Very nicely done, Armand."

Looking at Ciardis, she said, "Another attempt at an outburst by you will be looked upon unfavorably, Miss Weathervane."

"Now see here," Serena said, rising, "she didn't mean any harm." For once Ciardis was glad to have Lady Serena present. At least she was standing up for her.

Maree Amber's smile turned brittle. "Sit down before you also are forced to."

Serena balled her fists, again ready to object. The man to her right tapped her wrist and handed her a note. She turned as pale as a moon lily and sank into her chair.

"As I was saying, Miss Weathervane," Maree Amber continued, "your behavior has been a mark against the Companions' Guild in the eyes of the nobility since you came here a short time ago. You may have the favor of the Prince Heir now, but you'll need more than the boy to survive in the courts. You need the guild."

Ciardis's eyes had begun to water. She couldn't help it and was struggling to hold back her tears.

They were tears of anger, of retribution, and not of fear. She turned her eyes slowly from the Rithmatist to Maree Amber, asking silently for permission to speak.

The woman smiled cruelly, acknowledging the tears glittering in Ciardis's eyes. She thought she'd won. Far from it.

"Speak, Ciardis," Maree Amber said with a leisurely wave at the Rithmatist to get him to loosen his grip.

"The nobles here are useless creatures! They're arrogant, spineless, and they think they know everything."

"Those are your betters and you will respect them—"

The latest panelist who had yet to speak stirred. He'd been sitting in an elegant sprawl and leaned forward in interest when Ciardis had been allowed to speak. His rings were bejeweled and his golden hair was styled in loose curls. He said in a loose drawl, "Please, my dear, continue."

"They are my betters only by birth. I know what's it's like to truly live in the Algardis empire. They? They live the lives of fairytales," she finished in an irate huff.

Serena had grown progressively paler throughout Ciardis's speech.

The bejeweled man smiled and his eyelids lowered as he studied the defiant girl who sat on the stool as proudly as if she sat on a throne with the court seated below her.

Softly he said, "Untested power such as hers could be the spark that flamed the court."

"Maree," he said in a louder tone, "I think we've found her."

Meanwhile, Ciardis was furiously thinking to herself. This insufferable council was supposed to be on her side, to be her mentors, to protect her and advocate for her. From the start they'd been nothing but hateful. She thought of all the things she'd love to do to them—setting them on fire and drowning them figured prominently in her imagination.

Maree Amber's mouth thinned into a line. "Armand," she snapped, speaking to the Rithmatist, "Release her."

She stood, her seat floating silently back without a touch of her hand. The man with the golden hair also stood.

"Ciardis, you will come with us," said Maree Amber, venom in her words.

Ciardis stood warily. At Serena's signal, she walked around to the back of the panel and followed Maree Amber and the weird man.

The older woman turned to the man once the doors of the moon room had closed behind them. "You know of her family's history. We can't have another mistake like that. Are you *sure*, Crassius?"

The strange man folded his hands into his pockets as they walked down the hall. "Very."

Ciardis's shoulders sagged. She had a hunch that she'd gone from hell to high water.

CHAPTER FOURTEEN

Maree Amber guided them straight to her office. A suite with a huge balcony facing the beach, it was open and airy. Curtains framing the balcony fluttered in the wind as they took seats around her massive desk in the center of the room.

"Look at me, girl," commanded Crassius. His eyes, a blue as bright as his hair, narrowed as he tilted her head up with his fingertip. He stared straight into her eyes as his pupils began to enlarge.

Ciardis didn't move her head. Although she was tempted to bite his fingers off just to be ornery. She could feel his magic searching inside her with tentative pushes against her mage core.

"What are you looking for?" Ciardis asked.

Irritation briefly masked his face. "A sign."

"A *sign*?"

He dropped his finger from her chin and looked over at Maree Amber, who had sat back in her ornate office chair and watched them with intrigue.

He nodded at Maree Amber and Ciardis swore the woman closed her eyes in frustration.

"Crassius, even if it is *possible*…"

She stopped in mid-sentence and held up a hand to halt his protest. "I don't doubt your abilities."

She turned hard eyes on Ciardis. "What I do doubt is this person's ability to act as a vessel for the plans we've put into motion."

"Hey!" protested Ciardis. She wasn't as exactly sure what it was that Maree Amber was doubting about her, but blanket derision didn't look good on anyone.

"In time, we'll see," he said.

"Look at this," Maree Amber said. She grabbed another piece of paper from her desk and handed it along with the scroll to Crassius. He took them and glanced over their contents with a bored look in his eyes.

He tossed an amused look at Ciardis. "The head of the Musicians' Guild writes that you threw his prized poodle into the bushes. And the head of the Weavers' Guild says you unraveled every single bolt of expensive silk fabric in her warehouse. This is, of course, in addition to your rather strange affair in the gardens at the dead of night with the Duchess of Carne."

"Those were accidents," Ciardis stressed.

"Companions don't have *accidents*," said Maree Amber.

"Well, not the Duchess of Carne, but she tried to kill me!"

"More importantly, mages don't have accidents," Maree Amber continued, resolutely determined to ignore Ciardis's outburst. "It's time you were properly trained."

Glancing down at a note in the report on Maree Amber's desk, Crassius added, "Instead of just relying on your ancestral memory ball."

Ciardis raised an eyebrow. "Companions aren't mages. Companions have *talents*. I have a talent to enhance and improve upon others' abilities."

"On the contrary, my dear," said Maree Amber coldly, "we believe your Weathervane abilities go far beyond the talents of your ancestors. You've accidently enhanced the powers of other mages five times now. There will not be a sixth."

Ciardis bit the inside of her cheek to keep from retorting. "I didn't mean to," wouldn't go over well in this situation.

"You're a Companion, you're a mage, and up until this moment we were lax in reining you in. Your status as the newest Weathervane in almost twenty years had quite a bit to do with that," said Maree Amber. "It's time for a change."

"From this day forward you will be trained by me. Furthermore, you will not set foot into the palace for another month—not until I'm sure you're ready to handle it. Lord Crassius is correct in this: You need guidance."

What about Sebastian? Wait—Lord Crassius?

Ciardis looked ready to object on quite a few points.

"Be silent, Companion Trainee Ciardis," said Maree Amber. "I've heard tales of your rudeness. That kind of behavior will not be tolerated when speaking to your betters."

"In this case I mean your elders," she continued on blithely. "And it certainly will not be tolerated in this office."

Out of the corner of her eye Ciardis saw Lord Crassius roll his eyes. She almost smirked.

"Unless given explicit permission to voice your opinions, keep silent," Maree Amber said while standing up. "I will return in a few moments."

When Maree Amber left, Ciardis obstinately stared out the window. She'd never been talked down to like that before in her life.

Some days—this whole season, really—were enough to drive a person mad.

*****

Lord Crassius took in her profile. She was irate, no doubt of it. The girl couldn't hide her feelings at all. She looked like a porcupine that that been poked and had stuck out its spines in defense, just waiting for the next attack.

He decided to take pity on her. "Companion Trainee, I give you full permission to speak freely," he said. "Just don't make me regret it."

"It was an accident. You know the kind of things that happen in the Imperial Courts," she snapped. "There are thousands of mages wandering in and out at all times of the day. A wind mage could have pushed that dog. It could have been anybody," she practically whined.

"It wasn't anybody—it was you."

"How do *you* know?"

"Because every mage's gift leaves a special signature when used, an essence of them that is left behind in traces."

Ciardis wilted in her seat. If this trace stuff were true then her life had become just that much more complicated. She wasn't an imbecile; she had enhanced every nearby mages' powers in an effort to protect Prince Sebastian at the time. Regardless of whether or not he was speaking to her then, he was still her friend.

He continued, "That is how I know you were the one that pushed the powers of all those mages, in effect causing them to use their magic without a choice and how I'm certain that you need to be trained. Of course, a mage would usually be trained by one of like ability, but that's not going to be an option with your Weathervane powers."

Maree Amber walked in at that moment. "Lord Crassius is correct again. As such, you'll be under my tutelage henceforth."

If anything could be worse, Ciardis couldn't see it. The woman gave her the creeps.

Ciardis's eyelid twitched but she managed to restrain any comment.

Looking to Lord Crassius, Maree Amber said, "Will that be all, Crassius?"

"For now I leave her in your capable hands, Maree," he said while standing.

"Very well, may your trip west be fruitful."

He nodded and left.

"Stay seated, Miss Weathervane, I have orders to give you," Maree Amber said while pulling parchment out of her desk and inking a quill by her side. She busied herself writing out three missives while Ciardis stared out the window, wondering where her life had gone wrong.

"This first missive with the golden ribbon is for the head of housekeeping. Take it to her immediately—I have ordered her to reassign your guest quarters to my tower. The maids will pack your things. The second missive with the red seal is destined for the guild couriers—they are to take it to the Imperial palace immediately. The third missive is for the school for mages. It is to be sent by pegasi windrider. Give the letter to a courier and tell them the destination. They will make arrangements from there. Were my instructions clear?"

"Yes, ma'am."

"Very well. Go and don't dawdle. You are to meet me at my tower in two hours. We'll begin your training."

"Yes, ma'am."

Ciardis was tempted to ask her what the training involved, particularly since Maree Amber had already admitted that no other person's abilities came close to matching Ciardis's. What could she teach her that experience and the memory ball couldn't?

She took in the woman's expression and decided that for once forbearance would be the more acceptable tactic in this situation. The woman looked cold and cranky. Neither of which boded well for their lessons together.

She left hoping Maree Amber would be in a better mood in the afternoon.

*****

After quickly delivering the letters, she raced off to the White Horse Café. Sebastian, black hair a mess from the wind, sat in a corner booth of the bustling tavern. She recognized him immediately and was a bit surprised that he was sitting out in the open. Wouldn't the other bar crawlers notice him, as well?

As he saw her, recognition poured through the bond in place between them and quiet contentment flowed freely from his end.

Well, at least someone's happy with how this day is going.

He grinned as she slid silently onto the bench. Ciardis waved at the tavern girl for a tankard of cider. Sebatian put in an order of soup.

"A little overdressed for a bar crawl, aren't you?"

"Had no time to change after my court date thanks to an urgent meeting called by the Companions' Council," she said sourly.

He whistled in surprise.

"The Companions' Council? What'd the council want with you? They only convene for lord, ladies and important Companions, not trainees, particularly not troublesome ones like you."

The tavern girl brought his soup. As he reached up to take the offered bowl, Ciardis noted the dangling Mindas bracelet on his wrist. The one that could warp the perceptions of people who came across him. The woman thought she was serving an ordinary man, a handsome one, but not the heir to the emperor's throne. She plunked a mug of cider down in front of Ciardis with little fanfare.

When the tavern girl left, he started to eat his soup. Looking down at the green depths, he swirled his spoon around and managed to pick what looked like a wriggling centipede out of its contents.

"I *am* important."

"In what universe? Your position with me has gotten you squat." He paused. "Except death threats."

"Now hold on, I'm more than just *you*," she retorted, "As for the death threat—how did you know about the Duke of Cinnis?"

"I'm not blind."

"Could have fooled me," Ciardis said.

She shifted in her seat while fidgeting and continued, "Well, it's taken care of."

"What do you mean, 'it's taken care of?'"

She swallowed some cider and mumbled under breath.

"What? I didn't catch that," he said sharply.

"He sort of sent a man to kill me yesterday and I sort of had to take care of it."

For a long moment the Prince Heir just contemplated the young woman hunched over the tankard in front of him. He deciphered what she said and couldn't tell if he wanted to kill someone or kill *her*.

"And you sort of took care of that?" he asked carefully.

She bit a lip. "Yeah, with some help."

"Someone you can trust?"

"Absolutely possibly."

He blinked. "Right. Is the duke likely to retaliate because of what you did?"

"Nothing that I can't handle," she said resolutely. "I've got enough dirt on him that he can only rely on besmirching my character at court now. Speaking of which, have you heard all the rumors about me?"

He looked at her in amusement. "Such as?"

"That you're leaving me, for one?" she snapped.

He chuckled. "I've heard of that one, yes."

She glared.

"No truth to the matter, of course."

"Of course," she said smoothly. "But it'd be nice if you could do something about them."

He shook his head. "I can't. My father has forbidden me from declaring you as my Companion for now."

"Seriously?" she gasped. "You couldn't have mentioned this? For how long?"

"I'm mentioning it now. And indefinitely. But in all other concerns you are my one and only choice. Don't worry."

"You know what this means, right?"

He looked at her silently.

"It means I'm stuck with the shitty end of the stick."

"Smart woman."

She shot him a long-suffering look that bordered on anger.

He grimaced and choked down a post-bug bite of soup.

"So I take it the meeting didn't go well?" he said, shifting his attention back to the Companions' Council.

"They said they have received three reprimands of conduct against me from the palace protocol office." She paused and stared pointedly at him. "I repeat: *the palace protocol office*."

"I have no influence over protocol. They've been around for hundreds of years and don't care for my opinions," he said.

She sighed and grumbled, "I know. I just wish you did."

Clearing her throat, Ciardis said, "I won't be around for about a month—the council decided it was best I have formal mage training."

"With?"

"Maree Amber."

"Good, she's strict but a great mage."

"What kind?"

"You don't know?"

"Would I be asking if I did?" she snapped.

"She's the head of your guild."

"And?"

He muttered an unintelligible response.

"She's a telekinetic companion."

"Oh, well, that could be useful."

"Officially."

"Officially? What's that supposed to mean?"

"Unofficially, she's supposed to have other talents in service of the empire."

"Says who?"

"Says half the nobility, and my father."

"Oh. What kind of talents?"

"No idea. Only the ruling emperor and his closest advisors are privy to that sort of knowledge."

"Damn." Ciardis was curious. There were many talents a person could have, but to have more than one generally qualified a person as a master mage. And "in the service of the empire" was as revealing as mud. Another mystery to solve, then.

Sebastian tapped his fingers in a pattern back and forth as he thought.

"See what she can teach you. I'll call you into the Aether realm in a week's time so we can convene."

It was then that they heard a crier at the front door. "A summons has been issued to gather at the square for news of the day. Five minutes until the clock strikes the mid-afternoon."

Ciardis cursed a blue streak. "I'm late. See you at our regular meeting?" She barely saw him nod before she scrambled up from the table and ran out the door, nearly barreling over the crier in the process.

CHAPTER FIFTEEN

Hurrying into the street, she signaled for a fast carriage. The fact that the driver had to nearly run down an old woman carrying a basket of bread to get Ciardis where she was going was enough to earn him his tip. She took off in a flat out run before the wheels had even stopped in the courtyard. Tossing a small bag of coins at the man, she set off for Maree Amber's tower. Panting and out of breath, she made it to the base of the tower just a few minutes past the start of the hour. Ciardis approached the single-door entryway to the council head's chambers with some resignation.

Although it was called a tower, it was really a very large set of suites set together. She'd read that the original apartments for the council head had been in a tower. But an attack three decades ago had destroyed it. No one was quite sure if it disappeared entirely or fell into the ocean. The new set of apartments had taken on the name of the tower despite being only one and a half levels and in a fairly rectangular shape.

Loitering outside Maree Amber's door was only making Ciardis later than she already was. Sighing, she reached for the handle of the door and squeaked in surprise when the door not only shocked her with some form of electricity, but also swung wide open of its own accord.

Squeezing her hands together, she walked inside, slightly unsettled. She was getting used to magic, but only a fool would trust unseen magic. Inside was a wide foyer with a floor of marble, bookcases that lined each wall, and plush chairs arrayed in a sitting room style. Seeing no one there, she continued forward into the next room. There was a short hallway that made a sharp right into the council head's office. Ciardis walked around the corner and immediately stopped in her tracks.

Maree Amber, Head of the Companions' Council, sat perfectly composed behind her large desk. A few objects sat on the desk, but for the most part it was blessedly empty. She gave Ciardis a pointed look over the wire-rimmed glasses perched on her nose.

Ciardis wasn't paying the woman the least bit of attention. The beast in front of the desk sitting sedately, but Ciardis wasn't fooled, had her full attention. She began focusing on controlling her breathing, trying not to hyperventilate, and edging backwards through the door as fast as she could. Reaching it after three tenuous backward steps she put her hand back to find the corner for the turn. What she found instead had her nearly swearing a blue streak. The way was blocked by a barrier. It felt like the wind barrier on the ship, but she wasn't turning around to make sure.

She had to keep an eye on that monstrosity sitting in the middle of the room. It was practically salivating as it waited to attack her. It was covered in white fur and was easily the size of a horse. Pointed ears with tufts made of her think of a big cat, but its broad, curved tail and fluffy fur said it was a dog. Whatever it was, it's long and powerful legs would enable it to reach her in a single bound.

She wasn't fond of dogs or big cats. The former were mangy mutts with fleas and all manner of diseases. The latter were hunters that killed with impunity in the great forests of the North. She had some experience with big cats from her time in Vaneis. All the villagers had to some extent. The snow leopards there were so brazen that they'd been known to hunt the large oxen in the outlying farms and then kill the farmers who retaliated against them.

Looking at Ciardis with distaste, Maree Amber said, "Ranger, come."

The dog…cat…*thing* obediently stood and came and sat next to her desk.

"Better, Miss Weathervane?" she said caustically.

"Not really," said Ciardis.

"The dog is not leaving, so I suggest you take a seat." Her tone brooked no argument.

Wishing she were anywhere but here, Ciardis sat as she was told. For a few moments they just stared at each other. One a young woman who wished she were napping in her room. The other an older woman, wondering if this petulant girl could really be the answer to their problems. Ciardis was everything that the Companions' Guild wanted in its candidates: beautiful and talented. It was a guild of young men and women destined to serve as the partners of spoiled noble Patrons. For many of the companions the guild accepted into its halls, it was no more than that. But Crassius, for some reason, saw something more in this girl.

*****

He had seen past the soft and pretty, willful and obstinate exterior; apparently to a girl with some spine. Right now, to Maree Amber that spine seemed to be encased in sullenness.

Sitting back, Maree Amber knew it would take more than the usual to undo the damage done by rich food and a soft summer of parties and court functions. She needed to go from sullen girl to a warrior who could use her skills to fight. According to her portfolio she'd grown up in poverty; they would use that to their advantage. Strip her back to the basics.

With an inward smile Maree Amber knew what she had to. The girl would be going on a mission – a mission to Ameles. Perhaps after they completed their training in a few weeks.

Any other year Maree Amber would have told Crassius he was insane and to go out and find someone that wasn't so *soft*. She would have turned a primped and finished Ciardis Weathervane out to pasture, found her a suitable, perhaps even Imperial, Patron and washed her hands of her.

But the girl's powers stilled her hand. Unfortunately, they needed the Weathervane skills. The war in the North was only growing worse, and they were losing. The girl's adventures with the Prince Heir in the Aether realm had only served to further incapacitate their side. That blasted elemental, the one called the Land Wight, had been subdued for a reason. Now it was loose and wreaking havoc on both sides of the battlefield, fiery infernos showing up at unknown times, cracks in the earth turning into chasms, and crops turning to dust for miles. Unfortunately, there was no one to control it—not even the emperor, and certainly not his son. Maree was just grateful the elemental was content to leave its meddling to the North for now.

But it wasn't just the creature. Maree wished it were just that. The enemy on the other side of the northern barrier was growing stronger. They needed powerful mages to fight them. Maree wasn't foolish or starry-eyed. She didn't think Ciardis Weathervane was someone who could walk onto a battlefield and kill scores of soldiers. What she did think was that if the girl were properly trained and vetted, she could have the potential to be a part of the cohort they were amassing. If not, if they failed to train her…then other measures would be taken.

The idea of magically cauterizing the girl or killing her didn't hold any appeal to Maree Amber. But she was practical. That practicality had earned her a seat on the Shadow Council. She was a Shadow member, through and through. And she would do what she had to in order to ensure that everything that was threatening her civilization would fall.

She focused back on the girl who now quietly fidgeted in her seat. *Starting with her. It's time for you to succeed or fail, Miss Weathervane.*

"Have you ever been outside in the midst of a winter storm, Miss Weathervane?"

"Yes, many times, ma'am. I—"

"Yes or no is fine. What did you think of it?"

Not a yes or no question. "It was cold."

Maree Amber cracked a smile. "I suspect it was frigid."

*****

Ciardis lifted her head, wondering if she was being mocked. "But you're right, cold is an apt description. It's never nature's intention to make you cold or uncomfortable. It's just the way it was—natural. But nature has its limits, and those limits are broken when it comes to mages. Mages can manipulate anything and anyone. They manipulate people, objects, and the elements around them to their benefit. Do you manipulate those things to your benefit?"

"No."

"You don't think so? You didn't push that mind reader's talent over the summer? Just enough to spread his reach to a certain room? It exposed the Duke of Cinnis's infidelities to the world and made his wife a laughing stock."

Looking at Ciardis's flaming face, she laughed softly. "Oh, I see. You think what you did was for the greater good?"

"It was!"

"You did what you thought was best?"

"Yes!"

"Without training, without supervision…"

"There was no one else."

"There's *always* someone else."

"Of course." She snarled it.

Maree Amber didn't look as if she believed that Ciardis was agreed with her. She peered at her with a finger tapping on her desk occasionally.

Finally she said, "You have potential but it needs to be cultivated in service to the crown. Which will mean some sacrifices."

Ciardis looked at her uncomprehending. "Sacrifices?" she said.

"You can't be trusted amongst court officials for now," said Maree Amber, "So I'll ask you to stay away from the Imperial courts and I'm forbidding travel to the Aether realm."

Pulling out a box Maree Amber held out a hand, "Give me the bracelet, Ciardis."

Ciardis automatically clutched a hand over her wrist protectively. Her fingers hid a golden bracelet intricately designed with butterflies. What could the woman want with it?

"The other one. The bracelet that connects you to the Aether realm."

"How did you…?"

Maree raised an eyebrow. "I'm the head of this guild. It's my job to know."

"It's mine, given to me by my Patron, the Prince Heir."

"I didn't ask you for details on ownership, Miss Weathervane."

Ciardis decided to try another tactic. "I need it to make sure—"

"Now," the woman snapped.

Ciardis inhaled a calming breath. She carefully took it off her ankle and held it out. All the while she was fighting the urge to hurl the bracelet in the woman's face.

"I'm doing this for your own good," Maree said as she locked the bracelet inside the small box, and secured it in her desk.

"As of now, you're far too unstable to handle it."

"Am I dismissed?"

"No," she said.

"No?"

"No. Now, my dear, I think it's time for your lessons to begin," Maree Amber said as if she hadn't just stolen Ciardis's most prized possession.

Before Ciardis could think of anything to say, Maree said, "Ciardis, can you see what I'm holding?"

She was tempted to say "air," but held back.

"Look deeper. Open your core."

Ciardis gathered in her magic and prepared to drop down into her core.

"No, not like that. You're taking too long. Perhaps we should start with basic rules about cores."

Ciardis let loose her magic. "Too long?"

"You shouldn't have to gather your magic and then drop into a spiral, which was what you were doing, just to activate your mage sight."

"Oh?" she said hesitantly. "Then what should I be doing?"

Maree said, "Watch me. Watch my aura." It began to shift and shimmer, the power gathering slowly under the surface until it pooled like silver light around her eyes.

"You can see my power, yes?"

Ciardis nodded in affirmation.

"What did you do to access that sight?"

"Nothing," Ciardis answered truthfully. "Seeing power build has been something I could do since my powers came in."

She grimaced. "At first it was everywhere. Now to see magic as it is in a settled form, I have to call my core."

"That's where you're wrong, Ciardis," her instructor said. "You can call in your mage sight to see all forms of magic at any time without dipping into your core. You just have to build a reserve closer to the surface."

"Give me your hands—we're going to go into your core together. I will show you what I mean, but this is the only time you will allow another mage to draw from your core," she said firmly. "It's dangerous…more dangerous than you can imagine, Miss Weathervane. If another mage can successfully deplete your core, they can kill you. Your life force will dwindle and your body will die. Do you understand me?"

"Yes, ma'am."

"All right, good."

They grasped each other's hands.

"Close your eyes and focus on moving down into your core. It doesn't have to be fast. In fact, since I'm following you, it's best to go slow." Ciardis began the descent. She saw a tunnel of bright golden power leading down in a swirl to a bright ball of magic—her mage core. It wasn't precisely in the same realm as her body, but she knew where it was and how to reach it instinctively.

"Do you see the wave of magic curves along the walls of the tunnel? Like a spiral?" Ciardis turned to find Maree Amber, awash in a purple glow, following along behind her.

"Yes, is that why it's called spiraling?"

"Correct. A mage follows the trail their magic leaves along their core tunnel to reach the axis of their power seated in the ball at its center. The center being their mage core, and the tunnel being the magic taken from the core and used while the mage is in their corporeal form."

Ciardis looked ahead. "We're almost there." And indeed they were. As they leveled their ethereal forms out to hover alongside outside the core, Maree said, "Now, Miss Weathervane, reach toward your core. Skim a tiny bit of magic from the outside."

Ciardis moved her form forward and reached to grab magic from the core. It was a hasty attempt.

"Not like that. Slowly, until you have more practice. You don't want too much or you'll overwhelm yourself."

She tried again, this time reaching out slowly, and, with dexterity, she grabbed just enough to satisfy Maree Amber. "Good, now let's go back up. We'll stop close to the outer edge and I'll show you how to deposit what you've taken into a reserve."

Ciardis felt herself begin to rise. This time she followed behind Maree Amber and it felt a lot faster. It was generally easier to go back up the tunnel than to travel down to the mage core. As they neared the edge, Maree Amber's purple form stopped, an ethereal mass hovering just at the edge.

"Here, Ciardis, is where you'll place your reserve. Take the core and push against the wall. And then you're going to reach into the wall and grab small strings of power off of the tunnel. Wrap the reserve tightly. Now try."

Ciardis hovered and moved up against the tunnel wall. It thrummed with power and beat with the rhythm of her heart. It was melodic in its intensity. She pushed the orb closer to the glowing wall. Holding it in place with one hand, she reached around and grabbed first one string of power, then a second, a third, a fourth, and finally a fifth string of power was wrapped around the reserve ball. It glowed, a sphere encased by a glowing, pulsing web holding it snugly against the tunnel.

"Very good, Ciardis. Now, when you draw from your power, you can draw from here instead of dropping deep into your core. It will get easier for you do and you'll be able to tap a line of power from your core to your reserve to replenish it once you're ready."

Ciardis was surprised. "This is useful. I'm grateful."

"Let's go, then; we have work to do. Back to the regular realm."

CHAPTER SIXTEEN

"Tap into your mage sight," was the command given as soon as Ciardis resurfaced. She hesitated then dipped back to her core. Before she'd been gone for even a few seconds, she saw the bright reserve laying just on the edge. Edging closer to it, Ciardis pushed a line of power from herself into the reserve. She felt the magic rise immediately.

"Good, Ciardis, now concentrate on holding on to the power and open your eyes." Ciardis followed her command. Staring outward, she saw the glimmer of magic on her desk, in her clothes, and among the objects in the room.

"Where am I focusing my magic now, Ciardis?"

"Your eyes," said Ciardis, seeing the flare of power centering on Maree Amber's eyes. A shimmer of power had slid over her eyes like a veil.

"Now watch me." Maree Amber's magic rose in waves across her body until it came down slowly to center into a pool in her hands. She held her hands up. The pool of magic began to reshape itself into a web. The web began to twist and turn in on itself. The filaments of string multiplying and connecting until the surface of the web was smooth and the pattern was clear. A hazy image began to appear in the shape of a person.

"What do you see now, Ciardis?"

"A mirror," she said hesitantly. "A mirror of power. It glimmers and moves as if it's liquid."

A satisfied smile entered the woman's voice. "Very good."

"Now," she said softly, "reach forward. Cup your hands under mine as if you wish to hold the mirror yourself. Look into the mirror. Tell me what you see."

Ciardis took a deep breath, exhaled, and did as she was asked. She looked inside. At first it was just a mirror, rippling like liquid, but still just a mirror.

"Look with your sight, Ciardis," she said, her tone changing. "Not just your eyes."

"Right," she said, trying to change her perspective. Suddenly the mirror shifted; the glow moved to the center of the rippling water and disappeared inside. Images began to appear.

"What do you see?"

"Buildings, water, people…but nothing's focusing."

"Right—because I've introduced a limited amount of power into the mirror. I'm using my power only to scry and see images from afar. With our connection you can see what I can see. But there are limits on how much. Just as you would only be able to tap into any other mage's power as much or as little as they would let you."

Maree Amber slowly moved her cupped hands in a circle, dissipating the images.

"This time I'll call in more images with more power. Tell me what you see."

Ciardis peered once more into her cupped hands. A winding street in the midst of Sandrin began to appear. Buildings that looked like they would topple over, and a dark red cobblestone pathway that had seen better days.

"The bookbinders' district. I recognize the buildings."

Maree Amber smiled.

"Yes, that is correct." Slowly, she dropped her hands and let her power evaporate.

"You used your power to see what I saw, even to tap into what I saw," she said with satisfaction. "But know this, Ciardis: You didn't *enhance* what I did."

"No, I didn't."

"Do you see the difference?"

She nodded.

"Very well. That was the first test. Whether you could see the difference, and, more importantly, if you could do both. You did and you could."

"Why couldn't you just—"

"Ask? Have Crassius tell me? He *did* tell me. But sometimes it's more important for the instructor to observe, and, most importantly, it was good for you to do it yourself."

"Yes," Maree said, tracing a finger on a globe on her desk, "You could be very useful to us." Ciardis perked up a little at the praise.

Maree Amber smiled a cold smile and held up a warning finger, "But if you cannot be trained, if you do not *wish* to learn, you are a threat to everything we stand for, Ciardis. And we can't have that."

Ciardis wasn't entirely sure Maree Amber was speaking of the Companions' Guild in that moment. Her tone was far too deadly.

"I think that we've done enough for tonight," Maree Amber said thoughtfully as she sat back at her desk. There was a gleam in her eye that Ciardis didn't like, but if it got her out of her office that much faster, she wasn't going to question it.

She stood up uncertainly and asked, "Tomorrow, then?"

"Tomorrow I have a meeting with an Imperial representative," Maree Amber said pointedly.

As if Ciardis should know that.

Ciardis grimaced when she remembered why she was supposed to know such a small fact about the head of the guild's schedule.

Tomorrow was a petition day for the guilds across the city. An opportunity for each of the dozens of guild representatives in Sandin representing thousands of members across the empire to have their grievances heard by the Imperial Council. The petitions were given the night before to the Grand Vizier, the new one who had been appointed after the last one's unfortunate death. The head of each guild would be personally advocating for their community in the morning.

"The next day, then?"

"The evening will do."

Ciardis nodded and turned to leave.

"And Miss Weathervane?"

She turned back with dread.

"I meant what I said. I don't want to see you anywhere near the courts. If I do, believe me the punishment will be fitting." A glacial air overtook the room.

"I understand."

Ciardis left the room without another word.

After tracking down a servant who directed her to a maid, she was able to find out where her new room was. A square cinderblock with a small bed and cupboard, it looked smaller than the bathroom of the previous room she'd left. There wasn't even a bathroom in here. Ciardis sighed in irritation and flopped down onto the bed.

She sat up with an abrupt yelp as soon as she did. She pressed her hand into the firm mattress. "Firm" was a kind word for it. It felt like it had been made out of burlap and stuffed with horsehair; the bedding was that uncomfortable.

"What did I ever do to her?" Ciardis muttered into a pillow, her voice muffled.

Besides get the Companions' Guild on the Imperial censure list. She was sure she wasn't the only trainee with that distinction. Speaking of Imperial, she was supposed to meet with Sebastian tonight, but that dratted woman had taken her bracelet. The only way for her to connect to the Aether Realm.

Deciding that she wasn't going to wallow in self-pity, Ciardis took action. If she couldn't go to the palace, perhaps the palace could come to her. Looking around, Ciardis spotted towels folded neatly on top of her new cupboard. She grabbed a few and left. Casually, she walked out of her room and headed down into the dungeons as fast as she could without drawing attention. She was heading to the steam baths of the *hammam*.

Nodding nervously she undressed in the clothing station, putting on a towel and carefully wrapping her hair up in a second. She smiled at different Companions' Guild members as she walked sedately into the welcoming steam of the baths. Kept at over a hundred degrees, the steam was usually a pleasant and relaxing reminder of the end to a long day…just not today.

When she nearly bumped into Maree Amber—on her way to the facial room, judging by the brown gook caked on her face—Ciardis couldn't help but squeak in surprise. *Wasn't it enough that I just endured an entire afternoon with her? Does she have to ruin my evening too?*

The stone cold look the woman gave her in return made her want to sink into the floor. She stood silently as the Companions' Council head and her attendants glided smoothly around her. With a sigh of relief, Ciardis quickly slipped around the corner and behind a screen to a rarely used section of the baths.

Cracked walls and chipped molding gave testament to how long this small, round room had been left without maintainence. When Ciardis had first discovered the old nook in the back of the hammam, she had taken it as a good sign. It was clean and clear of debris and spiderwebs. So obviously *someone* knew about it. Even though it was off to the side in a secluded area. At first she'd used it as a place to practice her scripts when she didn't feel like being in her room and didn't want to be in the company of others wandering around the library, the main salons, or the outer gardens.

Sitting down on the ledge that ran along the circular wall at mid-height, she put the towel-wrapped bundle she carried in her arms down. When she'd first come to the baths with something like this, she'd had to unwrap it for bath attendants to inspect her provisions. Now they were used to her oddness and expected her to carry around the bundle filled with an inkpot, quill, and some used parchment.

But this time was different.

Quickly she pulled back the folds of the white towel covering the objects. Inside the bundle, instead of the usual writing tools, sat a chisel and a medium-sized round pendant made of wood with black squiggles carved into the sides. She had discovered the hidden function of this nook by accident, really.

It hadn't been more than two months ago when she'd been sitting in this exact same spot practicing her hand at the Sahalian script. She could read it, understand it, and speak it like a nobleborn now. But that ability didn't extend to writing. Stephanie's transfer skills were great, but they weren't infallible. Which was why she was stuck painstakingly copying line after line of the looping squiggles that served as letters for the dragon race. And she did it in whatever creative way she could, from writing outside, flat on her belly in the gardens, to holing up in the steam baths of the *hammam*.

Anything to break up the monotony of repeatedly looping those squiggles day in and day out.

One night she'd been nearly dozing off after hours of being cooped up in the steam of the baths. An invisible barrier dividing the air of this room from the humid, heavy steam of the outer baths let in less than five percent of the steam that drifted around in the regular baths. As far as she could tell, that was because of a protective spell, a layer, really, that existed all around the recessed room. A layer that was slowly failing. The steam had built up enough that she'd been succumbing to slumber where she sat. As she had drifted off with the Aether bracelet on her ankle, she'd heard a curious thing. It had been Sebastian's voice calling to her…from the Aether Realm.

Her memory of that night came back to her with all of the clarity of an event that happened just minutes ago. Ciardis remembered that she'd answered him, half-asleep, and he'd asked her where she was.

Where in the palace she was. At that point she had woken up from her slumber with a start. In disbelief, she had called out mentally, "*This can't be real?*"

"*I assure you it is,*" Sebastian had replied.

"*Are we in the Aether realm?*" she'd questioned while pinching herself.

"*No…I thought you were close by in the palace,*" he'd said. She'd hastily told him that she was nowhere near the Imperial grounds.

Ciardis had felt some confusion. "*Even if I was. We could only talk like this in our physical bodies if touching.*"

She had felt his bemusement and knew he had felt her confusion.

"*It feels like you're standing right next to me,*" she had said.

"*Where are you, then?*"

At that point in the conversation she'd stood up and spoke aloud. Testing the range of their conversation. "The steam baths," she'd said while looking around. She was speaking out loud, but he was speaking inside her head. How was this possible?

"Where are you?" she had queried.

"The Imperial nursery."

She had raised an eyebrow in surprise. "What are you doing there?"

"*Preparing for my unborn child,*" he'd said dryly.

"What?"

She had felt impatience flow through the bond. *"It's the only place I can find some peace now. Everyone wants something from me. And, well…they never think to look in the children's nursery."*

"Right, so…"

"*Hold on a second,*" he'd commanded. "*I think I found something. Your magic—I can see it in the wall.*"

"You can see my magic in the wall?" she had said slowly. Her disbelief was palpable.

*****

Miles away in the Imperial Palace Sebastian had ignored the slight censure in her tone and looked closer at the decorative wallpaper-draped panels that made up the Imperial nursery. He'd put his hand on the one wall panel in the beautifully decorated nursery which was glowing with Ciardis's innate magic. Tracing the flow of magic, he'd pushed firmly on the panel wondering what in the world was going on. He didn't have long to wonder, because as soon as he'd pushed the panel, his hand had gone straight through the wall. Off balance, he'd followed immediately after.

When a young man had come tumbling through the wall of the steamy room Ciardis had shrieked. Fortunately the barrier keeping out the mist from the baths also kept away sound.

The fact that he'd landed directly on top of her towel-clad body was just the sweet finish to an already tiring day. Kicking out, she'd kneed him in the groin and got to her feet, hastily rearranging her gaping towel.

"Ciardis," said Sebastian in a pain-filled voice, "did you really have to knee me there?"

"Sorry," she said, "It was reflex?" Another groan was her only answer.

He'd stood up and she could finally see his brilliant green eyes and black hair in the gloom of the steam. She had given him a brilliant smile and backed up a tad. He didn't look happy. In fact, he'd looked different altogether. Biting her lip, she had taken in his taller form and the fact that he was actually wearing something that didn't make him look like a toddler among grown-ups today.

Must be a growth spurt, she'd thought.

He had sighed and the rubbed the back of his neck. "Where are we?"

"The baths," she'd said, gesturing at the steam and her towel as if to say, "*Where else could we be*?"

Ignoring her towel-clad form after a cursory glance, taking in her curly hair pulled up into a thick ponytail and the gleaming bronze skin of her shoulders, arms, and legs, he'd turned back to the wall he came through and poked it tentatively. His finger hadn't gone through, and neither had his hand.

"Well?"

"It's a portal...a gateway between the nursery," he'd said, glancing specutatively around the room, "and the baths of your home."

"Why? Wait—don't tell me," she'd said. "The Royal Consort, right? The one who owned this castle—she had children."

He had nodded quickly and grinned over his shoulder. "You're catching on."

"I kind of have to," she'd said with dry wit, "constantly being dragged on one magical adventure after another with you."

He had turned around and smiled. "Well, yeah." And then there was an awkward pause. Awkward for a number of reasons that Ciardis Weathervane didn't even want to contemplate.

"So how do we get you out of here?" Ciardis had said.

"The same way I came in," he'd said. "I'd hate to see what the rest of your guild would say if I came out of your baths."

She had nodded and they'd set to work. It had taken them a couple of hours, but they finally found the trick to opening the gate back into the royal nursery.

Flashing back from the memory, Ciardis picked up the round pendant and the chisel. Sighing before the wall panel, she activated the gate. She anticipated the weird, itchy feeling that always came across her skin when she crossed through the gate. She didn't flinch, and came walking out into the royal nursery clad in nothing but a towel, carrying a necklace and what looked like a weapon. Hurrying, she raced over to the huge armoire painted with the same intricate details of the whole room—a sky blue color with golden filigree—while cradles and comfy cushions and small toys were scattered throughout the area.

Reaching for the smooth panel of the armoire, she realized there were no handles or doorknobs. Only a perfectly oval inset in the wood. She put the pendant in the oval inset and it fit snugly. Pressing the center of the pendant down, she felt the small center depress into the armoire and a corresponding *click*. The sound meant that the splints of the wooden pendant had extended outward and were now locked into place in the small holes carved into the sides of the inset. With a smile, she turned the armoire key and opened the door slowly while putting the chisel down quickly. Sebastian had explained that the pendant was a childproof way to keep the armoire closed. She hadn't disagreed. Hurriedly, she put on the simple dress she'd given to Sebastian to stash for her just in case she had to come in through the back way.

Locking the armoire, she hurried to the far wall and eased the chisel into an almost invisible crack in the wall's seam. Easing the secret panel open, she slipped into the dark corridor beyond and went in search of Prince Sebastian.

CHAPTER SEVENTEEN

Sneaking around the Imperial palace wasn't Ciardis's finest moment. But sometimes a girl had to do what a girl had to do. She hit a secret panel in the wall and ducked out of the servants' corridor once she made her way from the Imperial nursery and closer to the heir to the throne's living quarters. Warily, Ciardis kept an eye on everything around her.

The sun was setting and the sky was beginning to darken with the orange glow of the fading daylight. She eased around a corner silently and ran straight into a butler. Quickly, Ciardis stumbled back with an apology.

Before she uttered more than, "I'm sorry," the man interrupted her with a brusque tone. "Are you the new serving girl?"

Ciardis stared at him uncomprehendingly for a moment. Stepping back, he thrust a silver tray laden with cakes into her hands. "Right, yeah. Listen, you were supposed to be in the Turquoise Room one minute ago. You're *late*."

Too late she realized it was the dress. A serviceable dull brown, it fit right in with the dresses of the serving girls scurrying up and down the corridor.

"But I'm—"

"Lost? Yes, I know. Happens to all of us," he said, firmly turning her around by the shoulders.

"Down the hall, take a right, and head down the curved set of steps. You'll serve the Prince Heir first and the head of the Weavers' Guild second."

Ciardis had been about to protest his manhandling her, but shut her mouth with a click of her teeth when she heard the words "Prince Heir."

Well, I was looking for him. Seems I've found him.

Deciding to go along with a backwards glance at the butler who was already turning away to redirect another girl, Ciardis walked toward the Turquoise Room as directed. Her golden eyes were twinkling in mischief; she couldn't help it and wondered with amusement how Sebastian was going to extract himself from the meeting and get her out of the room at the same time.

Adroitly handling the silver tray she swept down the curved steps and prepared to step onto the landing into the Turquoise Room. And that was when she heard the voice.

The woman's smooth words floated up the steps toward Ciardis, and she froze. Maree Amber was inside. She'd know that voice anywhere.

Quickly realizing that her adventure was going to get her into a hell of a lot more trouble than she'd bargained for, she began to quietly back up the stairs, wishing the platter she carried was small enough for her to maneuver around in the tight space and flat out run.

"Hey," came a quick whisper in her ear, "what do you think you're doing?"

Ciardis hesitated. "I forgot some food for my platter. Need to go back up and get it."

"Doesn't matter, we can add it to the table later," was the girl's exasperated retort.

"But…but it's the Prince Heir's favorite."

"And how would you know that?" said the girl in disgust.

"Look, I just need to get…"

"I don't know what you're playing at, but you won't get me fired. Now *move*."

Seeing no alternative, Ciardis walked back down the stairs and into the room while trying her best to hide her face with the platter. Unfortunately the tactic wasn't going to work. It was a small room with less than five people inside. Ciardis included.

In the center of the room was a round table with glassware, plates, an overflowing cornupia of fruits and glazes for the treats. Around the table sat three individuals: Prince Heir Sebastian Athanos Algardis sat with his back to Ciardis; to his left was the head of the Companions' Guild, Maree Amber; and to his right, staring directly at Ciardis with an unsavory gleam in his piglike eyes, was the man Ciardis assumed was the head of the Weavers' Guild. The man never took his eyes off of her as she balanced the tray and kept a nervous eye on the occupants of the table.

Even in a simple dress her curvaceous figure showed through, and Ciardis felt dirty under his steady gaze; it was as if he were mentally undressing her. He probably was. Shakily, she came up on the prince's left and set the first entrée down on the table. Sebastian hadn't turned his head or acknowledged her presence.

But Ciardis knew that he was aware of her from the moment she had stepped into the room. Their bond had its useful moments.

Sebastian reached to pick up his napkin on his left side as she was withdrawing her right hand from the rim of his plate. His hand brushed hers and he sent his thoughts to her when they touched briefly.

You are not supposed to be here.

I'm quite aware. Don't suppose you could help get me out of here?

It was her only chance to reply before she turned to serve the head of the Companions' Guild. Hell, if she were going to get in trouble, she might as well follow proper table etiquette. The more powerful the guild, the higher in rank they were. And the Companions' Guild definitely outranked the Weavers' Guild. There was no way she'd be caught serving that pig before she served the Head of her guild, no matter what the butler said.

As she balanced the silver tray in her right hand and held the small platter on top with her left, she prepared to set it before the woman who was going to kill her for being here. But then she stopped. Before she could even move the small plate of food in the woman's direction, Maree Amber raised her hand in a commanding gesture. She didn't turn; she didn't speak. She showed Ciardis the back of her hand in a silent order to hold the food.

Ciardis didn't question her; she just moved to circle around the table and give the leering man his platter. She had just walked around the back of Maree Amber's chair when he smiled and also held up his hand. This time the head of the Weavers' Guild spoke.

"I prefer you where you are," said the guild head as sweat trickled down his forehead onto his fat jowls. He picked up a napkin to wipe his forehead and smiled at Ciardis – his lips stretched back over yellowed teeth and his beady eyes squinting from inside the fatty folds of a face too used to over eating. She felt like she needed a bath. She could feel Sebastian's disgust and anger as well. Although his face was expressionless.

Snapping back to her duties she had no idea what to do now that two of her guests had turned down the food. She hoped it meant she could leave the room. Quietly she began to back away towards the entrance she came in. The second serving girl looked at her with horrified eyes and shook her head swiftly with an angry look. Uncertain, Ciardis stopped and watched as the other girl set out silverware. After the serving girl had unfolded a napkin in the lap of each patron and set out the silverware within reach she began to back away from the table while motioning for Ciardis to do the same. Ciardis did as suggested, never turning around as she walked backwards while mimicking the careful pace of the other servant until she felt the wall behind her.

Over the next hour and a half, Ciardis's eyes glazed over and she fought to stand stiff as she watched Sebastian listen to the head of the Weavers' Guild make a case for the import of special cloth fabrics from the Ameles Forest at market rate. Curiously, Maree Amber did nothing and said nothing further the entire time.

Ten minutes after the hour and a half had passed, the butler opened a panel in the room and motioned for the two serving girls to follow him into the hallway outside. As he prepared to close the door, Prince Sebastian commanded, "Aaron."

The butler startled and whispered for the girls to wait in the semi-dark corridor as he hurried to the Prince Heir's side. When he came back after a brief moment, he told the other servant girl to wait in the kitchens. Before Ciardis could head off, he held her back and said, "You are coming with me."

"I don't think so. I really am not…"

"The prince has asked me to personally escort you to his chambers," he said. "I don't know what you said or did, but you're lucky. I know women who'd give their left arm to be in your place."

Ciardis paused, wondering what place he thought that was.

"Just remember. I got you there."

Really? He's going to take credit for my seduction or whatever he thinks this is?

"Remember that and I'll get you more assignments near him."

Right, like you have a choice.

Deciding that the conversation in the corridor had gone on long enough Ciardis said, "I think you'd better take me to those chambers now."

The man curled up his mouth in a snooty look but didn't reprimand her.

"Come with me." He held an old-fashioned candelabra in his hands. The kind used to light dark passageways without the aid of magic. As they wound their way through the servant's corridors with the occasional rat squeaking past Ciardis was glad to have the light. A mage orb would be better but beggars couldn't be choosers. He stopped in front of an elaborate doorway with glossy hardwood, the Algardis crest embossed in the middle and an actual door knob.

Staring in disbelief Ciardis couldn't keep quiet.

"Isn't this conspicuous? To have the Prince Heir's chambers marked so openly?" she said.

He turned towards her, the candelabra in his left hand as he said, "The servants should always know which door they approach and whom they should expect on the other side. Protocol demands it."

"I understand that," she retorted, "But any one can tell this door is different from the surrounding corridor. That someone *important* must reside here."

The butler's mouth had stiffened into a thin line, "That would be the point."

"You're asking for trouble. Assasins, thieves and the like."

He let out a suffering sigh, "The Prince Heir has the top guardians in the Empire at his side. Now perhaps it would be best for you to go inside…and keep your mouth shut unless the Prince Heir requests otherwise."

Ciardis sniffed and swept past him as he opened the corridor door into the Prince Heir's well-lit sitting room.

As the door closed behind her she sat for a minute. When ten minutes had past and Sebastian still hadn't come in she wandered around the room picking up objects and studying paintings. After another ten minutes had passed, the door to the formal sitting area opened and in walked a tired prince heir. Giving Ciardis a tired smile, he uncapped a decanter sitting on a side table near the door. Pouring himself a drink, he smiled and said, "Isn't this familiar?"

"Aren't you a little young to be drinking?"

"I'm sixteen," he said defensively, "and it's just an iced herbal tea."

She raised an eyebrow, not believing him. She'd heard that before. Not from a prince, though. Usually the village boys thought they were being smart by hiding their moonshine in water pouches. Stupid was a better description. After they put the alcohol in their water pouches they couldn't use them during the hunt. Too many animals, mage and mundane alike, knew the scent of alcohol in the North.

And they remembered what it meant. Those creatures would do anything to kill the person who carried the scent because it meant an evil which hadn't been seen in centuries was nearby. Focusing on Sebastian, Ciardis walked up into his personal space and took a direct and impolite sniff of his glass.

She didn't care that it was rude. She couldn't abide drunks, and she certainly wouldn't serve one. Not directly, anyway.

Fortunately for him, it was clean.

"If you're finished inspecting my nightly herbal mix," Sebastian said with dry amusement, "we have much to discuss."

She looked at him curiously and sat down on the couch, crossing her legs.

"You're not upset?"

"About?"

"Me inspecting your drink for starters?"

He looked at her with seriousness on his face. "Even when I was an Imperial outcast, there were very few people who cared to cross me at court. They all wanted me dead. But—at least in this realm—they were as polite as could be when they saw me."

He poured a second drink and motioned to an empty cup. She nodded.

"You, on the other hand," said Prince Sebastian, handing her the second cup and sitting back, "say what you think, don't guard your feelings, and are even…disdainful toward me."

Ciardis snorted. Polite semantics.

"I can't say I always enjoy any of those three things," he said wistfully, "but for the most part I appreciate it."

"Anything else you're not upset about?"

He snorted. "Nope, the rest of the night's going to be righteous indignation about your continual need to disrupt life in the Imperial courts and not observing the protocols before your betters."

Ciardis looked at him pointedly. He looked back at her over his cup, eyes laughing. And then they burst into gales of laughter. Neither could help it. It was the exact speech given to them by the new grand vizier after another incident.

Face twitching as she fought to get her response under control, she said, "I suppose I semi-deserved that."

"Right. So I hear you nearly killed a duchess? That's a step up from implicating a duke in a torrid affair."

Ciardis paused. "You do know the duke wasn't trying to kill me just because of that affair nonsense, right?"

"Yeah, but it certainly didn't help your case when you added a power struggle for my attention on top of it."

Ciardis put her glass down, kicked off her shoes, and tucked her feet under her comfortably. It was going to be a long night.

"I didn't almost kill her. She almost killed me," she confided. "And then the dragon almost killed her."

At that, Prince Sebastian sat up.

"Wait—dragon? The ambassador tried to kill the Duchess of Carne?"

Ciardis nodded. "Something about me being her *sarin*."

There was incredulity plastered on Sebastian's face.

"Don't ask me how she knew where I was," said Ciardis truthfully, "because I have no idea. And then that minstrel said the same thing happened to my mother."

A flicker of coldness flitted over Sebastian's face before he smoothed his expression over and shook his head in confusion. "Why don't you start over? From the beginning."

She did and she told him everything she'd learned up to meeting the minstrel at the inn. Explaining the duchess's attack on her in the garden was more difficult – not only because it was so brutal that her body was still recovering.

Prince Sebastian bit his lip. He immediately released his bottom lip from the hold with a frustrated look, "I knew about the duchess and the locket from the reports I received this morning from the Magistrate's Court. But the dragon—that I didn't know."

Ciardis shrugged. "The enforcers didn't seem inclined to question her. I guess they didn't include much in their reports about it."

"Besides aren't you supposed to have spies to tell you all of these things?" she continued with a wicked smile.

"Spies," he said laughing. "I just got back into my father's good graces and it's only been two months since I was almost disinherited. Let's take it slowly here."

"All I'm saying is you might know more about the going-ons at court if you had people listening in."

"Or knew where to put my ears to the ground," he pointed out.

This time it was her turn to sit back in contemplation.

"Those other two that you mentioned—Stephanie and Christian," he said. "Who are they to you?"

"Friends," said Ciardis while hesitating. She'd already told Sebastian about everything they'd done for her, minus the dead body. But she wasn't sure yet if she should tell him about the Shadow Council. She didn't even know what it was. Or who was behind it.

"Do you think they'd be good listeners?"

"Maybe. Let's think on it. Stephanie, at least, has good connections among the nobility."

"Now, about that dragon. You know what *sarin* means?"

"Yes," Ciardis said, "and right now I don't want to discuss it."

"But—"

"Sebastian, we've got a lot more problems to be thinking about than an issue that may or may not turn into a problem."

She paused, "This isn't about the fact that a *sarin* is supposed to be a bond mate to a dragon is it?"

He spluttered, looking uncharacteristically flushed as he said, "No! Why would it be?"

She narrowed her eyes, "Just…asking."

"This has nothing to do with that. It's my job to think ahead, Ciardis. For my Empire and for my people." Uncomfortably he continued, "And this could be a major problem diplomatically for my people."

She raised an eyebrow, "Okay, but there's a problem staring us in the face right now that we need to fix."

He ran a hand through his hair messily and refilled his tea, "Then we can come back to this. So what did Maree Amber want?"

Ciardis mouth dipped downward and she grimaced involuntarily.

"To punish me for court issues and to say that I wasn't allowed at court functions for a month while she trains me."

Sebastian raised a curious eyebrow. "And yet you're here?"

"Functions, not meetings."

"This woman isn't someone you want to play with, Ciardis," he said – his shoulders stiff and his eyes firmly on hers.

"Besides, how do you know she isn't tracking you?" he continued.

"If she was, wouldn't she have recognized me?"

Point taken.

"All right, it's your turn," she said.

"My turn?"

"What's the deal with the *kith*? Is the treaty still going to happen between Algardis and Sahalia?"

For a moment Prince Sebastian was silent. Just watching her. Then he stood and he paced. Back and forth.

Ciardis watched quietly for a few minutes while reaching out to catch his feelings. He was wary, distressed and conflicted. She had a hunch that it was because this was new territory for them. They were friends, they discussed assassination plots, but they never discussed politics. Ever.

"I know you think that these political maneuvers are best kept secret but I'm in the middle of them. I have been since we met three months ago and since I've thwarted not two, but three attempts on your life."

"You could at least tell me what's happening on your side," she said with a hint of hurt in her voice. She tried to hide it, but he could feel it and that pushed him forward.

Quietly, he said, "The treaty is at an impasse. The ambassador is adamant that we end the killings in the forest."

"Have there been more killings of *kith* in the Ameles Forest since we last spoke?"

"As far as we can tell, no. Just a few isolated incidents and some dead patches in the forests. Nothing that warrants huge concern. Kinsight will be leaving within a week to take care of that."

"His journey has been pushed back?"

"Protocol in the way again," he murmured. "Plus, the courtiers don't want a big fuss."

"And yet the ambassador is concerned."

"And yet." A grim air hung between them.

Ciardis sat back with her arms folded across her chest. She wasn't convinced. Not at all.

Prince Sebastian didn't look so sure himself.

A few minutes later, he stirred. "It's getting late."

"I should be getting back."

He escorted her back to the Imperial nursery under the cover of darkness, and Ciardis slipped back up into her room without a further word.

CHAPTER EIGHTEEN

A week later, Ciardis and Maree Amber were continuing their one-on-one lessons in the head of the Companions' Guild's office. This time they were working on magical interference. Maree Amber wanted Ciardis to interrupt another mage's magic. After two hours of non-stop tutoring, Ciardis was ready to tear her hair out.

She was rubbish at it. Every time she tried to stop Maree Amber from reaching out with her magic, she only succeeded in enhancing her powers. And the lady didn't let up with her magical onslaught. So far, Ciardis's chair had been pushed over, books had been thrown in her face, her cloak had been ripped, and she swore her hair had turned green at one point.

She was tired, frustrated, and it was chaotic.

"We're not through Miss Weathervane."

Ciardis turned miserable eyes on her. Her eyes felt bloodshot and she was pale with exertion. Ciardis gripped the seat cushion on either side of her body to keep from doing something she'd regret. Like lurching up and stomping out of Maree Amber's office.

Maree Amber sighed and stared at the girl in front of her. Ciardis's bottom lip stuck out like a petulant child's while she sat staring at her knees with her hands gripping the couch beneath with her a ferocity that said there might be half-moon shaped puncture holes when she got up.

"Normally I would not keep pushing a trainee like this Ciardis," she said with kindness in her voice, "But you *must* learn this as a basic defense technique. If you can interrupt my flow of power you can interrupt another's. It's useful in many scenarios…"

"And stopping mages if they're in the act of doing something bad," said Ciardis repeating the lesson extoled at her for the past two hours, "Yes, I know. But *knowing* it is a useful tactic doesn't make it any easier for me to produce what you're asking for."

"Very well," said Maree Amber while narrowing her eyes and standing up.

"Perhaps we're going about this the wrong way," she said while walking around her desk with a pursed mouth.

Ciardis cocked her head and stared at her with a wary look in her eyes, "And what other way would there be?"

"Using your talents in the ways that you know best Miss Weathervane. Stand up please."

Ciardis stood and faced the petite head of the Companions' Guild.

"Now here is what I wish from you. I want you to *enhance* my powers. Keep pushing them until I say for you to stop."

Ciardis nodded. She was tired but this would be easy. She'd learned that pushing another's power wasn't difficult. It was the holding back part that was hard.

Standing in front of her teacher she felt for Maree Amber's power. She saw the solid mage core sitting in her mind sedately.

"I'm not going to do anything Ciardis. I won't use my power. The point is that I want you to push me even though I am not doing anything." Ciardis listened to her with half her mind as she watched the woman's core in her mind's eye. She began to poke and prod it with her power. When she touched the core, flare-ups would occur. Maree Amber's magic would react to her own and draw out from the core a little bit and snap back when Ciardis pulled her magic too far away from its orbit.

After a few minutes Ciardis was confident she knew how to accomplish this task. She grabbed at Maree Amber's core and then pushed a chain of her magic in the center. With a direct link she began to enhance Maree Amber's power.

As she enhanced she waited for something to happen. For Maree Amber's magic to react and her powers to manifest. Wasn't that the way it worked? The other mages she had enhanced had certainly done so. When she had tapped that mind mage at court in order to expose the assassin sent by the Duke of Cinnis, his telepathic powers had extended far beyond his usual limits. Ciardis's push had allowed him to read the minds of many of the courtiers present and relay the information about the assassination plans, as well as the affair between the Duke and the woman, to the correct authorities.

She grimaced remembering that. All mind mages had telepathic partners who received any of the messages they sent. Regardless of the content. And all messages were written down in court records. She hadn't know about the Duke of Cinnis's liaison until it was too late. But she was glad she had caught onto his assassination plans.

As she kept enhancing Maree Amber's powers, Maree Amber seemed to be growing uncomfortable. She was still standing tall but her face was strained with lips tightened and her eyes wide in pain until finally Maree Amber slapped her palm on her desk to their right and shouted, "Enough."

Ciardis stopped. Stumbling back Maree Amber put her back to the desk with both hands holding her up. She closed her eyes briefly and licked her lips, "Do you know what just happened Miss Weathervane?"

Ciardis shook her head. "No."

"You almost killed me."

"I...what?"

Maree Amber stood up from leaning against the desk and crossed her arms in front of her as she faced Ciardis, "You were told you can enhance magic and that is true. But for the most powerful Weathervanes, the ones that venture into the territory of mages, you can override a person's magic, command it, and even kill the mage with it."

Uneasy silence descended upon them.

"I don't understand," said Ciardis. Maree Amber had her full attention. She was actually scared now.

"When a person exerts too much magic usually their body will shut down. Because that much power is too overwhelming for them. It's a defensive tactic."

Ciardis nodded.

"But when a Weathervane uses their enhancement powers as you just did the body cannot shut down. The mage core will not

stop building. It will keep going until the magic overwhelms that person – stopping their heart or worse."

"What could worse than killing someone?

"A great many things Miss Weathervane," said Maree Amber with a dark look on her face, "A great many things."

They stood in silence until a loud bark interrupted both of their thoughts.

Ciardis startled. She had forgotten about that monstrosity sitting beside the desk. Looking over, she saw that its white fur was standing up every which way as if stood in the midst of windstorm. It was looking at the glowing orb on Maree Amber's desk.

"So soon?" she murmured as she took in the red glow.

Quickly moving around her desk Maree Amber gathered her satchel, "It's time to go."

Ciardis watched as Maree Amber hurried around the desk with the dog following her as she grabbed her cloak.

Looking irritably over her shoulder, Maree Amber stopped upon seeing her protégé still standing in front of the desk.

"Well?"

Ciardis scrambled to the door. Apparently the night wasn't over yet.

They headed outside and caught a carriage to the weave dyer district. It was on the edge of city where the smell of the dyes would go downwind and over the ocean. Once there, they exited the carriage and walked into a large building. Inside it was a warehouse with no partitions or doors. Just wide open space and a peaked roof with large, square holes in it to let in sunlight.

Maree Amber walked forward into the middle of the room where a cloaked person stood waiting for them. To either side of the middle pathway were very large vats. Ciardis walked past the vats sunk deep into the floor. The colors swirled together with every push of a dyer's mixing staff. Soon they made it to the center.

Beside the cloaked figure stood a fat merchant—she could tell by the moneybags weighing down his belt and the counting beads he had on his tablet that he was either a merchant or a tax collector; she wasn't very fond of either, to tell the truth.

The merchant cleared his throat as they approached and said loudly, "Clear the room." All of the women around them vacated their stations and quietly exited.

"Please activate the wards," Maree Amber said.

The merchant did so with wary glances around. His nose was twitching like a rat's. A fat rat's.

"Of course," said the man with the hood as he pushed the dark fabric back from his brow. Ciardis bit the inside of her cheek. Secret location, secret meeting—what would be next? Maree Amber looked over at her as if she could read her mind. She raised an eyebrow and motioned for her to come forward and stand by her side.

Ciardis could see that the uncloaked man had bland features. He had dull brown hair and brown eyes. His face was round and average, the kind of non-descript individual who could fade into a crowd at a moment's notice. She didn't trust him.

The merchant muttered something. Ciardis saw his magic flash faster than she thought possible, and there was a small *pop* in the air.

"The concealment is in effect. Our voices are muted and we cannot be seen," the merchant said. "But we don't have much time. I can't keep this up for more than a few minutes."

Maree Amber stepped forward to the formerly cloaked man and raised her hands. She called on her power and concentrated it. Ciardis watched as the magic from Maree Amber washed over his form. It started at the tip of his head and moved down to the soles of his feet. When the power dissipated, a woman stood in his place. Her hair, golden like wheat in the fall, fell down her back like a waterfall. Her eyes were a magnificent dark brown. But there was something odd about her ears. They stood straight and angular, peeking through her golden hair.

With shock, Ciardis realized that they were not only pointed, but they also had tufts of fur on them. Which meant she was inhuman, a *kith*.

"I didn't know there were more like the Ansari," Ciardis said with wide eyes. The woman turned to Ciardis, "We are not like the Ansari. Although my people respect the winged species highly."

Maree Amber interrupted. "We risk our lives by meeting this early, Alexandra. What could possibly be of such urgency?"

The woman turned her brown eyes, the shade of loam on a dark forest floor, to them and said, "Thank you for coming, Maree. There are two things that could not wait."

She turned to the nervous merchant, who was wiping perspiration from his brow. "Have you brought it?"

He nodded and reached with sweaty hands into a pouch at his waist. Fingers trembling, he picked up a small cloth-wrapped bundle. He attempted to hand it over to Alexandra but she motioned for him to give it to Maree Amber. Maree's face grew still. There was blood dripping from the cloth. Ciardis eyed it with unease.

Taking the small bundle in one hand, Maree Amber opened the cloth, glancing into Alexandra's mournful eyes.

On the cloth lay one of the *cardiara*, a mythical race of creatures which were human in all appearances except for the huge gossamer wings they possessed. This one had been stabbed, and not by its own kind. The wound in its chest nearly bisected it. This female *cardiara* had been impaled upon a human-sized weapon. Her mouth gaped open where she'd coughed up a small amount of blood, and her eyes—a stunning baby blue—stared open blindly.

"May the gods have mercy," said Maree Amber, her voice unsteady.

"The gods?" said Alexandra. "The gods have nothing to do this. It was murder…murder of one who has not left the Ameles Forest in decades."

Maree Amber glanced sharply at the fallen *cardiara's* wrist. It was true: She bore the intricate tattoo of the homebound, those of the *cardiara* who would not leave their forest voluntarily.

Ciardis stared at the tiny body blankly. This was a tragedy, but what did it have to do with them? The merchant, who'd escaped Ciardis's attention, said, "This won't stand…not one of the *kith* will let this go."

"Why?" said Ciardis.

"Because the *cardiara* are the guardians of the Ameles Forest. They ensure the health of the ecosystem," said Maree Amber her eyes jerking away from the body before her.

He continued, "It's why I brought the body here and informed Alexandra. This is just one of the many deaths in the last few months."

"Of *cardiara*?" questioned Maree Amber.

"Of many forest inhabitants," said Alexandra, "The only thing they have in common is the background as *kith*."

"Surely it is the venue of the Imperial courts to deal with this," interjected Ciardis. She cast a nervous glance at Maree Amber, waiting for a reprimand, but the woman said nothing to rebuke her.

"No," said the merchant, shaking his jowls violently. "The emperor will send his messengers, but they will do nothing but spout nonsense. They don't understand the *kith*. Maree, you do. That is why we have come."

"I have obligations—"

"To safeguard your empire and ensure its inhabitants' safety. All of the inhabitants."

Maree Amber gave a deep sigh. "Have you at least spoken to the Imperial courts about this, Alexandra?"

Ciardis was wondering why a merchant and a *kith* were pleading with the head of the Companions' Guild to intercede in their conflict. What could she possibly do that the Imperial courts could not?

"They've agreed to send Lady Vana as an envoy and lord mage Meres Kinsight to represent the Imperial courts ahead of the Prince Heir's visit. Even though I believe they hope to have the killings solved by the time he arrived, it will change nothing, of course."

Ciardis's ears perked up upon hearing the two names. Lady Vana was Terris's sponsor, and where Vana went, so did Terris.

"Very well," said Maree Amber, "I will take the time to see this through. To end the bloodshed. But I cannot go immediately."

"Maree, I cannot stress to you, and I shouldn't have to, how vitally important it is to get on top of this immediately."

"I would not delay this any further than I have to, Alexandra, but I have to be in Sandrin for another few days on an urgent matter." She paused. "Ciardis will travel ahead with you; I will follow as soon as possible. Hopefully within three days."

Alexandra turned considering eyes on Ciardis. "Very well."

CHAPTER NINETEEN

The meeting ended as quickly as it had begun. When they arrived back in front of Maree's tower, she stopped and exhaled.

"Do not think I've forgotten our month of training, Ciardis. You will not be going near the courts again until you have had that training and can sufficiently contain your power. I will make sure of that."

Ciardis nodded. "Of course."

"We'll continue where I left off in three days' time. You'll travel by horseback with Alexandra in the morning. Do not contradict her, follow her orders, and do not interact magically with anyone until I arrive. You are there to observe only. Is that clear?"

"Yes."

Maree Amber began walking into her office. Ciardis cleared her throat to get her attention.

"Why are we traveling by road?"

Maree Amber turned back to Ciardis with eyebrows raised. "Because you're going to the Ameles Forest."

Ciardis shifted her feet. That hadn't answered her question.

"What should I wear?"

"Boots, tunics, and pants," Maree Amber said in a caustic tone.

Ciardis straightened her spine, getting a little angry. This woman was dropping her into a whole new world. One which she was unprepared for. She'd already left her home once. She wasn't sure she was ready to leave another.

Maree Amber turned to her – an expression of pity on her face but it wiped away as quickly as it came.

"You will be fine Miss Weathervane. I trust Alexandra to take care of you," she said, "And what's more – I hope you grow and learn in the days you are away from me. I believe you have potential to be one of the Empire's greatest assets but only if you can find the strength to persevere in adverse situations. Of all kinds."

"Why me? Why a *forest*?"

"Good question. Because you may be needed. I definitely will be needed, and I also need to keep an eye on you."

"The death of that *cardiara* means more than you're saying."

"Much more."

"I—"

"There are things that I don't have the time or the inclination to explain right now," Maree Amber replied. "There is much that I need to do over the next few days. Please stay out of trouble and obey Alexandra's wishes."

"Yes, ma'am."

Ciardis turned to go to her room.

"One more thing, Ciardis," Maree Amber said with a tired look. "This is not to be discussed with anyone else in the guild. It is a private matter, and you will leave in the morning under the cloak of darkness."

"Very well." With that, Ciardis departed for a short night's sleep.

As Ciardis departed Maree Amber stayed behind in her office. Hours passed and she worked long into the night writing correspondence, scrying far across the empire and worrying about the possibility of the empire hosting a war on two fronts. But as she went to sleep, her last thought was not of conflict. *We really need to find a better way to weed out our candidates for the Shadow Council before they become the insipid twits the Companions' Guild so loves to foster.*

*****

As Ciardis left Maree Amber's office she didn't head to her rooms. She hurried to the baths, seeing no other way to contact Prince Sebastian from so far away and without the Aether Realm bracelet. Moving through the portal and into the Imperial nursery, she followed the directions he'd given her to get to his quarters undetected. As she slipped into the sitting room, surprised that there were no guards or servants around, she tiptoed to his bedroom door.

Easing it open, she called out to the dark bed that took up a large portion the room, "Sebastian".

A confused voice echoed out, "Ciardis?"

"No, it's the maid with your midnight sandwich. Yes, it's me! Now get up. We need to talk, and quickly."

As they went into the sitting room she launched into a detailed recall of the night's events without leaving anything out. By the time she was done, he looked as if he was holding back a yawn. Straightening from a relaxed pose he said, "She volunteered you? That doesn't sound good."

"I know. I'll be away from the courts for far too long. What if someone attacks you, or…"

"It's not me I'm worried about it. The forest is a dangerous place, and it'd be easy for an accident to occur. One sponsored by your court enemies."

That hadn't occurred to Ciardis, and now she wondered who was really behind her exile from the Imperial Courts.

"What can I do?" she implored.

"You have to go. Stay as close to Vana and Meres as you can once you meet up with them. I'll follow as soon as I'm able to convince my father that the Imperial delegation should be a priority."

Ciardis nodded and swallowed.

"Well, I guess this is goodbye."

"For now."

Before she could stand, he reached forward and pulled her into a deep hug. Still encased in his arms, she heard him whisper into her ear, "Stay safe. For me, okay? I need you around."

With an awkward laugh, he continued, "Without you, court is just going to be boring."

She smiled and stood quickly. With a nod, she left without a word. She made it out of his sitting room doors just as the first tear fell down her cheek.

*****

The next morning came quickly for Ciardis. She barely had four hours of sleep before Maree Amber's personal valet stood over her bed saying the lady had sent her to wake Ciardis immediately. Ciardis hurriedly dressed and rushed down to meet Alexandra.

Alexandra sat in a carriage outside, cloaked and confident. A few minutes later, Ciardis was looking out the carriage window, taking in the sleepy city of Sandrin as it passed by. Early morning mist twisted around the cobblestones, a chill laced the air, and a few early morning sellers were preparing the shops to open. The bakery's fires had already begun for that morning's bread, and the farrier was already shoeing a gleaming chestnut in front of his stable.

The horse's owner caught Ciardis's eye as the carriage momentarily stopped to allow a herd of large oxen pass in front of them. He was tall, easily six feet, with the bulging muscles of a man not unaccustomed to hard work. He wore fine linens and his hair was tied back and braided in a design that she'd only seen among the soldiers of Sandrin. He turned briefly from the farrier's work as she peered curiously from the cabin.

Hurriedly, she sat back in the carriage, embarrassed at being caught staring.

"You're a very curious young woman," Alexandra said, leaning casually forward to rest her arms on her knees as they exited the city gates. Turning to her, Ciardis couldn't help but be fascinated by the pointed edges of her ears that peeked out from the long strands of blonde hair.

Alexandra reached down and grabbed a short blade from inside her high boots. The edges gleamed as she turned it around in her hand. Ciardis leaned back into the plush seat cushions. The woman looked at her with knowing eyes.

"Have you ever traveled by road before?" she asked, still twirling the knife.

"Of course," Ciardis said proudly.

"From?"

"Vaneis to Sandrin."

"Those roads are paved. The path is even. There are no holes, large or small, to mar its way. It does not wind in and around obstacles, and it certainly does not buckle under pressure. That is the emperor's road."

"This," she said, gesturing outside to a road heading east, "is the *kith* road. And your journey will not be so easy."

Out the moving carriage window, Ciardis could see both roads. One laid and paved with orderly bricks, the other a flat path of brown dirt cleared of vegetation. In her opinion, neither one of them looked very hard.

As if reading her mind, Alexandra sat back and smiled. "You will see."

When the city had disappeared, the ride went from smooth to extraordinarily rough, and Ciardis began to see what she meant. The ruts in the road meant that the carriage was constantly jumping and banging, the occupants in fear of being thrown every which way if they didn't keep their hands on the handles inside.

It was misery after two hours. Her back hurt, her head throbbed, and her arms felt sore from being jerked around.

"How long did you say this journey would take?"

"Three days."

Ciardis closed her eyes in horror.

"Let's do something about this, shall we?" said Alexandra with a mischievous glint in her eyes.

"Something?"

"Something magical, of course."

"I can't. Maree Amber was very clear that I'm not supposed to—"

"As the person in charge of your care and your instructor over the next three days..."

"Instructor?" Ciardis said.

"Maree instructed you to obey my wishes, did she not?" the woman said authoritatively.

"Yes, but—"

"My wishes include a thorough instruction on the use of stabilization tactics through my air magic." She hesitated and added, "Of course, this is a subject I wouldn't force. What do you say?"

At that moment they hit a particularly bad rut in the road and were thrown to the left side of the carriage. When she impacted the wall, Ciardis felt her sheathed knife jab her cruelly in her stomach and her head banged against the wall. Shifting back into her seat while cradling her abdomen, she didn't hesitate.

"Let's do it."

"Very good."

Ciardis didn't have anything against using her magic, and Maree Amber's commands had been quite explicit. If this woman wanted to make their ride more comfortable while teaching her something, she wasn't going to say no.

"Has Maree taught you to look for another's power?"

"Yes, through mage sight."

Alexandra looked out of the window for moment. "This is how we'll do it then: I will call upon the air to form a light stream underneath the carriage. The carriage will then move forward on the air. Then we will use your power to create a stabilized feed. This road will go on for another five hours using that technique. But I warn you: the air must be constant underneath the carriage or we will go tumbling. I'm going to teach you not just to enhance a gift, but to steady it, and allow it to run on a power base far below normal output. Because the task we're doing is simple, we can redirect the wind's natural predilection to follow the currents and push it to follow the carriage."

Ciardis was a little hesitant. "Isn't that going against the natural order?"

"It is," Alexandra said, "but this will also get us to the forest at a rate five times as fast. You cannot use the pegasi to fly to the Ameles Forest or gate in by portalway. It must be by this road, and time is of the essence."

Weighing the pros took less than a second. "Let's start on that lesson then."

"In order to stabilize anyone's power feed, you first need to know how much power they're capable of pulling in to a task. What can they give over a long amount of time to feed the stabilization link? How much is too much power to take? And what is too little?"

Ciardis nodded. "How will I know?"

"Stabilization feeds are uncomplicated but need a dedicated source. They are usually done with teams of mages, but for this output only one mage is needed. I can do it, and because you're unversed in this I will put a limit on how much magic can be drawn from my core."

"Like a reserve?"

"Sort of, but more like a withdrawal with no option to increase the flow. It will be more than enough to serve our needs. All right, watch me." Ciardis turned her mage sight on Alexandra. Ciardis watched while Alexandra drew power from her core and set the power aside in a neat ball that became visible without mage sight. It glowed like a small sun in the confines of their carriage. Inside the golden sun was a much smaller silver core.

"That small silver core is the last of the magic in this withdrawal. Once reached it will either have to be replenished or we'll be riding on dirt again. I set it to silver to give us warning."

"Not bad," Ciardis admitted.

"I'm glad you approve," Alexandra said with a smile.

"Now for the stabilization feed. See how I'm drawing power from the core sitting beside me?"

Ciardis nodded as a thin but fluctuating stream of power began to flow from the core through the floor and out to the underside of the carriage.

"I'm sending it into the air below to form a wind pathway for us, but it's not stable. The power flow is fluctuating and becoming too big or too small depending on the air flow. It is responding to magic's natural tendency to be fluid. I can stabilize it myself. But having a second mage on hand will help. I don't deplete my resources as much and you can learn how to control power flow."

"Now, Ciardis, I want you to tap into the stream of power. Not into me or my core. Reach out with your magic. Concentrate."

Ciardis had never done anything like that before. She reached and reached…but there was nothing to grab the stream with. She could see the stream, she knew where it was, but using her magic to manipulate it was another thing altogether. It felt like she was missing a key step in the process.

"Here," said Alexandra as she reached for Ciardis's hand. She noticed momentarily that her hands were as cold as ice, but she focused on Alexandra's instructions instead.

"Feel the pulse of my magic throbbing through my hands. Yes, like that. Now look through your mage sight and follow the path. The magic is flowing directly from my core—it pulses with the beat of my heart. Do you feel the withdrawal core beating with same intensity?"

"Yes."

"Good, reach for it."

Ciardis felt for it, but there was a barrier around the core. She couldn't touch it.

"Keep going. If you can't touch the core, see if you can hook into the stream."

"Got it."

"Keep hold and relax. Now you can feel the thrum of the power going through the stream. It's pulsing erratically, with bits of magic large and small flowing through it. I want you to smooth it out, restrain it from taking too much magic at one time. Stabilize it."

Ciardis blew her breath out slowly. The stream felt slippery, like a live snake in her grasp. She was beginning to sweat in the confines of the carriage and her curls felt heavy.

"Can you open a window?"

Alexandra opened the window and watched Ciardis while she sought out the coiled knots of too much magic flowing through the thread and the empty pockets of too little magic flowing out. Alexandra had put a barrier over her withdrawal core to make sure the girl couldn't access or tamper with it. What Ciardis would deal with was the stream. She needed to learn to control her power, and, in doing so, learn to control her use of another's.

Slowly, little by little, she used her magic like a rolling pin. Ciardis evened out the bumps and pockets in the stream, redistributing the flow of magic inside. When that was done, she said to Alexandra quietly, "Now how do I make it stay like this?"

"Think of your magic hold as a bottleneck; as long as you have a grip on the stream of power flowing into the underside of the carriage, you can control how much magic is released. Do you feel the magic flowing inside the stream?"

"Yes."

"Keep monitoring it. Smoothing it out consistently. Restrain it when necessary. Soon it will become second nature and you won't have to focus on it continuously."

Ciardis didn't take her eyes off the stream. Smoothing the flow took some finesse at first, but now it was mostly monitoring and hitting occasionally abnormalities when she saw it. After fifteen minutes, she sat back with a tired sigh. Her eyes still took in the stream, but she knew that the stream was flowing regularly.

"The trick," Alexandra said, "is not to fall asleep while monitoring."

Ciardis laughed. "Right."

Then she noticed how smooth the carriage ride had become. With surprise, she looked out the window. They were floating a few inches above the ground and speeding along. This was so much faster. Comfortably monitoring the stream's flow with just her magic, she watched the scenery go by. Now that the road was smooth, the carriage had picked up speed. They had long ago passed outside even the large towns on the outskirts of the city of Sandrin. The hamlets they passed through now reminded her of Vaneis.

The huts were square, some with multiple levels, but they were generally small in stature and made of brick with thatched roofs. They spoke of homely inhabitants and farming communities. She saw men and women in the fields off in the distance, digging and irrigating their land.

Occasionally they would drive over a river and the carriage would move up and down as if on a sharp hillside. "The air outside had to be compressed and pushed upward," Alexandra explained, "while moving over rushing water." But for the most part it was just the road, the trees, and nature for hours.

"Will we be reaching Ameles sooner?" Ciardis questioned.

Alexandra nodded. "By the end of the day you shall see the forest rise above you."

CHAPTER TWENTY

They continued along the road. Villages only popping up sporadically, as the carriage cast its shadow on open fields in the noonday sun. Ciardis shook herself out of her stupor as the day grew closer to dusk. Alexandra was watching the scenery go by.

The carriage stopped at dusk. "I go no farther," said the driver.

Alexandra got up and exited the carriage. Ciardis, still reeling from using her power over such an extended period of time, was slow to follow her.

The driver unloaded their two knapsacks and a very large trunk.

With a crack of his whip, he turned the carriage around and was off in a storm of dust.

"How will he get back without us?" Ciardis questioned.

"He'll make it. It will take him a long time and he'll have to stop in the local villages, though," Alexandra said dispassionately.

Alexandra didn't look like she was ready to move in the next few minutes. Ciardis glanced down at her knapsack resting in a pile with Alexandra's own pack and decided to take her spyglass for a look around. They stood at the base of a small hill, and the road curved around it to disappear on the other side. Grabbing the metal instrument, she walked forward to see what she could see.

When she rounded the curve, dark forest stretched as far as the eye could see. The path ended at the curve of the hill. In between the hill and the forest stretched a flat, open plain. It was devoid of life. Empty of trees and plants, the land looked barren. Ciardis put the spyglass up to her eye. She focused on the woods before her.

Alexandra came up beside her.

She pointed to a spot in the middle of the trees. "There is our ride."

Ciardis saw a rider emerge from the trees. One man rode in front with two saddled but riderless horses following behind him. She saw horses emerging from the depths of the trees, beautiful black horses with glossy manes and coats that shimmered like liquid midnight. Alexandra turned sharply and returned to their packages. After a few moments, Ciardis lowered the spyglass but continued to stare out at the barren landscape. What could cause such devastation? Particularly just feet from a forest that so obviously teemed with life?

As he got closer Ciardis was surprised to see that they were no ties between his horse and the two riderless ones. They followed on their own. Once he reached Ciardis and Alexandra, the man spoke to each of the horses in turn, but didn't attempt to tie them up. The horses trotted over to the hillside and munched grass. Their tails, long and flowing, occasionally swished back and forth to beat off flies.

As he walked towards them Ciardis saw that his hair was closely cropped and black. His eyes were the darkest brown she had ever seen.

"Lord Mage Meres Kinsight, I wish I could say it was a pleasure to see you," said Alexandra, "but…"

The man cracked a sarcastic grin. "We've never been on good terms."

He nodded to Ciardis in greeting.

"If there's no need for delay," he said in a leading tone.

Alexandra took his cue while replying, "There's none. No other travelers are coming with us. I assume Lady Vana arrived with you?"

"She did. Let's mount up then," Meres said. "We'll reach the campsite by dark. Terris and Vana are waiting for us there."

They mounted up on the midnight horses and rode toward the trees. When they rode amid the forest, it was almost like being underwater. The tree canopy was so thick that sunlight barely reached the forest floor and it was already getting dark.

"Dismount," said Meres as they reached a fjord. "We'll walk across." Water sloshed across her boots as she waded into the moving water while leading her horse by the reins. Smooth stones on the banks turned into thick mud, which grasped as their boots as they went across. The horses had an easier time of it. But the water was up to her hips by the time they reached the middle.

"Grab on to the horse's mane, girl," Meres Kinsight said. "Let him guide you." Stumbling, Ciardis hurried to turn back and grasp the horse's mane. With his weight pulling her forward, she made it across. Deep moss covered the bank in front of them as she reached shore. It squelched beneath her boots. She realized it wasn't moss with her second step. It was too green and slimy.

Alexandra said, "Keep going, and don't stop." Her voice sounded different. High and melodic. Ciardis looked at her with a frown, but the horses were blocking Alexandra from view. Ciardis had a suspicion that Alexandra was performing magic. She could feel currents of air magic moving around her, but couldn't tell what Alexandra was trying to accomplish.

Ciardis marveled at the trees they met on the other side of the river. Huge trunks the width of five men grasping hands arced upward into the night sky. She wanted to see what the forest looked like in the dawn, but for now she would enjoy the night forest. She crouched low momentarily to stare at a blooming flower, a deep red with glowing white tendrils rising from it. It was as if the plant were magic incarnate.

"That is a red moonflower," said Alexandra. "As you can see, they bloom at night. They have hallucinogenic properties and also work as an anesthetic."

Standing, Ciardis saw other flowers she wanted to touch and admire. But she did not. She heard the howls of night wolves roaming the forest. They were pack animals; where there was one, there was always more. She told Meres and Alexandra. They made no comment and continued forward.

After a few minutes they reached a clearing. It was filled with lush soft grass and tents had been pitched in the center. Strong, tall trees ringed the clearing like guardrails with very little space between the trunks except for one opening. As they walked through the entrance, Ciardis felt a tingle down her spine. As if the trees were recognizing her. She didn't like it.

Moving forward they came to the campfire in the center of the ring. Terris and Lady Vana sat waiting for them in front of the fire with small gourds baking in the hot coals on the edge. While the three settled their horses and walked over to take a gourd, Lady Vana continued to speak to Terris in a low tone. The gourds were medium-sized, with the textured skin of branches woven into a bowl. Lifting the gourd to her lips, Ciardis took a sip, expecting water. Instead a rich soup filled with leeks, carrots, and juice met her lips.

She finished the soup in minutes, famished from their daylong journey over land.

"All right, is everybody finished?" questioned Alexandra. When everyone nodded, she said, "Good, let's pack up for the night and—"

A scream tore through the silence of the night. A knife appeared in Alexandra's hand in seconds. Ciardis sat frozen. She looked over at Meres and saw that he held a sword. Where had that come from?

A second scream echoed through the night, this time it was closer. Alexandra stood and began issuing orders.

"We can't stay here," she said firmly. "Grab only what you can carry and let's go."

"But—" protested Lady Vana.

"*Now.*"

The gaze she turned on all of them was that of a warrior. Ciardis didn't miss the fact that Meres had already gathered his knapsack and stood close to the entrance with his sword out.

He began cursing and turned quickly to them. "Hurry. The packs are coming. Leave the horses."

"Packs?" questioned Ciardis as she hurried to his side, Lady Vana and Terris beside her and Alexandra bringing up the rear.

"Vana, can you cast an orb? There's no point in us running in the dark only to trip and fall into a sinkhole," Alexandra said, her voice grim.

Without further words, the three adults created a light orb. Meres led in the front and Ciardis followed behind him with Vana in the middle, Terris behind her, and Alexandria last. As he carefully chose his path, Ciardis wondered what kind of pack it was that they were running from. Now didn't seem the opportune time to ask.

As they maneuvered around giant tree trunks and hanging vines, the voices of animals chattering overheard ceased. Ciardis heard Meres curse again. Animals in the woods, especially small mammals like squirrels, chattered when they were frightened. Their silence indicated an even greater fear. The hunters were close enough to them that the animals were trying to hide.

"Ciardis and Terris to the center," Vana said quickly. Alexandra, Meres, and Vana, who'd knocked an arrow in her bow, surrounded the two girls in a circle as they eyed the surrounding forest warily. Ciardis could feel her heart beating fast. It was throbbing in her ears as she strained to hear any sound of movement.

"What are they—"

Then the bushes around them erupted. A night wolf came barreling out of the forest, snarling and white teeth bared in the moonlight. It hit Meres—or, rather, it tried to. His sword gleamed as it arced through the air to slice into the night wolf's chest. The wolf howled in pain and kept coming. Two others emerged from the trees and ranged around their small group, preparing to attack. Meres began to speak, not in the language of humans but in the language of beasts.

He was trying to reason with the wolves. It wasn't working.

Vana edged forward. "Alexandra, take the one closest to you. I'll take care of the other two."

Vana gathered magic and shot the arrow in her bow. It split in two. Not when it hit its target, but before. The split arrow had reformed into two perfect arrows. One arrow angled left and the other angled right to target the two remaining night wolves. Ciardis was expecting the arrows to inflict a small wound on the large wolves. They were the size of horses, with heads as large as oxen's heads. She didn't think they'd go down easy. She was wrong.

The wolves were thrown back into the woods. Ciardis heard distinct thumps and yelps as they landed. Without pause, Vana knocked a second arrow as she waited for them to return.

Alexandra had called in the winds while the fight was focused on the other two wolves. The winds surrounded the third wolf in a gale storm of harsh winds. The poor night wolf was picked up like a stuffed puppet. With a flick of her hand, Alexandra tossed it far off into the woods.

"We need to keep going," said Meres.

"Why?" said Terris. "We've defeated the pack."

Alexandra pulled out a second knife from her waist. "That wasn't the pack."

CHAPTER TWENTY-ONE

Vana quickly assessed all of them and said, "No one's injured. Good. If we don't start moving soon we'll have more trouble than we can handle." Ciardis heard rustling in the woods and felt unease. As the group moved forward again in their original arrangement, Meres called back to Alexandra at the end of the group, "Alexandra, it might be good if you could contact your friends." Ciardis couldn't see him, but she definitely heard the biting wit in his tone. He sounded angry.

"They're too far off," she said. "What about yours?"

"The animals in this forest are too frightened to come out of their hiding places and too angry to help a group of humans anyway," he said, hacking viciously at vines with his sword.

They reached the river they'd crossed before, although this time they were much farther upstream.

"Vana, could you scry for the Panen warriors? If we could head in the direction of a roving group of Alexandra's people then we'd be safe." Meres asked.

"In rushing water?"

"It's water, isn't it?"

"Could you be any more of an idiot?"

"I could if I tried."

Vana gritted her teeth. "Try not to."

Alexandra had ranged upstream during the conversation. She came hurrying back.

"We need to do something, and fast. They're coming."

"Damn wendigos," cursed Meres.

"Wen-what-digos?" said Ciardis her voice rising at the end.

"Wendigos," answered Terris from beside her where she held her hand. They'd clasped hands awhile back. It made it difficult to walk fast but they'd stopped walked at the rushing water minutes ago. Ciardis could tell that Terris was frightened – her hands were clammy. Which was strange. Like Meres Kinsight, Terris had a bond with creatures; she was able to speak the mundane and the magical ones alike. Not many animals or *kith* would frighten her.

"They're flesh-eating *kith* that developed a taste for humans hundreds of years ago during the Initiate Wars," Terris continued.

"Meres, *you* can thank your ancestors for these bloody monstrosities," Alexandra said.

"Now, now, Alexandra." Meres tutted. "Your people allow them to live here. Wasn't there some kind of treaty between the two? Aren't these wendigos supposed to be peaceful?"

"Do they sound peaceful?"

"All right, Ciardis, I'm going to need your help. If I'm going to get anything out of this water. We're going to have to work together," Vana said.

Ciardis disengaged from Terris and reached for Vana's hand. But Meres raised his hand and said sharply, "Hold up, Vana. I hear something."

They waited a moment and then they all heard it. Bells.

"Good ears," Vana said.

"Do you think it's them?"

This time, Alexandra answered. "Yes, it's them. My people are coming."

Meres whistled. "Great, now where are those damn wendigos when you need them?"

"Enough," said Vana.

Meres gave her a flat look, his hand gripping his sword, but he said nothing further.

Alexandra laughed while twirling her knives. "Probably backed off as soon as they heard the approach." She flashed a sinister smile. "Happy to leave you out here if you'd prefer."

This time Ciardis saw the creature first. It came out of the trees in a blur of movement and went straight for the most defenseless: Terris, who stood off to the side. It almost looked human—a wrinkly, hunchbacked, nude human. But the creature, upright on two legs with claws as long as knives and serrated rows of teeth in its jaw, was the stuff of nightmares.

What was worse was that it immediately latched its teeth onto Terris's shoulder. Her scream rent the air and blood blossomed down her chest. Meres Kinsight leaped over Vana and brought his sword crashing down on the creature's back.

It was cleaved in half. Ciardis noted numbly, *That's one sharp sword.* And then another wendigo came out of the bushes. Vana and Alexandra worked together, Alexandra throwing her knives and Vana calling in liquid fire. The weapons hit the creature in the shoulder and the chest respectively, but it wasn't enough. It had slowed down but it was still coming.

"Fire doesn't work on wendigos!" shouted Alexandra as she hurriedly dodged a swipe of the creature's claws.

Meres had crouched down over Terris, desperately trying to stem the blood flowing from her shoulder. He would be of no help against the wendigo. Alexandra's magic wasn't really helping here, and Ciardis hadn't the slightest clue what Vana could and couldn't do.

The wendigo, ugly as sin, was turning back for another run at Vana and Alexandra. Ciardis stood in between the creature and its two intended victims. She gripped her knife tightly in her hand, knowing it wouldn't make much difference in the scheme of things. Then a spear—tipped with silver—came sailing overhead. It hit the wendigo dead on, piercing it through the heart and pinning it to the tree trunk behind it. The creature died instantly.

Ciardis turned around and saw warriors on horseback riding their way. They looked a lot like Alexandra – perhaps more of the Panen people that lived in the forest. Ignoring them for the moment, she rushed to Terris's side, fearing the worst. Meres said, "She'll live, but she needs a healer."

He whistled sharply to get the rider's attention. It was the kind of whistle that would pierce through the noise of an angry crowd brawling in the streets. It definitely caught the rider's notice. They bundled Terris up and had the others ride double.

By the time they reached their community, Terris was unconscious from blood loss and her brown skin was uncharacteristically pale. Ciardis feared for her friend's life.

Dismounting quickly, the entire riding party rushed to follow the man carrying Terris into the healer's compound. That compound was one of the few on the ground and had lights all around it. As steady crimson drops of blood dripped from Terris's shoulder, Ciardis sent up a string of prayers to all the gods she'd ever believed in.

Please don't let her die.

They took her through a carved wooden door and into a second room off to the side. Healers bustled in and out of the room assessing her injury, cleaning out the wound, healing the flesh, administering medicine, and bandaging the shoulder. Ciardis saw that it was black with the poison of the wendigo's digestive system. They had to draw it out with magic, letting the poison leech out of her shoulder and drip down into a bowl below Terris's bed until the water inside the bowl was as black as tar.

The healers tried to clear the room, growing more impatient by the minute. Ciardis ignored them and planted herself firmly at the head of Terris's bed. Out of their way and with fingers lingering on Terris's forehead, she poured what magic she had into her friend. Her magic pulse would not stop beating, not on Ciardis's watch. The healers would tell her later that she had helped. The continuous recharge of Terris's magic allowed the young mage to burn off fever. But after a while Ciardis slipped so far into her trance state that even the sharp smell of vinegar under her nose didn't awaken her.

As they left, one of the healers lit sticks of bitter weed sitting in wooden incense burners to cleanse the room. The smell of the bitter weed was enough revive Ciardis from the tired slump she'd adopted while watching over Terris. She wrinkled her nose and shot up from her crouched position by the bed. Bitter weed was the foulest smelling thing she'd ever come across. Unfortunately her legs were so tired from the crouch she had adopted that they had locked in place and she fell backward. She expected a hard, cold floor to meet her head, but was surprised when instead she fell back into a warm robe and a hard body. There was no mistaking it: She had fallen into a person. She wasn't sure what was worse—falling to the floor in humiliation or almost crushing another person while she was at it.

Straightening up, she turned to apologize and noticed with confusion that the rest of the room was empty.

"Your friends have been sent to their beds," said the man who stood behind her.

"I am Rainburn," he continued. "You have traveled a long way to be here, Ciardis Weathervane. You should rest as well."

"I'm not leaving Terris."

He paused and turned slightly to gesture to a large armchair with blankets and pillows making a comfortable nest. "I assumed you wouldn't. Your bed will be here tonight. By your friend's side."

"I'm not tired."

"My apologies. I assumed the long journey would be stressful even for a Weathervane."

"You assume a lot of things."

Reaching down, he said, "But perhaps the chair would be comfortable anyway."

Ciardis was too tired to feel the soothing tendrils he sent through her mind, the push to sleep. She didn't argue as she settled into the chair and, with one last look at Terris's resting form, collapsed into a deep sleep.

*****

The next morning she awoke to Alexandra standing over her. She carried coffee and a sandwich. Brusquely, she said, "All of us need to go to the Greeting Hall." Ciardis turned quick eyes to Terris, who was still asleep.

"With the exception of the wounded," Alexandra continued with a sip of her own coffee.

"It's required. We need to present our party to the representatives. Come, Ciardis, Terris will be fine in the healer's care," said Vana.

Ciardis quietly stood. Her mouth tasted like shit that even the coffee couldn't disguise and her eyes felt gritty. She was well rested, but that was the extent of her feel-good self this morning. She stank.

"I need a bath," she said irately. She wasn't sure if she was mad at Vana for getting Terris into this situation, Alexandra for putting her in this situation, or that damn healer for putting her to sleep last night. She decided it didn't matter. She had enough ire in her for all of them.

"You'll get it later," said Meres with a smirk. He had clearly had a bath and wore new, clean clothes. Ciardis extended her ire to him, as well, for good measure.

They all walked out silently, with Ciardis making sure to tell the healer on staff to come get her immediately when Terris awoke. As they walked in the morning sun, light shining brightly down upon them, Ciardis noticed they were in some kind of tree city. Homes were built high up in the branches of massive trees. Except for a few buildings at the base of the giant tree trunks like the healing center, the world of the Panen was in the skies.

Turning in a circle, she took in the people walking along elaborate bridges and walkways up above her. Of course their destination was on the ground, located not too far from Terris's bedside. She didn't have the time or the inclination to investigate further before they arrived at a large meeting hall. But she put it on her to-do list for later.

The four of them walked side-by-side to the front of the hall where three men awaited them. They bore the same slender body structure that Alexandra and all the Panen did. They had the same pointed ears with tufts of fur and chestnut eyes, as well. But their skin was weird. It was as if an artist had taken a deep, rich brown and a verdant green and swirled them together. But the swirl hadn't been completed, and they'd been left with mottled brown and green skin.

As they walked forward, Alexandra cursed. "These are my people's warriors. I was hoping for the village council. Say nothing; I'll do the talking."

Hmm. I guess that explains the skin that looks like living camouflage. I wonder if it rubs off.

Meres tilted his neck until Ciardis heard an audible *crack* and felt the barest hint of magic from him. Vana had her hands folded across her chest, an impolite gesture for a companion, but cleverly put her hands in position to grab the knives she had hidden up her sleeves.

Am I the only one not prepared for a fight?

The man in the middle stood ramrod straight. His long hair was pulled back and he had a stony expression on his face. Without warning he was in motion. He had no sword or knife in his hands, but he didn't look like he was running to them for a hug, either.

Alexandra moved just as fast. She met him in the middle of the room with a swift kick. He was faster. He dodged the blow like lightning. She was crafty and had already dropped to kick his feet out from under him. As he fell backwards she dove towards him with a knife. Grabbing his throat, she moved behind him and held the knife against his neck. His pulse beat steadily in his jugular vein just under the tip of her knife.

It should have been over then. It wasn't. The second man came forward. Sword raised, he headed for the three humans. Meres pulled a sword out. Vana's knives appeared like magic. Ciardis grabbed a hardwood staff that she'd been eyeing for a few minutes. They began to position themselves to surround him and face off against the third one if he joined in.

And then a voice called out from the entrance, "Stop! Immediately."

They all turned to see a man with pale skin and long gray hair staring at them from the entrance to the building.

His gaze swept over the scene and he abruptly dismissed two of the warriors.

They sheathed their weapons and left the meeting hall without a word. Alexandra released the one she held at knifepoint. That one didn't even glance back at the woman who held a knife at his back. He stepped forward and bowed briskly as he said, "Grandfather."

The old man leaned on his cane and continued to stare.

"Such reprehensible behavior. From both of you. Julius, why didn't you properly greet our guests?"

The warrior gave them all an unhappy stare.

He turned to Alexandra and stiffly, "You are once more welcome at our hearth."

With a cold glance at her companions, he said, "Your guests, on the other hand…"

"That's going to be a problem, Brother," Alexandra replied through gritted teeth, "as I brought them here to settle the war on the *kith.*"

"Brother?" echoed Ciardis.

CHAPTER TWENTY-TWO

Alexandra ignored them. "Thank you for coming, Grandfather," she said. "Before you stand the envoys from the Algardis Emperor: Lord Mage Meres Kinsight, Master of Beasts; Lady Companion Vana Cloudbreaker, Master of Codes and the Unknown; and Companion Trainee Ciardis Weathervane."

The old man chuckled. "And by the envoys' faces, you've left out a lot of details with them."

He looked them over carefully, then turned around and began walking to the door. "Let's get them up to speed, shall we?"

The siblings looked at each other uncomfortably and then Julius followed the old man out. Alexandra motioned for the group to follow.

As they walked the Panen patriarch said, "Lord Mage Meres Kinsight, I assume you know of the death of the *Cardiara* female. What you don't know is that there are more deaths…many more."

Ciardis flashed back to her conversation with the merchant, Alexandra and Maree Amber in the middle of the night. They had been warned to expect worse numbers than the reports conveyed but apparently Meres had not.

They came to very large and open plain. It was clear of trees and shrubs but not bodies. From end to end, the area was filled with death. But not humans—*kith*. The ones who weren't dead lay moaning on the ground in agony. Amid it all, dozens of healers in blue and white—human as well as *kith*—raced back and forth attending to patients.

"For weeks injured *kith* have been appearing in the field," the old man said.

"They have two kinds of wounds," said Alexandra, stepping forward. "Long, diagonal strikes, like those done by a knife, and singes and burns, as if the victim were set on fire. The burns we have been able to mend, but ..."

She hesitated and her grandfather continued for her, "All of the diagonal strikes resisted all of our forms of healing. It is as if the wound just fills with poison again when the healer is done."

"When it first started, we feared hunters had entered the Ameles Forest and left their murdered victims to be found in the open field. But day after day more injured and dead have appeared with no reason from what we can tell. No portalway exists here, and this area is no more magical than any other."

Stepping forward, Lord Mage Meres Kinsight asked, "Have any of the victims been able to tell you who attacked them?"

"They all come from different parts of the forest and the surrounding area. But all of their stories have the same two things in common: they were all taken unawares. None heard a sound or knew they were being watched until the moment they were attacked. And they were all tortured by a figure that they call 'the shadow man.'"

"Who is this shadow man?" questioned Lord Mage Meres.

"We don't know if it's one person or a group of people," said Alexandra with pain stretched across her face. "If we did know who was responsible, they would not still be in the land of the living."

"Some of my people believe the shadow man was conjured by a mage," the old man said. "A human mage of immense power."

"Dark magic such as that has not been seen since the Initiate Wars," pointed out Lady Vana. "Are you sure a mage is the cause?"

"We are sure of nothing except that our people are dying," spit out Alexandra.

"Now that you have seen the killing fields," said the old man solemnly, "what will you do about them?"

Finally Lord Mage Meres spoke. "May we speak with the survivors?"

Alexandra's grandfather nodded.

Turning to his group, Meres said, "Vana, Ciardis, and Alexandra, we shall split up and converse with the fallen here. Understand their stories, see if we can find out more about the shadow man, and, most importantly, see if any residual magic lingers from the attacks."

Julius said angrily, "You don't think we've done that already?"

"It cannot hurt to have a second set of eyes," said Lord Meres.

"Let them," commanded the old man.

As Vana, Ciardis and Alexandra walked among the victims they each spread out to cover a different section. At first Ciardis was hesitant. She'd never dealt with victims of war before. Everyone she saw had some kind of wound marring their bodies and all had grief-stricken eyes. It was enough to send her running from the area. But she mustered her courage. If they could survive such brutal attacks the least she could do was speak to them, hear their stories and perhaps help them with their grief in a small way.

As hours passed Ciardis spoke with dozens of individuals from griffins to *cardiara* to sylphs, but the one that struck her most was the tiny merchild lying listlessly in a pool of water. She looked down into the face of a young girl who had lost everything—her memories, her passions, herself. Her eyes were vacant even though her body responded. The healer who cared for her said, "She was attacked so brutally that she retreated inside herself. We believe she saw her family die, as well. She's been like this since we found her in the river."

As the noon sun faded, Lord Meres took note of all of their stories. Ciardis and Meres walked away from the grounds and along a small path. He asked her to expand on her visit with the mergirl she had seen.

"That's the only one of an aquatic nature that I've noted," Lord Kinsight said.

"Is that significant?"

"I don't know," he said, heaving an irritated sigh. "I wish I did. There are just too many unknowns about these incidents. But if we knew *why* the mergirl was the only one attacked in the water, perhaps we could postulate on the limitations of the creature or person attacking the others…this shadow man."

"But with her unable to answer questions…"

"We can't even do that," he said. "But I will still alert Imperials authorities in Sandrin of what has been found so far."

Ciardis nodded and prepared to walk back.

"Ciardis…" Meres Kinsight said hesitantly. "There's one other thing."

She stopped and turned to look at him, hearing the uncertainty in his voice.

Shifting on his feet in obvious unease, he nevertheless looked her straight in the eye as he said, "As you know, a few months back I was ill. I'm better now, but at the time I withdrew my petition to act as your Patron."

Ciardis was surprised this was what he wanted to talk about, and a little uneasy. She wasn't looking for a new Patron.

Hastily, he added, "And I don't want to renew that interest."

At her raised eyebrows, he amended, "Not that you aren't lovely. I'm just…not in a place in which I can assume those responsibilities now."

Ciardis face twitched in amusement, but she kept her composure.

"Of course, Milord," she murmured soothingly.

He cleared his throat. "Very well. I'm glad we were able to speak about this."

They were joining the others when the patriarch of the Panen – Julius and Alexandra's grandfather – caught up to them.

With a heavy sigh, he said, "There is one other thing you must see."

Vana raised her eyebrows in question. "More death?"

"Not precisely," he said with a gaze that could read souls. "But it is just as important to the forest and the people."

"Grandfather, do you mean at the center?" said Alexandra.

"Yes," he said while coughing, "If there's any chance that a journey there will help *kith* survive we must allow them to go there."

"Very well," said Julius, "We will escort them."

Vana muttered to Meres, "Do you know what center they're talking about?"

"No," he whispered back with a furrowed brow.

"Perhaps it's best you tell us more about what you want us to see first," Meres said aloud.

Alexandra and Julius exchanged hard glances.

"It might be best for you to see for yourself rather than have us explain it. But know it is important to the pact," Julius replied.

"If we are going we must do so quickly before the day passes anymore. It's a long walk," said Alexandra.

At Ciardis's hesitant look, Alexandra said, "Terris will receive the best care in the healer's center. What she needs is rest and quiet. You can provide that by coming with us."

Ciardis nodded, "I'm ready then."

They gathering their hiking attire and followed Alexandra into the forest.

After a short while Ciardis fell back to walk beside Meres. "What pact?" she asked him.

"The bond between the Imperial family and the Ameles Forest is among the strongest natural bonds in the entire empire," Meres responded, pushing past heavy vegetation. "Each time a descendant is born—"

"They receive a piece of land and imbue it with their powers and care for it for eternity, yada, yada, yada," said Ciardis with an eye roll.

A smirk crossed Mere's face. "So you've heard of the bond? Not surprising, you being the Prince Heir's Companion."

"I'm not his Companion," said Ciardis. "I'm just a trainee assigned to the Prince Heir's service."

"Assigned by who?"

"Myself, for now."

Meres's snort of disbelief was audible, but Ciardis chose to ignore it. She looked ahead to glimpse the others, who had ranged quite a distance in front of them. Vana had paused and bent down to examine a beautiful flower with wide, thick pink petals as large as Ciardis's waist. As they caught up to her, Ciardis caught her first unpleasant whiff of the plant.

Wrinkling her nose and backing up a step, she said, "Vana, what is that? It smells like death."

"Carrion flower," said Vana, eyeing it with immense interest. "I've never seen one in person before. It's quite good for masking scents."

"No kidding," said Ciardis sarcastically. "Can we leave the plant be?"

Scrapping off a sample, Vana stood and held out a mocking hand in front of her. "After you."

Ciardis walked quickly to catch up with Alexandra and Julius, taking in the surrounding forest. It was a sea of greens, browns, reds, and colors she could never put a name to. Her feet moved automatically, crushing fragrant flowers and releasing their fragrances in the air.

"It feels as hot as summer here," she said to Alexandra.

The woman smiled back at her. "The Ameles Forest is what you would call a rainforest among your people. It is always humid and hot, with plants that grow year 'round."

"But we're not more than fifty miles inland from the coast and the city of Sandrin," Ciardis said in disbelief.

"Does that matter?"

"I don't know," admitted Ciardis. "But shouldn't it? If I were walking the city streets back on the coast now, it would be cold. I mean, without the tricks the Weather Mages can produce."

"That's true and possibly the very reason you have such unnatural weather," said Alexandra.

Ciardis was sure she'd just been mocked, but she was more concerned with whatever her cloak had just gotten tangled in. Tugging on it with increased might wasn't working. She finally turned and prepared to manually disentangle it from whatever shrub had caught hold of it, and then she saw the long, furry legs that were currently encroaching on the bottom of her blue cloak. She screamed bloody murder.

Unfortunately, the eight-legged monstrosity that was currently staring up at her with its pincers of doom didn't flinch. She grabbed the cloak again to give it another tug, hoping to displace the five-pound spider from its perch but having no such luck.

"Ciardis," Alexandra warned. "Stop tugging; you're going to annoy it. You don't want to do that."

She released the cloak with a whimper as Alexandra walked in front of her and stared her in the eyes. "Stay still. I'll cut your cloak. If it goes for your neck, I'll stab it."

Comforting words, that.

To distract herself while the cutting was going on, she looked over Alexandra's shoulder at Julius.

"They go for the neck with a paralyzing toxin in their fangs," he said in answer to her unspoken question.

Except she hadn't asked and she hadn't wanted to know. Whatever happened to delusional blindness?

Alexandra cut through the left shoulder of her cloak with ease and switched over to the right, where the spider was currently perched.

"You cut the cloak and hand it over quickly," said Meres quietly. "I'll fold it over the spider to keep it from running at anyone else."

"Can't you talk to it?" said Vana sarcastically. "You know, since it's not moving or anything."

Meres's eye twitched, "Wouldn't be a bad idea, but moon spiders are notorious curmudgeons. Even if I did talk to it—him—he'd probably just get angry."

Ciardis was really not appreciating the jokes right now.

"See the design on its back?" said Meres excitedly, pointing out the white crescent shaped on its back.

Nor did she appreciate excitement over a thing that might possibly kill her in the next few seconds. And then it was over. Alexandra snapped off the edge of the cloak shoulder and tossed it quickly to Meres, who quickly wrapped up the struggling spider in its depths and tossed it into a deep crevice in the forest floor.

They walked farther until they saw something that shone with the glint of metal in the sun. A square enclosure appeared in the midst of the forest, conspicuously out of place with its straight wooden posts. From inside muffled cries came. It was the sound of a hurt creature.

"There's a griffin inside," Alexandra said, resting her hands on the wooden enclosure.

"A griffin?" asked Ciardis curiously. "What's that?"

"A *kith* with the body of lion, the long, daggerlike claws of a *hurak*, and the wings as well as head of an eagle," Julius explained. "She's the last of her kind in the forest and carrying kits, which makes her extraordinarily valuable."

Frowns were beginning to show on the faces of Meres and Vana. They didn't like where this was going.

"How do you know it's a griffin?" said Vana.

"Because we put her in there," said Julius.

"What?" snapped Meres as he pushed forward, angry and defensive. "Griffins are sentient creatures. How dare you."

"Of course she's sentient," Alexandra said turning to him.

"This is the mate of the dead griffin in the killing field. Griffins are magical creatures and we couldn't restrain her in her grief," she continued. "She attacked *kith* and human alike indiscriminately in her rage. Two of our people died under her claws."

"If she is maddened by the attack—" said Vana slowly.

"She is not without her sense," said Alexandra, "but she will also not respond to our efforts. She must rise from the fury she is in."

Julius said, "She is the last of the griffins in the Ameles Forest. The others have been wiped out in the shadow attacks."

"All of them?" asked Ciardis while looking over at them with a startled look on her face

"There were over thirty mated couples of griffins in the forest a few months back," Meres said his hands balled into fists and teeth gritted. "How can this be?"

"Are any of the other *kith* races facing such dire straits?" said Vana.

"No," replied Alexandra. "It's just the griffins.."

"Now you see why we have done all that we could to protect her," Julius said. "It's your turn to act Kinsight. If she stays in this battle rage, the kits inside her will die."

"And I suppose you brought me here to speak to her?" said Meres with anger in his voice.

"That's the idea," said Alexandra.

"Well, we have a problem. This enclosure is blocking my reception," said Meres. "You need to open the gate."

"Can't do that," said Julius, leaning against a tree. "This is the only thing keeping her contained. If it's opened, she'll be released magically and physically. One more chaotic episode could leave more individuals dead as well as agitate her enough to remove all chance of saving those kits."

Ciardis was aware that she'd been brought along for one primary reason. She was a portable amplifier of sorts, and she didn't feel offended. Stepping forward, she put her hand on the wood, looking for the griffin's mage core. But all she could see was a web distorting her vision like a cloth had been put over her eyes.

Ciaris turned away from the enclosure to say, "This enclosure. If feels as if it was built to keep individuals out as well as well something confined inside. Why can't I feel the griffin's magic?"

Julius and Alexandra exchanged wary glances. Alexandra said, "The Princess Heir used this enclosure to keep something trapped inside. She never said what and we didn't question her. Her mages came and made sure no one could pry magically or physically from the outside and whatever it was couldn't escape from the inside. The enclosure emptied on the same night of her death."

"And this whole mess with the shadow creatures started," said Julius bitterly.

"You think one had to do with the other?" asked Lady Vana.

"I think it's a hell of a coincidence."

CHAPTER TWENTY-THREE

Meres looked at Ciardis and put his hand on top of hers.

"At least you can feel the barrier," he said. "Perhaps if you act as a conduit we can broadcast my thoughts through to the struggling mother inside."

Ciardis nodded and put her hands back on the enclosure. She closed her eyes and opened her mind to the protective invisible barrier that vibrated under her fingers. She couldn't feel the griffin or see it in her mind, but she saw the wild burst of magic emanating from the griffin's core.

It wasn't so much a sign of agitation as it was the feel of natural, wild magic. Human mages trained, pruned, and bound their mage cores so much that the presence was muted. In fact, it was considered a social affront to leave your magic leaking in a presence of another. *Or a sign of a pompous twat*, Ciardis thought with satisfaction while she remembered a certain count's son who took joy in puffing up like a peacock and displaying his magic for all to see.

Outside of the wild magic of the griffin, she felt the cautious and steady beat of a complex system of magic surrounding the fence. It was built layer upon layer with all the efficiency of a seamstress's prized cross-stitch. She wouldn't be able to get around it; it had been built too well. Ciardis began to grow frustrated as she searched for a way in. She could hear the griffin's magic and feel the distress in its mind. Both called to her, but in different ways. The magic felt like a power she could meld with, enhance, and push to greater heights. The mind was one she wanted to soothe and comfort through its agony.

Ciardis surfaced and looked behind her. Meres Kinsight couldn't help her push through the barrier, but she had a hunch who could.

"Vana," she called as she caught the woman's eye. The mage was watching her with a cautious expression, legs crossed as she sat on a large rock conveniently placed nearby.

Sighing Vana asked Ciardis, "Do you know what you're asking for?"

"Yes," replied Ciardis, but she was beginning to wonder whom she was asking. She didn't know much—okay, *anything*—about the background of the woman known as Vana Cloudbreaker. She knew that she was mage of the unknown—a dark specialty of mages whose powers took unique forms. But exactly what the extent of Vana's experience was happened to be information that she didn't know and she doubted anyone else knew, either.

Walking forward, Vana came to stand to Ciardis's left. Over the girl's head, she caught Meres's eye and shook her head slightly.

To Ciardis she said, "I'll help you get through this barrier, but understand this: we will not *break* it. We will only unlock it."

Ciardis nodded in acceptance.

"Do you understand?" Vana repeated slowly with a glint in her eye.

"Yes," Ciardis said, returning the look with a firm gaze.

Assured but wary, Vana latched onto Ciardis's other hand and melded their magic.

Taking the lead, Vana formed a purple spear of magic in her mind. She mold the purple spear until it touched the edge of the enclosure. Wriggling it gently, she helped it ease a slight bit further into the barrier's magic. Built by powerful mages, the enclosure's magic resisted her advances and already sought to push the invading magic out of its meld. But the key was that Vana was in, and once she was in she could break anything. This she didn't want to break, though. She just wanted to peek through for a second.

Focusing on that intent, she sent tiny tendrils of her magic out. Carefully pushing magic into the opposite end of the spear, she began to widen the end that sat in the barrier meld until it resembled a trumpet with a wide, shallow end inside the enclosure and a hold tube piercing the enclosure's magical barrier to the outside. Smiling, Vana opened her eyes and looked over at Ciardis.

"Your turn," she said while looking at Meres and Ciardis.

Ciardis and Meres poured their magic into the enclosure through Vana's tunnel. When Ciardis reached the interior, she felt and heard a warning cry.

Warily, she halted, not backing up but not pushing forward, either. And then she heard Meres's voice in her mind.

"The griffin is alert and she's wary. Too many mages are surrounding her. Pull back, Ciardis. Now that I'm through, as long as the tunnel is here, I can get through on my own", Meres said.

Ciardis felt like a child that had been shown a prize that had been snatched back immediately. She wanted to pout, she desperately did, but she restrained herself and did as he had asked. As she opened her eyes and saw Vana watching her, she said, "Meres said—"

"I know what he said," said Vana curtly. "Just stand still and wait."

Ciardis was miffed; why was she being so cold? Deciding not to bother with it now, she closed her eyes and leaned on the barrier physically. She might not be able to be inside the fence, but she might be able to hear what was going on.

Slowly, Meres's voice began to trickle down the tunnel. At first it was distorted, but as she listened carefully she understood more and more of what he was saying.

On the other side of the fence, Meres stood facing an angry griffin imprisoned in a fence, its hackles raised and feathers fluffed. Standing firm so as to not give the appearance of fleeing, he began to speak using soothing words and a quiet voice. The pregnant griffin wasn't really in the mood for the lullaby. She screeched and moved forward, raising her forearm in an intimidating manner and clawing the air in front of him.

"Let me go!" she screamed in his mind, enraged.

Time to change tactics.

"We're trying to help you," he pleaded.

"No, no."

He crouched in pain, not from the mental shouting, which did hurt, but from the images she was sending through the link. She and her mate in flight. They'd been hunting and had dived down on unsuspecting prey—a juicy deer that they had torn to shreds with relish. Without warning, shadows had come from nowhere, a human walking behind them. He had ordered his creatures to attack them. She had barely gotten away.

She bore resentment for what she saw as one of his village warriors' attacks.

"It wasn't us, Queen of the Air," he protested.

"Human, I saw—it was human!"

"There are many humans," he said, *"Many different ones."*

A gleam came into her eye. Meres continued to talk to her. To placate her, all the while using his mind magic to calm her down imperceptibly, to push the anger back and allow reason to flow through.

Finally she trembled and lowered herself to the ground. With all four legs beneath her and her wings smoothed along her back, she was beautiful, a radiant golden goddess of the air.

"Raina," she said. "*My name is Raina."*

"Raina, then," he replied. *"Your kits have been fueled by your rage. Are they well? Can you feel them moving inside you?"*

She tilted her head quizzically at him, as if trying to understand his query, and then quickly stuffed her head under her wing and looked at her stomach.

Looking back at him, she said, "*They move. They are whole.*

"May I help?"

"Help? Help how?"

"By giving them energy and life."

"Take me from this prison first."

He raised an eyebrow. Griffins were intelligent and she knew how to bargain.

"I can only do that if you keep calm," he said, *"If my companions can speak with you and see that you are back to being of sound mind, they will free you so that you can birth your kits in freedom."*

She nodded.

Meres left the enclosure and retreated back to his physical form. Sighing, he stretched his neck to let out a crick in the side. Looking over at Vana, he said, "She wants out."

"That wasn't part of the deal."

"She's better now. Sane."

"I don't care."

"Excuse me," said Alexandra, venturing forth. "She told you this? Is she truly well?"

They all heard an angry shriek inside the enclosure when Meres removed his hand from the barrier.

Vana shot him a look and said, "Sane, huh?"

"She just doesn't want to be left alone in silence in that stupid cage," he retorted.

"Can you prove it?" Alexandra asked with an unwavering stare.

Meres nodded and said, "Take a look for yourself."

She stepped forward to touch the barrier and he guided her down to speak with the imprisoned griffin. Julius followed after that, and then Vana took a brief look inside. Finally, when they had all emerged once more, Meres said, "So can we release her?"

"It is possible," said Julius reluctantly.

"More than possible," said Alexandra firmly. "No creature of the Ameles Forest shall be imprisoned against their will when it's clear their mind is whole and well."

"I suppose the deaths are just going to be forgiven?" said Julius sardonically.

"She was driven by rage at the death of her magic."

"By that logic, if someone killed you and I decided to kill five sylphs in retaliation, I would be freed?"

Alexandra sighed and rubbed her forehead.

"Is there a council here?" Ciardis ventured. "One that your grandfather is part of? Now that she is well, they can decide."

As all four adults looked at her, she added, "Can't they?"

"It's true," Alexandra said slowly. "They can do it."

"Until then she stays inside the cage," said Julius firmly.

"A twenty-foot cube is no place for a pregnant griffin or any creature of the skies," said Meres tightly. "In fact, I'm surprised she has survived this long."

"What would you have us do?" snapped Julius. "Kill her?"

"Even if this imprisonment were a punishment for crimes committed rather than an attempt to keep her from harming herself or others, it could not last forever."

"We can feed her, make sure she has nutrients and is as comfortable as possible."

"It will kill a person's mind," Vana interjected with shadowed eyes. "It would take longer in a creature with the magic and mind of a griffin but it would happen."

They all looked at her, flabbergasted. "What?" asked Alexandra.

Vana sighed and said, "I'll tell you this much and no more. During the Initiate Wars, prisons were created to keep enemy combatants in. For the strongest mages, it broke them down over time. It wasn't really designed for *kith*, hence the size. What the Princess Heir was doing with it, I don't know."

"How she got it is what I want to know," demanded Meres.

"And why in the seven hells is it in our forest?" demanded Julius.

Vana shrugged.

"After the wars, a lot of the artifacts were left out on the battlefields. It wasn't until the school of mages made a concerted effort, ongoing even now, to clean up the sites that we truly saw all of the atrocities of the war," said Ciardis.

At a surprised look from Vana and Meres, she gave a sheepish grin. "I read a lot."

"Right, well—"

"No," interjected Alexandra. "It's time. It's time to get her out. *Now.*"

Alexandra looked over at her brother firmly. This time he didn't object. Even he couldn't condone an individual being stripped of their mind and magic slowly; it was torture.

Vana, Serena, and Meres backed away as the siblings strode forward to take their place. Alexandra lifted a necklace out from under her robes. At the end of a long silver chain was a beautiful key made of polished metals with intricate detail work.

She and her brother put their right hands on the wall, careful to keep the rest of their bodies at a distance. The fence began to pulse with a white light. Alexandra took the key and inserted it directly into the glowing wall. As she turned it, they all heard the *click* of a lock springing open, and then a portion of the fence began to dissolve. The siblings backed up in haste, preparing to face a potentially angry griffin.

When Rania stepped out in the sunlight, she blinked at the natural light shining in her eyes and dipped her head at Meres in thanks.

"Now," he said slowly after bowing to the silent griffin, "I'd like to check on your kits."

After all was pronounced well, Rania spoke, "I leave for my nest."

As she turned, she spread her long wings to fly.

They watched silently as she flew away.

CHAPTER TWENTY-FOUR

As they walked back toward the village, Meres said, "I'll check on Raina as much as possible."

Turning to Julius, he said, "I assume you know where the nest is?"

"About twenty miles north, in the cliffs above the waterfall," Julius said.

When they arrived back Alexandra called the council of elders to a meeting. Since the meeting hall was on the forest floor and fairly large, Ciardis saw no reason why she couldn't attend. Vana left, whether to avoid being asked more questions about the prison in the middle of the forest or to take a small rest, Ciardis couldn't tell.

A few minutes into the conversation, Ciardis was beginning to wish she'd taken the chance to leave, too. No one could agree on anything, but they all thought Julius and Alexandra had made an impulsive and potentially reckless decision to allow the griffin to be set free.

A woman with long feathers in her golden hair and the wisdom of ages in her eyes stood and said, "This is a grave decision that has repercussions for us all. What if she returns in a fury as she did before?"

"Then we will aid her, heal her," Alexandra's grandfather countered before Julius or Alexandra could speak.

"But—" protested another gentleman.

He was interrupted by a loud *bang* as the outer door of the meeting hall burst open in a gust of wind. When Ciardis looked over at the door, she reassessed her previous impression—it was more like a gust of angry woman.

In the doorway stood a stocky human woman, very unlike the svelte Panen people around her. She put her hands on her hips and angrily demanded, "What have you lot done to that poor griffin?"

Alexandra stepped forward. "She was imprisoned, but she's gone now."

"Gone?" huffed the woman. "I should hope not, since I just got her bandaged and fed in my healing center."

The entire room stared at her in confusion.

"You have a griffin?" said Julius slowly.

"Here, Helen? Now?" said Alexandra.

"Ain't that what I just said?"

"What color is it?" This came from Meres.

"I'm not here to answer ten question from you lot. You want to know about the griffin? Come see for yourself."

As they all rushed down the aisle, she held up a warning finger, staring up at the Panen who all towered at least two feet above her. "But I'm warning you lot. Disturb her rest and I'll have your heads."

To a person they hastily nodded, and she turned and slowly walked out of the meeting hall, the group behind her following like recalcitrant children.

When they arrived at the healing center, it was as she said. Raina was looking a little bedraggled in a nest that took up half the room. "What happened to her?" demanded Meres.

"Something attacked her and that's all I know," replied Helen. When the group tried to question her, the healer further hustled them out with admonishments about the griffin needing rest.

*****

The next morning, Terris awoke alone in her room confused. She spoke to the healers after they came in and asked after her friends. Ciardis rushed in minutes later to see Terris sitting up and looking around. Terris gave her grin.

"How are you feeling?" Ciardis asked.

Terris shrugged. "Whole." She was hesitant to add that her magic felt *weird.* She felt like she could hear other minds as well – animals perhaps but she wasn't sure what they were. And while she'd been asleep, she'd felt awash with flames, as if she'd been burning alive and nothing could quench the white fire in her veins. It was probably the poison from the wendigo, Terris decided. They must have some kind of severe hallucinogenic properties like the giant land lizards on the Western Isles. One bite from the land lizards on her home island would give a person a high fever within hours along with delusions and muscle spasms. The creatures used the forced movement in their victims and the high fever to track them in the dense forest, and then devoured their prey once the poison had done its work to fully immobilize them.

Terris sighed and rubbed the back of her head, looking around the room she was in. It was clean and spacious, with new linens on the bed and what looked like vines woven into the ceiling. Sunshine came through the wood-carved windows and a breeze wafted through. Wistfully, she thought, *Reminds me of home.*

"Where are we?" asked Terris.

"The city of Ameles," Ciardis said.

"Feel up for a walk?" said Terris.

"You're asking *me*? You're the one who just nearly died."

Terris shrugged, "Pretty sure there's nothing wrong with my legs." Testing herself she swung her feet over the edge of the bed with Ciardis hovering over her anxiously.

Standing up tentatively she jumped up and down a little, "See? Feels fine!"

Ciardis blinked and said, "Alright. If you insist. But the minute you feel tired we're coming back here."

As they walked outside, she looked at Ciardis with raised eyebrows. "City?"

"That's the literal translation of the Panen word for the place," Ciardis said as she looked around ruefully. Compared to human cities, it really didn't look like much of one. While humans carved their territories out of the surrounding nature, it looked as if the inhabitants of the Ameles Forest had done everything in their power to incorporate their 'city' into the forest. Huge, spiraling trees with large trunks that testified to centuries of existence served as the platform for an interconnected network of vine-crafted bridges and natural paths high up in the trees. On broad branches the size of normal city streets, the inhabitants had built or carved homes out of the trees upon which they stood. Natural light filtered in and out of the branches, with carefully placed mirrors reflecting light into darker corners of the thoroughfares.

As Ciardis and Terris walked along one of the footpaths, they took the time to look over the edge as they carefully held on to the vine barriers that prevented accidental falls. They were more than twenty feet off the ground, and they were currently on one of the lowest levels. As they wandered Ciardis told Terris of yesterday's adventures and the victims they'd seen on the forest floor.

As they neared a rounded hut, Terris began to feel unwell. Eventually her head began to hurt so much that she clutched it in pain. "What it is?" asked Ciardis in alarm.

"I don't know," Terris said, wincing over the pain.

"Perhaps we should go to the healer,"

"I think perhaps you're right, but—"

And then the pain intensified. Terris fell to her knees and folded her head down. Nothing was helping. Closing her eyes, she wished fervently for this to end. Deciding that she needed help, she clutched Ciardis's hand and tried to mind-call for Vana's aid. But something interfered. As soon as she open her mind to the mental connection, another voice entered.

"*Who? Who?*" questioned the voice in a weird manner.

"*Who are you?*" responded Terris.

Ciardis could hear the exchange, as well, as Terris had opened her mind and magic to her friend with her touch.

"*I am Flightfeather. Flightfeather needs help. Come, come,*" the voice commanded. It pressed an image into their heads. An image of the home in front of them. The voice was urging them to walk inside.

Ciardis looked at Terris, and Terris at Ciardis.

"My headache is gone," whispered Terris.

Ciardis raised an eyebrow at her. "Then let's see what it wants."

"It?"

"Did it sound human to you?"

Terris grimaced and stood. "We're going in and out quickly. No lingering."

To the door she called out, "And no funny stuff! We've got knives."

"We do?" whispered Ciardis.

"The healers took mine," admitted Terris.

When they walked into the home, they saw it was a single large room. Next to the far wall stood a perch with a large gray owl resting on it. Next to its perch was a large bed with thin curtains. The owl flapped its huge wings in warning when they entered and tilted its head.

They heard the same voice in their head when they looked at it. "*Who? Who?*"

Deciding it couldn't hurt to humor the thing, Ciardis pointed to herself and said her name, then pointed to Terris and did the same.

And then the light in the room shifted and curtains moved with the wind. There was a young man in the bed. As they moved closer, Ciardis could see slashes on the man's neck. The same ones seen on the stricken that she spoken to the day before. But this was man was comatose, not dead.

"*Help him, help him,*" demanded the owl.

"Help him?" queried Terris.

"How?" asked Ciardis.

"*Listen for his heart in the shadows, his heart in the shadows, his pulse through their darkness, his pulse through their darkness,"* said the owl.

For a long moment Terris stared directly at the owl. Ciardis got the feeling that she was speaking to it on a different level. Then she reached down to grab the young man's hand.

A loud *crash* sounded behind them and they turned to see glass shattered on the floor. A woman with a long braid down her back and age lines on her face stood in the open doorway with glass scattered at her feet.

"What do you think you're doing?" she shrieked.

The owl screamed and flew at the door. Unfortunately Ciardis and Terris were in front of the door, and they rushed out, nearly knocking the woman over as they hurried to get out of the angry owl's way. Once they were all outside, it circled in the air once and swooped right back into the home.

"I'll ask you again," the woman said, her face pale, "What were you doing in that home?"

Ciardis and Terris rushed to explain to her that the owl had invited them in. She listened to their tale and didn't interrupt.

Finally, she said, "That owl has not let anyone else besides me near my son for the past five months. It hasn't spoken to anyone, either. And yet you were there."

Suddenly they heard a commotion from inside. Rushing in, they saw that the boy's body on the bed had begun to shake. It began with tremors in his hands and spread throughout his body. He curled in upon himself, his head buried in his hands and screams erupting from his mouth. Ciardis and Terris backed up with their hands over their mouths and eyes wide in fear.

The woman didn't hesitate. She rushed over to the bed and grabbed her son from behind. Soothing him, she pulled his head back as he relaxed. Mopping his brow with a cloth from the bedside and patting his head, she said through sobs, "Barren, my Barren. It's all right. You're safe. Come back to us."

Soon he was limp again, as if he'd never moved. His mother rearranged him back in his bed and pulled the covers over his chest.

Clutching the cloth to her chest, she said, "Our best healers aren't able to help my son."

"Are either of you a healer?" she said with hope in her voice.

"No, ma'am," answered Terris softly. "We just heard the voice—the owl calling out to us in our heads."

As if on demand, the owl mind-spoke again. *Let them come. Let them come.*

The woman started and put her hand to her throat in surprise. She looked from perch where the owl roosted to the two girls standing before her.

"There is nothing that hasn't been tried to revive my son. I am grateful that he is still alive, but I want my son back," she said, her tone wavering into pleading. "The bond owls of Panen are sacred to my people. They know things when their human bond mates don't. If Flightfeather thinks you can help, then please can you at least try?"

Ciardis and Terris looked at each other uncertainly. They weren't healers and couldn't do anything for the young man trapped inside his own mind.

Ciardis said, "We would try if we knew *what* to do but we don't. Perhaps it would be best to call a healer from below."

"You don't think that every healer in this community hasn't tried to help my son?"

A bitterness entered the mother's voice as she wiped her son's brow, "They've all tried. They've all failed. All I'm asking is for you to give your best. The bond owls are often wise to many things we don't know."

Gulping Ciardis and Terris walked forward to the bed.

Returning to his side, they saw that his eyes were closed and his arms lay by his side on top of the blanket. He was still and pale, with wisps of hair coming down over his forehead. Someone had recently trimmed the sides and back, though. *Perhaps his mother*, thought Ciardis. She stood behind them solemnly, her hands folded in front of her, watching their every move.

Terris reached out to touch him, but her hand fell short of his face to grab a hand at his side. Hoping to give the mother some comfort, she asked, "What is his name?"

"Barren," the woman tearfully replied.

Terris loosened her grip on his hand, preparing to let go. But she felt something in his touch. A whisper of magic. A whisper of his mind. But it felt like it was cloaked, hidden by another presence—a dark mind.

"*Yes, yes,*" said Flightfeather. "*Bring him out. Bring him out.*"

He was there; Terris could feel his presence. But he was locked away, far away. Unconsciously, she reached out her left hand for Ciardis's right.

I need you, Terris said mentally.

I'm here, responded Ciardis.

And then they fell. They fell into a spiral of magic and power, searching for the boy named Barren.

As they reached his core, they felt a wall. But it was like no wall either girl had ever seen. It moved and twisted with a litheness that spoke of darkness. It was as black as ink, and, as they pushed on it, flexible. "*It's like it was built of shadows,*" Terris whispered. It was strong but flexible, and yet it also had a quality that made it feel like vapor.

"*He's behind it,*" Ciardis said. "*But it's like a barrier—similar to one that Alexandra put up when we were riding together. It's preventing his magic from releasing and those seeking his presence and his magic from finding him.*"

Pushing against the barrier was no use. So Terris felt for cracks.

There must be a way in here, Terris thought with frustration. *I wouldn't feel his presence otherwise. A tiny crack, a tiny slip in the barrier.*

She forced herself to calm down and methodically search the moving shadows for a crack in the seams. For a long time there was nothing but silence in the room as the two girls dove deep. And then a loud shout of glee echoed throughout the room in excitement. They had found the crack.

Wedging her essence into the small crevice, Terris widened it. She knew instinctively that she had to break it. Gathering her magic and Ciardis's enhancement, she pushed and pushed until she felt like she was exploding. And then the barrier dissipated and his power and his presence rushed out. Terris and Ciardis were thrown back into their bodies forcefully, and they fell back onto the ground in disarray.

When they arose again, both sported fierce headaches and identical expressions of confusion.

Before them on the bed, Barren had sat up and he looked no less confused they did. His mother let out a cry of joy and raced to her son's beside to gather him in a hug.

Seconds later Barren's mother dissolved into the tears.

Flightfeathers sent his thoughts to Terris and Ciardis. *Good, good. Thank you. Thank you. Barren, my Barren, is back!*

"Yes," said the mother, simultaneously crying and hugging her son. "Thank you. Thank you so much."

From that moment on there was no peace. People, neighbors, friends, family, and healers poured into the tiny home, all eager to see Barren and hear the story from Terris and Ciardis. They explained over and over what they had done, but they couldn't explain how they had done it.

CHAPTER TWENTY-FIVE

The next morning Ciardis and Terris were surrounded again by well-wishers and curious mages. It wasn't until Alexandra's grandfather chided everyone for overwhelming the three young people that they pulled back at all. Barren's mother, Olivia, with a glare on her face and her hands on her hips, managed to get rid of the rest of the stragglers.

After everyone dispersed, Julius wandered up to the group.

"Grandfather?" he asked as he approached.

As the Panen patriarch, Meres, Vana, and the two young women turned to greet him, they quieted at the tired look in his eyes. "There's been trouble," he said curtly. "On the southern border of the forest I've had reports of a pillar of smoke coming from the town of Borden."

"The human village closest to the forest?" asked Meres. Ciardis caught his expression. He did not look happy; dark thoughts were running through his head.

Grimly, Julius nodded. "It's not only smoke. We haven't received trade from the villagers in many days. Usually they would have brought their shares of milk, cream, and meat in exchange for our fabrics by now."

"Have any of your people seen them?" questioned Vana.

"No," replied Julius stiffly. "They prefer to come to us. We meet at the forest edge and barter there once a week."

"This is troubling, Julius," said Alexandra, coming forward.

"I seek permission to ride with four of my best warriors to survey the village," Julius said while looking at the patriarch of the Panen.

"Permission given," replied the old man, raising a stalling hand before Julius could take off. "The representatives from the Algardis Empire will ride with you."

Thank the gods, thought Ciardis, *We need to know what's going on with those villagers. If they've been attacked by the* kith, *heaven help us.*

"Very well," replied Julius, looking to Vana and Meres. "Are you ready to ride?"

Meres turned to looked Vana, Alexandra, Ciardis and Terris, "Are we?"

Various affirmations met his inquiry.

"Then let's ride. Everyone gather a pack and meet at the entrance in twenty minutes. We don't know how long we'll be gone so pack necessary items but keep it light."

As Ciardis and Terris trailed Vana back to their homes Vana spoke to them, "I know it's been an action-packed time for the two of you in just a few days. I hope you're holding up well."

They nodded as Ciardis commented, "I can't imagine it getting even busier but Maree should be here within a day. A lot of the responsibilities will fall to her."

"And you'll be trailing behind her the whole time," murmured Terris in commiseration.

Ciardis sighed. There was nothing she could say to that. She wasn't looking forward to more of this.

Gathering their things the group was soon on its way to the village that was a mere hour's ride from the forest border. Even before they reached the village, Ciardis could smell the smoke. As they drew closer and her eyes began to water, she drew up a scarf around her nose and mouth. There was nothing she could do for the sting in her eyes, however.

Riding onto the village main road, they were met with a stillness that was uncanny. There were no children in the streets or people going about their daily shopping in the market, and the homes had the empty look of abandoned buildings. Ciardis couldn't help but shiver. Meres motioned for them to keep moving forward. Julius's demeanor was alert. They rode toward the village square not knowing what they'd find.

In the center over what had once been the village's pride and joy—a central stage for entertainment—rose a pyre at least ten feet tall with smoke still rising from it and flames that flickered in the vast pile. As they dismounted, they took in the horror before them.

Hundreds of bodies were thrown haphazardly onto the huge pile, wooden logs interspersed between bodies. Some of the flesh had escaped the inferno by falling to the base. The bravest of the group, including Julius's warriors and Vana, took a closer look at the pyre. Even they couldn't stay near it for very long – the stench of the burnt bodies lingered even now. But they all reported the same thing – slashes from that thrice-damned shadow creature marked every visible body.

"This must have burned for days," whispered Vana, her mouth covered by a cloth.

"We would have known about it," said Julius in denial as he walked around the pyre.

"No," said Vana. "A Weather Mage has been here. I can see the remnants of the spell. It contained the blaze with walls of wind to this spot."

Ciardis trained her eyes on the ground where a perfect large circle was outlined on the ground with black scorch marks.

"After they were through with their torch," said Alexandra, "the wind was shifted, right?"

She looked to Vana for confirmation. The woman, who had turned a ghastly shade of white, nodded.

"There are very few villages between here and Sandrin," Meres said thoughtfully as he dug a finger into a clump of ash on the ground.

"No one would have seen the smoke or alerted the courts," he continued while dusting off his fingers. "Not from so far away."

"What did you find?" said Alexandra as she looked at him sharply.

"The dead. The living dead," he said finally.

"What?" whispered Terris.

Straightening his shoulders with a weary look, he said, "This mage, whoever it is, has trapped the souls of the dead in the ash of their bodies."

"Mother light," cursed Alexandra, backing away.

"Impossible!" said Vana. "No Weather Mage could do such a thing."

"Which is why it wasn't just a Weather Mage," he said. "There's a necromancer among us."

CHAPTER TWENTY-SIX

On the other side of the empire, Maree Amber lit a large torch. She was two stories below the Imperial courts in the catacombs reserved for members of the Imperial families. She watched as the flames threw long shadows on the high walls and tombs around her. In front of her a gatekeeper brought out a large set of keys. She could see at least a dozen iron keys dangling on the large ring he shifted around. Finally finding the one he was looking for, he thrust the key into the old, iron gate. It opened with a long creak as he waved her through.

Shutting the gate behind him Maree Amber and the gatekeeper walked down a narrow slope to the banks of the underground river. Maree knew this river supplied all of Sandrin's water supply as well as acted as a secret network of transportation under the city. While this was the main branch, a vast number of smaller rivers existed across the city. Many, she had no doubt, lay unexplored or were used by criminals for nefarious purposes. As long as the criminals left her alone she had no cause to inform the guard about them. Besides, she needed to keep the river network open. It was one of the many ways she

was able to get informants and special deliveries in and out of the city.

Taking her seat on the old boat, she directed her power to push the skiff along. After some time she came to another dock, this one much more elaborate than the last. It had been landscaped with steps carved into the cliff, and a stone entrance awaited her at the top. When she reached the top, she noticed a pike man in passing. His gray attire and stiff stance made him appear to be part of the wall. Maree ignored him and waited for the door to open.

Swiftly she walked in and climbed the stairs, removing her hood. An empty room awaited her with a roaring fire at the head. Maree Amber took off her gloves as she moved forward to rub her hands before the fire. Minutes later she heard steps behind her. She turned to meet the brown eyes of the Emperor of Algardis, and dropped to the floor in obeisance.

"Get up, Maree Amber," he said quietly. "Much is to be discussed tonight, and time is of the essence."

Well, I guess formalities are out the window, she thought.

"Very well, Sire."

She hesitated briefly before continuing on, "If I may ask—why are we meeting here? The Shadow Council has always met in secrecy, but never in such darkness."

"The answer is very simple. I do not trust all of our council."

"Milord, they are all loyal and would die for the cause of the empire."

He chuckled. "I think their definition of 'the empire' might not always consider myself or my heirs necessary."

"I'm certain—"

"The Sahalians heard of the *kith* concerns from someone in this empire, Maree. I will not have further concerns spread beyond those necessary. What I'm about to show you could destabilize all that we have worked for."

She waited for emperor to say anything further, but he just stared into the flames, watching the red, the gold, and the orange colors flicker.

He turned to face her, his face lit in profile by the flames, his high-collared military uniform cast in shadows with every movement of the fire, but nothing touched the weariness in his eyes, and the grim set of his lips.

"Milord?" she said.

"Let us go," he said, leading Maree to a small door on the far side of the room. It was built in the stone and had escaped her notice before. A shadow peeled off the wall, one of the night *gardis* that protected the emperor from dusk until dawn. They were mages with the ability to blend and merge into any shadow, taking their weapons with them, and as such were well-suited to being the night guardians of the Imperial family. Without a word, the shadow man preceded the emperor to the door and then slipped underneath. A second night guardian smoothly opened the door to allow the emperor and Maree Amber to pass through to the small room beyond.

The room was filled with bodies. Humans laid out on tables in neat rows. They were at every stage of decomposition.

"How many?"

"Ten women and children," the emperor said solemnly.

He pointed to the urns that lined the opposite side of the room. "And twenty-four men."

Maree turned her eyes from the bones and fragments of hair still attached to the decayed skin to the urns that the Emperor had pointed to.

"Do you mean…?"

"They burned the men until they were nothing but ash and then tied their souls to the remains. I called in the Ashlord to confirm."

At that name Maree turned pale as snow; the Ashlord was one of the most feared men in existence, a necromancer with command over the dead and dying.

"I thought he was ordered to the battlefields of the North." A question that was really a statement. As close as she could get to reprimanding the man who ruled the entire empire.

If the emperor noticed the reprimand, he didn't say anything about it. "Extraordinary circumstances," he said in a voice that was too quiet.

Pursing his lips, the emperor continued, "Furthermore, the Ashlord was quite clear: he'd never encountered anyone with the power over the living and dead like this. Other than himself."

"There's another with the power to reanimate the dead and their souls?"

The emperor shook his head. "As far as we can tell, this person is only able to manipulate souls. They are living dead only in the sense that their souls have been trapped in the ashes of their corporeal forms."

A quiet pause as Maree Amber took this in. "Are you saying a Shadowwalker has risen?"

"I had hoped otherwise, but—"

"Is this a killer that you wish the Shadow Council to remove?"

"Rather a systematic murder that I wish you to solve. All of these bodies come from the village of Borden ten miles west of the Ameles Forest," he said.

"May the heavens protect us," she whispered.

"They were sent as a warning from the *kith* that if the killings among their people don't stop, the deaths of humans will continue."

"Does anyone else know about this?" she asked quietly.

"I've brought my son here. He will go with you to the Ameles Forest. This must end before more blood is shed."

She nodded, and as he turned away she asked, "Sire, does Sebastian know? About the Shadow Council?"

He gave a heavy sigh and replied, "Not yet. It will be time soon, but that time has yet to come."

*****

In the palace the Prince Heir in question was staring down at a book on the legends of the *kith*. For centuries researchers had learned what they could about the inhuman races that lived in the empire, but most were reclusive creatures and preferred to keep their secrets. The books held drawings, diagrams, and written backgrounds on all those who had been catalogued but he had yet to find a creature who killed in the manner of the 'shadow man' described in Meres Kinsight's missive.

Perhaps if he could see the wounds up close it would be easier to diagnose. Perhaps they were wrong and it was a form of mass hysteria; there were more than enough potent flora and fauna in the Ameles Forest to cause such a disturbance. Shutting the book with an angry sigh, Sebastian rubbed his tired eyes and sat back.

He'd been at this since dawn, when his father had shown him the human village that had been massacred and given him the letters to read.

He knew full well that if the *kith* murders weren't solved soon, then this could blow up into another mage-*kith* war. In fact, he was surprised news had yet to get out about deaths of all of the villagers in Borden. It had been an act of retribution, and the only reason he thought hysteria hadn't spread was because the bodies had been dumped on the emperor's doorstep—literally. The guardians on watch had been smart enough to secure the scene and await orders from the commander of the Imperial Guard. It had only taken one look to assure the Imperial healers than every person in that courtyard was long dead, and then the remains had been whisked away underground until it could be determined where the bodies came from, who they were, and why they were sent.

Now it was up to Sebastian to figure out how to stop it. His father was deploying a regiment—ostensibly to guard the Prince Heir outside the capital of Sandrin, but really to ensure that no skirmishes erupted between the human settlers and the *kith.* He packed up a book and grabbed several maps of the region. It was time to meet with the regiment commander.

As Prince Heir Sebastian was heading through the palace into the military barracks, the regiment commander was making some decisions of his own.

*****

Regiment Commander Gabriel Somner stood at the head of the table poring over a map of the empire of Algardis. It was richly detailed with depictions of natural occurrences, major villages, and cities, as well as the largest thoroughfares. To his left stood Stephanie, a nervous look on her face. To his right stood Christian, his younger brother.

"Even if I wanted to take you with me, what's so important that the two of you need to come on an official Imperial visit to the Ameles Forest? Hell, there's nothing out there but trees and *kith*."

"Perhaps I just wanted to spend some quality time with my brother," Christian said, giving him a winning smile.

"I have dozens of dead men, women, and children, plus a regiment of men heading into uncharted territory," he replied with no warmth.

Christian dropped his pretenses. "We have someone inside—a girl named Ciardis Weathervane. And quite frankly we fear her powers might erupt just when they aren't needed."

"Curious," said a voice from the doorway. "Many people, including a certain dragon, have Ciardis Weathervane on their minds recently."

Three heads snapped up from the map, and instantly Gabriel Somner leapt out from behind the table and stood at attention in front the Prince Heir to the realm, Sebastian Athanos Algardis. Sebastian acknowledged him with a quick, "At ease, Commander."

"The question is why you are so interested in Ciardis?" Sebastian said with piercing green eyes fixed on Christian.

Taking a deep breath and once more ruing the responsibility that came with being an older brother to a headstrong man like Christian, Gabriel said, "Forgive me, sir. This is Christian Somner, my brother, and beside him stands Stephanie Copier."

Christian gritted his teeth just before he spoke. There was no good way to tell the Prince Heir that the mage who'd saved his inheritance was being set up as the conduit for a war, particularly if the Prince Heir was also sixteen and just entering a growth spurt. Young boys never tended to react well. It would help if he knew if the boy was infatuated with her or simply interested in her as a powerful ally. Half the courts couldn't figure out their relationship, and the betting odds in the parlors said infatuation.

Christian wasn't so sure.

Deciding that there was no time like the present, Christian tested the waters. He told the Prince Heir of their adventures, of the girl's actions in court, and of the dragon's interest in her as *sarin*. He watched as the Prince Heir's face revealed no emotion. He waited for surprise to kick in.

But he was the one who was surprised.

"And?" asked Sebastian crisply. "All of that is very nice, but a good portion of that can also be attributed to an inept mage-in-training. Particularly one with Ciardis's powers. Why would her small pushes start a war?"

Sebastian was eyeing the man with keen interest. He could see Christian Somner sizing him up like all of his opponents and allies did. They usually came away with the conclusion that he was young, excitable, and foolish. They were always wrong.

"Milord," said Gabriel Somner solemnly, "I apologize; my brother has woven quite a tale, but I'm sure nothing of the sort is happening." Gabriel had his private doubts on the matter, but nothing of substance that he could bring as evidence to the Prince Heir's attention.

Stephanie cleared her throat. "If I may speak?" All three male heads turned to the woman who up until this moment had been silence incarnate.

Stepping forward at Sebastian's nod, she leaned over the map spread out and pointed at a town on the outskirts of the Ameles Forest that was close enough to the *kith* road to receive trade from travelers. "This is Borden. There have been reports of widespread disappearances in the area, but no deaths."

Sebastian knew that only he, his father, and the regiment commander had been privy to knowledge of any kind of disturbance in the area. He had to wonder how she had gotten hold of it.

Continuing after a pause, she said, "That could mean that the villagers decided to relocate to an outside town and leave no notice right in the middle of fall harvest, or they're all dead somewhere. Regardless, Borden is the town closest to the Ameles Forest, and one of the few with all human residents."

Reluctantly Sebastian spoke while moving forward to eye the ten-mile distance between Ameles and Borden. "You seem to know more about the situation than anyone else outside of my father's inner circle."

Before anyone could issue denials, he raised a halting hand and said flatly, "I don't care for platitudes right now. Let's suppose the bodies were here at court. What does that tell you?"

"That someone wanted the court to find them, for the nobles to know about the massacre," Stephanie said without hesitation.

"But why?" said Gabriel Somner. "The nobles don't care for the poor."

Hastily, he added, "Not to include yourself or those close to you, Lordship."

Sebastian ignored the comment and said, "It gives them a reason—a reason to invade Ameles. The nobles have been trying to annex that forest since my forefathers set it up as an independent principality centuries ago. They want the forest."

"And Ciardis is the oil to light the flame," Christian concluded, "They didn't need her before. But now the bodies are gone, out of the nobles' reach. They need another reason to start a war. What's a better way than sending the Companion of the Prince Heir to her death?"

"Who ordered her there, Milord?" asked Gabriel Somner point blank.

"I did," said an authoritative voice from the doorway.

The regiment commander was beginning to get a headache. Where were his guards and why weren't they guarding the blasted door?

After a pause, Stephanie smoothly stepped in. "Your Highness, Regiment Commander, and Christian Somner, may I present Maree Amber, Head of the Companions' Council and Guild?"

Her presence filling the room, Maree Amber stepped forward. "I sent Ciardis to the forest ahead of me to build fortitude. I see I may have made the greatest mistake of all."

Turning piercing eyes on young Christian, she said sharply, "You believe she is to be murdered?"

"Or forced to use her powers to kill more humans," he said.

"Where is the second nearest town after Borden?" she said crisply.

As one, Stephanie, Sebastian, Gabriel, and Christian pointed to Hartspoint, which sat just southwest of the forest.

"Very well," she said, "Milord, you'll send a detachment of troops to the town immediately to secure the premises and evacuate all residents if necessary. We will go directly to the *kith* forest to end this foolish war before it begins."

Eyeing them all and turning to Prince Heir Sebastian, she said, "If that suits you, Milord?"

What could he say to that? He knew that Lady Amber had been handpicked by his father, and besides, she was right. "It does," he replied.

Turning to the Regiment Commander Sebastian asked, "Sir, how soon can your regiment be ready?"

"On the move by morning."

"Good; there's little time to lose."

CHAPTER TWENTY-SEVEN

An entire week went by before Ciardis and Terris felt well enough to venture outside their guest homes again. When they did, Ciardis decided to have a quiet day exploring the noonday market. As she stared down at the intricate fabrics laid out on a blanket outside a weaver's shop, Ciardis was impressed. She picked up a particularly beautiful robin's egg blue piece that had golden thread stitching on the border in a rose pattern. Footsteps behind her warned that someone had come up next to her, and a hand slipped into the crook of her elbow. She was quick to show Terris the beautiful design she'd found.

"Yes, yes, it's beautiful," said Terris, impatient with excitement. "But we need to go. The golden griffin is birthing her kits."

"Hmm," murmured Ciardis as she appreciatively looked over a deep red scarf that would go perfectly with the red ball gown she already owned. She wasn't ready to go yet. But Terris wouldn't take no for an answer, and alternatively tugged and cajoled her into heading to the healer's birthing center. When they reached the door and stepped into the airy facility, they saw the laboring griffin in the corner.

By her side was the head midwife. The same stout human female with a thick waist and no-nonsense attitude who had hustled the group out of the healing center when Raina had first arrived. Helen had her sleeves up to her elbows and her messy hair thrown into a bun on top of her head as she positioned herself to ease the delivery of a third griffin cub.

She turned to face the door as they walked in. She pursed her mouth as she saw Ciardis. The girl was dressed in spotless attire that looked easily dirtied.

"I'm about to be arm-deep in a griffin, girls. This had better be important," she said pointedly.

"I know," stammered Terris. "We came to see if we could be of any help."

Ciardis raised an alarmed eyebrow. *We did?* Blood, birthing fluid, screaming—this was not going to be good.

Helen looked them over for a moment and finally said, "I can't handle the two cubs over there and take care of their mama. And she seems to like you, so come over here and lend a careful hand." Terris was practically vibrating with excitement, while Ciardis was more inclined to start backing away slowly.

"Like us?" said Ciardis in a whisper, "How does the healer know? The griffin hasn't said a word."

"Precisely. If she had disliked us, we wouldn't be standing here. She can project a powerful screech that will echo through your body in a wave. It's so powerful that the shock has been known to crack bones," whispered Terris.

"What?" said Ciardis in a harsh whisper, "And the kits?"

"Don't be silly," replied Terris. "They're *babies*."

Ciardis noticed that she hadn't said they couldn't project the shock screech.

As they walked over, Helen, the head midwife said, "Your clothes. Change them." As they both turned, she said, "Just Ciardis. Terris, your practical ones are fine."

As Terris came over and Ciardis was directed to a back room, Helen said, "And no speaking during this process. I'll need to soothe Mama Griffin with vocal magic."

Ciardis took in her options in the workroom and opted for the cleanest. She changed into patched brown breeches and a too-large, far-from-immaculate tunic. They were plain and clearly belonged to someone who was indifferent to measuring tape when cutting hems.

Oddly enough, these remind me of home. It's been so long since I've worn something so...simple. She felt free for the first time in a long time. Irritated with where her thoughts were going, Ciardis hurried back outside. Going to a bowl at Terris's indication, Ciardis rinsed her hand in the healer's mixture of vinegar and rose water to cleanse them. Walking over to the griffin kits, she copied Terris's motions. While holding each griffin kit in a thick blanket, Ciardis was careful to avoid the claws on its feet as she wiped it down from head to tail to get rid of the birthing fluid surrounding it.

Looking over at Ciardis, Terris motioned for her to first wipe the fluid from its eyes and to use an inflated pig's skin to suck out the fluid from its nose. As she finished that task and slowly wiped down its body, the little griffin raised its head blindly search for the human holding it. Terris cooed in awe. Ciardis was less inclined to praise it, but her hands stayed gentle and focused. Standing up once their kits were clean, Terris motioned for her to follow her and they walked over to a large fenced-in area in the corner.

It was lined with blankets and thick scarves that had been sewn together and stuffed in odd shapes. Carefully, Terris laid her kit right next to one of the odd pillow creatures and they watched as it snuggled up to it, clutching the thing with its claws. Ciardis did the same and they walked back to their station, taking on the newly birthed kits. Hours later, the mother griffin had given birth to eight kits, all told. All healthy and some even beginning to mew.

"Kits are hungry," said Helen in tired satisfaction. "Let's leave them to their mother now."

The mother in question had already gotten up and begun to move over to the nursery area where her kits lay. It was large enough for her to comfortably lie down in a corner.

"In a few weeks they'll be crawling and crying," said Helen fondly.

When Raina passed by Ciardis and Terris, she spoke. Ciardis nearly jumped when words came flowing out of her beak. It had been long since she'd heard from the griffin, and even in the forest it had been mind-to-mind.

"You have my thanks," she said. Carefully, she picked two shining golden feathers from her wings. Holding them in her beak, she motioned for Ciardis and Terris to take them. And then she turned her focus on her kits mewling for milk.

With a smile pasted from ear to ear, Helen shooed them to their baths with thanks of her own. Tired, aching, and covered in birthing fluids, Ciardis was happy to be gone. Terris, with a lingering look over her shoulder, followed less eagerly. As they walked outside, Ciardis took in the scenery. Next to the healer's center was an herb garden, ordered and organized with a military general's precision. It lay mostly bare now, but she suspected in would be vibrant with rows of green herbs and plants in the summer. She was surprised to see some very large bushes cordoned off to the side of the herb garden. While nothing else was much taller than her waist, these arched up above her head.

Poking Terris, she pointed them out. "Hart's birth," the girl replied with a yawn, "They're incubators for the *cardiara*."

Ciardis sighed in relief as they finally reached the cluster of low buildings on the forest floor that served as housing for the soaking and bathing pools. Walking in and taking towels from the stack laid out in the center of the open atrium, they could feel the steam wafting in from the hot spring on the other side.

An attendant said with a chiding smile, "Been at the birthing center, I take it?"

They nodded with tired smiles.

"Well," she informed them, "the steam room is on the other side of this wall. You'll be able to discard your clothes for washing and loosen up the gook in your hair."

Dismayed, Ciardis reached up with a tentative hand and felt her locks, hoping in vain that there wasn't any birthing fluid in the curls. It would be impossible to get it all out. Unfortunately she could feel her curls already stiffening in the goop.

Damn, she thought. Even though she was irritated, she still felt mildly impressed at the stiffness of the curls; the stuff could double as holding spray for hairstyles. If you could get past the "ick" factor.

"Beyond the steam room are the shower stations and bathing stations, and after that you can relax in the soaking pools." The attendant quickly added, "There are bathing pool attendants who can help you with your hair. They have a special shampoo that they use whenever Helen comes in—works every time."

Ciardis felt her shoulders relax in relief. *Thank the gods.*

Standing under the pounding water of the shower did much to relax Ciardis and Terris. They decided to head to the bathing pools after that just for the hair treatment. Once past a screen of thick trees that separated the two areas, they were treated to a complex of three bathing pools, one large enough to fit dozens of people and two smaller ones that were more intimate. The attendants took one look at the towel-wrapped girls' hair and beckoned them over. They proceeded to untwist the braids that Terris had wrapped in elaborate loops in order to get to the goop inside the mass of hair.

For Ciardis, they released her curls from the ribbon binding them and manually applied a cream to each section. They explained that the fluids would harden under the cream until they could crack the outer layer surrounding their hair. Then they'd be able to wash it with a normal shampoo. Happy, the girls let them continue and relaxed in the hot water. After that, with wooden skewers holding their hair in place, they headed over to spend a good hour in the soaking pools.

When they arrived, it seemed as if they were not the only ones who had had the same idea. Meres and Vana already lay up to their chins in the hot mineral water. With surprise, Ciardis noted that all of the soaking pools were co-ed. They went up to Meres and Vana's pool and eased into the hot water.

"Where were you two all day?" asked Vana.

"Giving birth to kits," mumbled Ciardis.

At a raised eyebrow from Meres, Terris explained, "The golden griffin gave birth today. We soothed the kits while Healer Helen did the hard work."

"Griffins have a long birthing process once started," commented Meres. "Each kit can take up to an hour to pass through the birthing canal."

"You're telling me," said Ciardis with a groan.

"Doesn't seem so bad," commented Vana with a wicked grin.

Terris snorted, "Yeah, compared to humans who can take two days, I'll take it."

After the girls had their fun poking at Meres, they turned to other more important matters.

"I've sent word to the courts and asked for further assistance," he said.

"What was their response?" said Vana in a serious tone.

"A regiment was deployed days ago alongside Maree Amber and Prince Heir Sebastian," he replied.

"It seems that the emperor is not taking this lightly."

"Yes, but it could be a few more days before they arrive," he replied with a grimace. "As you know, the road is horrible and that many soldiers will not be able move quickly."

"Undoubtedly."

Ciardis and Terris tried to look solemn and attentive while also hoping that Meres and Vana wanted them included in their conversation.

Tentatively, Ciardis said, "With Prince Heir Sebastian by your side, perhaps the attacks on the *kith* can be stopped."

"The problem remains: Whom do we negotiate with? Why are they doing this?" Meres said while running a frustrated hand through his hair.

"I think it's time we had a deeper conversation with the old man," Vana announced. "We need to know as much as there is to know from the Panen people before the Prince Heir arrives."

He nodded and they stood up to reach for the robes that the attendants had laid out for all of them.

"Terris and Ciardis," Vana said while eyeing the girls, "I think you've both had a long enough day. Retire to the guest quarters, please."

They nodded, wishing they were going with them to meet with Alexandra's grandfather but not willing to push their luck.

As they headed back, the sunset wasn't that perceptible through the dark canopy of trees that housed the homes of the forest people. But the quiet of the forest, the gradual disappearance of daylight, and the general restful atmosphere told the girls that the sun was going down. Bedding down in the guesthouse that had been given to them in their twin cots, which had been heaped with blankets for the cold nights, Ciardis could think of nothing better than a restful night's sleep.

Curling up in her bed with a "Goodnight," to Terris, she dropped into a deep sleep.

*****

Hours later she was roused roughly from her slumber by an excited Terris. Ignoring her, Ciardis snatched the covers over her head and did her best to burrow back into the comforting warmth of her bed.

"Ciardis," snapped Terris while tugging the blanket back. "Flightfeather's here."

"Tell him to go away," came the muffled response from under the covers.

"He needs help," pleaded Terris.

"*Help, needs help*," echoed the large gray owl in both their heads.

Irritated beyond belief, Ciardis sat up and pushed the covers away. Rubbing sleep from her eyes, she saw the large gray owl perched on a bird stand above Terris's bed.

"Help with what?" she muttered sourly as she looked out of the guesthouse through the open window. Seeing the moon still high in the sky, she cursed and fell back into her bed.

"He says Barren needs us," said Terris, looking at the bird to confirm.

"Do you know what time it is?"

"A quarter to midnight," Terris said. "But Ciardis, I have a bad feeling about this. The images from Flightfeather aren't good."

This time Ciardis sat up, leaning on her elbows as she squinted first at the bird and then at Terris. "Images?" she asked suspiciously.

Terris sighed. "I can hear him in my head."

"Yeah," said Ciardis with a yawn. "So can I."

"I mean I can hear full thoughts from him Ciardis—more than the short phrases he can push into a human's mind."

"Oh."

"Yes, oh."

"Is it just owls? Anything else more interesting – can you talk to the nightwolves too?"

"Now is *not* the time."

"Right, okay. What's wrong with Barren again?"

"Flightfeather was startled earlier tonight when Barren got up out of bed on his own. He's been weak since the healing and usually needs help. This time he got up and walked out without assistance."

"That's it?" Ciardis said, her eyes throwing daggers at the bird. "Maybe he had to go pee."

"No, that's not it. If you'd shut up and listen, I'd tell you the rest."

There was silence from Ciardis's bed, which Terris took as assent.

"He got up and left in nothing but his pants. It's been raining. Flightfeather says Barren always wears his boots in the rain because he hates mud between his toes."

"I'd hate that, too," muttered Ciardis while plucking at her blanket and wishing she could fall back asleep.

"Barren didn't stop walking when he left the house," Terris said, ignoring Ciardis's muttering. "He walked to the forest and he just stood there."

"Right, okay. So where is he now?" said Ciardis, not up for a midnight hunt for a boy in the forest.

"If he's in the forest, we need to alert the warriors," she continued in a hurry, finally worried about the boy. Standing up, she shucked her sleeping clothes and put on a warm shirt and pants and dropped to the floor to look for her socks. She could never keep them in one place.

"I am not going out to that forest," Ciardis said with her butt sticking in the air and her head under the bed while she rooted around for the missing pair.

Terris cracked a smile and even Flightfeather turned his head sideways, eyeing the girl in that odd way owls do.

"Well, that's good," said Terris. "But we don't need the warriors."

With a triumphant "Gotcha!" and a startled yelp as she hit her head on the underside of the bed, Ciardis emerged victorious with the dirty socks to ask, "And why is that?"

"Because he's standing outside."

Ciardis looked at her already-dressed friend warily. She put on the socks and hurriedly stuffed her feet into boots. She stuck her head out of the house to confirm that Barren was, in fact, still out there and popped back in with a sigh.

"Yes, so he is," Ciardis said, arms crossed. "What does the bird want us to do?"

"Follow him," Terris said.

"Follow him?"

"Flightfeather can sense that Barren needs to go somewhere, but he needs us to go with him."

"The bird told you this?"

"He shared his bond with Barren so I could decipher the feelings."

"All of this happened while I slept?"

"Something like that."

Ciardis sighed in irritation. "Why can't his mother do it?"

"He needs us."

"Dammit, Terris."

CHAPTER TWENTY-EIGHT

As they snuck out of the guesthouse, Ciardis took a closer look at the boy.

"Have you noticed his eyes are closed?" Ciardis asked caustically.

Terris nodded. "He's sleepwalking. That's why I think he needs to show us something. If he's in a dream sleep, his subconscious could be leading us to a clue about the attacks."

Ciardis bit her lip in uncertainty. She had a bad feeling about this, but she also could see that Terris felt it was important. Besides, they'd probably be back in their beds within the hour. The owl took flight in front of them as they followed Barren without a word. A light misty rain began to fall, but Barren didn't slow down. If anything he picked up his pace.

They jogged behind him as he detoured along the ornate bridges and around the silent homes in the trees. He kept going farther down to the forest floor until finally they were running along the cleared dirt pathways on the ground to the outskirts of the village. Before long they saw the dark forms of trees that

marked the natural forest. Barren went straight for the trees and disappeared into the forest. Before Terris could follow him in a headlong rush, Ciardis grabbed her again.

"We can't go in there," Ciardis said pointedly. "There are things in that forest with teeth and claws. Things that eat humans. Don't you remember how you got here?"

Terris wrenched her arm out of Ciardis's grip. "I'm not leaving him out there. I can't!"

Ciardis shook her head. "I told you, I don't like it. This is as far as we go."

"Wrong," Terris said. "This is as far as *you* go."

Before she could argue with her any further, Terris took off after Barren. Ciardis stood im open-mouthed shock. Where had that come from? Terris was the sponsor's pet. She did everything Vana asked and excelled at her training. She never got in trouble and she never talked back.

Lucky me—she gets a streak of independence and it just happens to be now.

Ciardis knew that every second counted here. Hesitating, she turned to look back over her shoulder at the winking lights of the village overhead and considered running for help. But by the time she got back, Terris and Barren would be long gone. Cursing her luck, she followed behind Terris. After a few minutes of slapping large fronds back and stumbling over hidden roots and vegetation, she called in a mage light. She knew she wouldn't be able to track Terris in the forest, let alone Barren and his damn owl. But she didn't have to. Ever since she'd helped Terris—followed her, really—into Barren's mind, she could sense when she was near. Careful of her footing, she followed that sense.

Hopping over what suspiciously looked like a very large snake, Ciardis pushed aside a large number of hanging vines to find herself next to a rather large tree trunk. She could feel Terris now; she was close—very close.

But there was someone else here, she realized suddenly.

Ciardis stooped into a crouched and edged forward around the trunk. Trying to find Terris as well as staying out of sight. Unfortunately she misjudged her footing, and suddenly went tumbling into the clearing. Head over heels. This was one of the few places in the forest were the canopy of the trees had left an opening. Moonlight shone down on the small clearing where Ciardis lay on the ground, cursing.

When she got to her feet and looked around she wished she hadn't. That was when she saw him. A man in dark clothing hidden in the shadows. He came forward with his hand outstretched, chanting. She had no time to defend herself and soon was falling into a deep sleep. As she slumped over and fell back onto the forest floor, Ciardis noted something unique. The man's shadow. It was moving. But it was moving independent of him, walking by his side as he moved closer to her.

In the dense shrubbery of the forest, Terris suddenly felt her link with Ciardis twang in Fear. There was something wrong. Ignoring her search for Barren at the moment, she backtracked in search of her friend. She arrived at the clearing just in time to see Ciardis fall to the forest floor with a tall man standing over her. With a shout of anger Terris surged forward to defend her friend. At least she tried to. From behind her a hand appeared out of nowhere and clamped over her mouth, while a strong arm gripped her waist and hauled her back. Struggling, she tried to get them off of her, but she was at a disadvantage facing away from the perpetrator. Pissed off, Terris half turned and kicked the person in the groin.

As he released her, she looked back at the clearing to see that Ciardis was gone. Vanished into thin air. Terris raced into the clearing, hoping it was an illusion, that her eyes were playing tricks on her. But Ciardis wasn't there, and there was nothing to show that she had been. Leaves crunched behind her as the person who'd stopped her came forward. With an animalistic growl, Terris whirled around with her hand balled into a fist.

She was ready to get some answers from this person. If they were in on this, not even the gods would be able to help them. For a moment she stared, her jaw dropped, her fists still balled. It was hard to comprehend that the person in front of her was working with the shadow creatures. More than the shock of seeing who it was, she felt hurt. And that hurt didn't lessen when the large gray owl in the tree above her hooted.

Barren stepped out of the shadow of the tree that he was leaning on. She hadn't kicked him *that* hard.

He came into the light of the clearing clutching his head. When Terris got a look into his eyes, she froze. They were black—as black as the shadows around them.

He fell to his knees, clutching his head and panting for breath.

And then Barren stood up and the shadows in his eyes were gone.

Barren stood before her, holding out his hand defensively. "Wait," he whispered.

"We saved your miserable life," shouted Terris, "and this is how you repay us?"

The owl hooted again and mind-spoke. *Flightfeather is sorry. Flightfeather—*

"Shut up, you miserable bird," said Terris, anger clouding her voice.

She continued forward to Barren and prepared to hit him so hard he would see stars.

"It's not what you think," he said, backpedaling fast. "Can't you trust me for a moment?"

"Hell no. I don't know you," she said bitterly.

"I'm not here to hurt you," he said. "I didn't bring you out here for the shadow man."

"At least, I didn't mean to," he continued.

Terris stopped, "The shadow man? *That* was the shadow man?"

He nodded.

"How dare you," she whispered in fury. "That man—that *creature*—is killing your comrades, and you gave Ciardis to him."

"I didn't give anybody to him," he said. "It was like I was in a dream, following the sound of his voice. He told me he chose not to let me die. That I had purpose—to bring the Weathervane to him. I fought him, but as long as his magic lingers in your system, you can live at his will or die. There are no other options."

"And you chose to live," Terris said bitterly.

"I chose to find out as much as I could about him," he countered, "for my people. But when he finally decided I needed to serve my purpose, my will was gone."

She dropped her fist in disgust.

"And now my friend is gone."

"I know." He nodded. "But I know where he's taking her."

Terris looked at him, wary disbelief etched on her brown face. Contemplating her options, she decided she didn't have much of choice. Not if she wanted to get to her friend in time.

"Well, then," she said, "why didn't you say so in the first place? Let's go!"

"We need backup," he said firmly.

"While that man does gods-know-what to her?" Terris replied angrily. "No, we're going now."

With Terris standing firm, Barren sent Flightfeather back to the village for the warriors and to alert their guardians to where they were going. And then they were running in the darkness and the night, hoping with all of their might that Ciardis Weathervane was still alive.

*****

The world folded and time stood still.

When Ciardis awoke, she was no longer in the clearing. She lay in a makeshift bed of vines. She twisted and turned, trying to see more. Her head was the only thing capable of movement, her body from her shoulders to her feet bound by the moving vines. The vines were twisting, never still, and a dark color that shifted like smoke. Stifling a scream, she saw that the vines were made of shadows.

The man must have brought her here, but where was here?

Looking up, she saw more trees, but they were different. The trees had huge trunks and red leaves falling to the ground. She looked around but couldn't see much else. The shadow man walked out of the darkness of the surrounding forest.

"Ciardis Weathervane," he said softly. "I've been waiting to meet you."

"Who are you?" she said while trying to fight against the vines. But every movement just caused them to tighten, cutting into her blood circulation and making her feel faint.

"And can you call off your creepy vines?" she snapped.

He looked at her with unreadable eyes.

"It's not like you're going anywhere."

She glared at him. "I'll ask again: Who. Are. You?"

"I go by many names. None of which are important to you. Just know that I work in the service of the empire."

"By killing *kith*?" she said sardonically.

"By doing whatever is necessary to right the wrongs against *me*," he hissed back.

She watched him impassively. He was very focused on his anger.

"You and the Duchess of Carne?" she questioned more cautiously.

"Who?" he asked in genuine confusion.

Guess that means she had nothing to do with the kith *deaths. Guess that means I owe the duchess an apology. She still tried to kill my mother, though.*

But Ciardis had more immediate problems to deal with. The Shadow Mage had decided that they had talked enough. He released the shadow vines. Before she could even comprehend that she was free, he'd moved swiftly and grabbed her wrist, twisting it in his grip and smiling as pain flashed through Ciardis's arm.

She fell to the floor screaming, her wrist still in his hand.

He said, each word distinct, "And I will do anything to accomplish my goals."

Maybe angering him isn't such a good idea, she thought when the pain arcing through her body like fire had been subdued enough for her to think.

He released her wrist and smiled down at her.

"And you, my dear, are my key."

Snatching her wrist back, she fought hard not to let the tears welling up in her eyes fall down her cheeks. He'd think it was because she was weak. Because she was afraid of him. She was anything but. Furious, angry, tired, but never scared.

"What do you mean I'm the key?"

"You're calm for a girl who thinks she's going to die."

"Am I *not* going to die?" she asked hopefully. "I mean, I assume you wanted me here to help you increase your powers, but it'd be nice to get some assurance."

When in dangerous situations, Ciardis tended to be flippant.

He looked at her as if she were crazy. With a motion he called forth his shadow. Out of the darkness of the trees behind him it came, first a dark indistinct blob moving on the forest floor. When it reached a bright pool of moonlight in the clearing, it began to rise up. The blob elongated until it was as tall as a man, and then it began to take a human shape with arms and legs, a head, and a chest. Ciardis watched in detached fascination. And then the shadow man extended its two middle fingers into a long, pointed shape. Ciardis knew she was in trouble. It was a sword.

Ciardis began to backpedal across the grass. Stumbling and looking around for an escape, she noticed her way was blocked by the shadow vines, which had grown shoulder-high and were writhing together to form a wall.

"Damn vines," she muttered, turning desperately in a circle.

The man watched her dispassionately as his shadow stalked her.

"It's not personal," he said lazily, "but with your death I can spark the war. It's funny, really, how one death among so many counts for everything. Maybe then you'll amount to something bigger, something great."

"What do you mean?" she asked shakily.

Seeing the shadow pause as he contemplated her, she asked again. Desperate to get more time.

"What do you mean?" she repeated. "Why does my death mean so much?"

"There are bodies and there are bodies, Miss Weathervane." He shrugged. "I've been killing for years—at the behest of the emperor, at the behest of the nobility. But they don't care if the job gets done with casualties. Especially non-human ones."

"So you're one of the emperor's men?" she said, trying to sound calm while eyeing him and his shadow. If she could keep him calm, then maybe, just maybe, she could reason with him.

He laughed cruelly. "The emperor's man? No, never that. I do my work for the empire, but I was never good enough to be called the emperor's man. I do the Empire's dirty work and disappear into the shadows."

"What kind of dirty work?"

She noted that although the clearing they stood in was devoid of weapons of any sort, long vines were hanging loose from the trees above into the clearing below. If she could reach them perhaps she could climb over the vine barrier.

Assuming the shadow man stays where he is and assuming the living vine barrier doesn't grab me. Lots of assumptions there.

"Assassinations and disappearances mostly," he said resentfully.

She took note of his tone. "And you wanted to be more? To be recognized for more?"

"Impossible," he hissed. "Always impossible living in the shadow of my brother. I was never good enough to be a true mage. I could do parlor tricks calling shadows and fading into the night, but now I can do more—so much more."

His mouth curled distastefully. "The mages had no use for things like that after the wars. Well, now…now they will." He said it in a tone that gave her the creeps. The man was insane.

But he was still talking to her, and as long that kept up she was still alive.

"There's another war," she said. "One in the North. You can go there and be the important person you're supposed to be."

He laughed. "My brother's war, you mean?"

"Who's your brother?" she said, fishing for a name, anything to link him to a place, a time, or a family.

He continued furiously, ignoring her query. "He never wanted me by his side. Never thought I was good enough. Well, we'll see who is good enough now."

Looking at her in surprise, he admitted, "You've been a good listener."

Ciardis smiled, relieved that she was breaking through his barriers.

He smiled back and looked over at his shadow man to give a single order.

"Kill her."

CHAPTER TWENTY-NINE

Barren had successfully tracked Ciardis to the clearing.

Biting his lip, he whispered to Terris, "She's in there."

Terris didn't bother replying; she could hear Ciardis speaking now and was looking for a way around those damn vines. The best way seemed to be to climb the tree trunks. Surging forward, she tried and fell on her ass just as quickly. Her people were great swimmers and divers, having lived on small islands their whole lives, but tree climbers they were not.

"Quiet," whispered Barren. "I'll go over the barrier. Once I get those shadow vines down, you come in as backup." Before she could object that she hated his plan, he was up and scaling the large tree like a squirrel. As he disappeared into the leaves, she hoped he got over the barrier.

She paced around the perimeter, keeping an eye out for weaknesses and hoping for a fallen branch that arced over the side. *A girl can dream, right?*

A crunch of leaves was her only warning that something was behind her. She felt something hit her across her back and push her face first into the dirt and leaves. It felt large. She tried to get up. Whatever it was still lay on top of her. Maybe it was just some dead forest thing that had fallen on her. She raised herself up on to her hands and knees, trying to roll it off. And then she felt its warm breath on her neck.

Her heart pounding as the thing moved, Terris looked at the clawed hands resting on either side of her own and she almost sobbed in fear.

Then she heard its voice.

"Human. Food," it cooed.

"No," Terris corrected desperately. "Friend. Not food."

"Food," it insisted.

Terris was frightened beyond belief. Any second now it was going to bite down on the back of her exposed throat.

Feeling the wendigo on top of her, she prepared for death, closing her eyes and hoping it would be over quickly. And then her eyes snapped open. How had she known it was a wendigo, and why did it feel familiar?

Tapping into her power silently, Terris sent her feelers out. There was a bond there. However slight, she could feel a tenuous connection between her and the disgusting creature that was crouching on top of her, ready to eat her brains.

Pushing for more, she realized that it was the same wendigo that had nearly killed her that first night in the forest. Then it began to hum deep in its throat. Why wasn't it chomping down on her neck yet?

She felt its confusion and its hunger. It wanted to eat her, but it also recognized her.

Second shock of the night: The thing was sentient. Most *kith* were but she never expected a cannibalistic carnivore that howled in the night like a banshee and looked like the living dead to be intelligent.

She tried once more to reason with it. "Up! Get off me. Not food. Friend." It stayed put, still humming with hunger, confusion radiating from its mind.

Talking wasn't helping. Maybe magic would. Her talent was supposed to give her the ability to assume control of any creature, magical or mundane. As the wendigo's drool crept down her neck and it sniffed her, she felt like there was no time like the present to figure out if her ability to assume control of the practice dogs in Sandrin extended to *kith*.

Silently hoping that Barren and Ciardis were doing okay—Ciardis was still talking, after all—she mind-merged with the wendigo. Just as she lost herself in the creature's mind, she heard the shadow man say two chilling words: "Kill her."

Barren managed to drop from the trees at the exact instant the shadow mage announced the death sentence. With the strength of a childhood spent in the Ameles Forest, he tackled the shadow mage, bringing him down quickly. Unfortunately Barren had no weapons on him and the shadow mage was no slouch—he clearly knew hand-to-hand combat.

As they struggled on the ground, the shadow creature raced from where it stood over Ciardis Weathervane and maneuvered to defend its master.

"Barren!" cried Ciardis. "Watch out! That shadow is coming and it's got a sword."

Barren was too busy trying to unwrap the mage's fingers from around his neck to answer.

The mage stared down at the boy in confusion in the meantime.

Narrowing his eyes the Shadow Mage spat out, "Who are you?"

Barren smiled through a bloody mouth—courtesy of the mage on top of him—and said, "What? Don't recognize me? You nearly killed me."

When recognition flowed into the mage's eyes, Barren head-butted him, sending him tumbling back and clutching his forehead in pain.

Unfortunately that didn't take care of the shadow creature; it was almost on top of him. Ready to defend its master.

And then their world dissolved into a high-pitched screech.

*****

On the other side of the barrier, Terris had used one large push to force herself into the wendigo creature's mind. It was sentient, but not much smarter than a dog. Which made this easier. Without too much effort, she located its consciousness and sent it to sleep with a whispered command. Unfortunately she had underestimated it. It might have been as simple-minded as a dog, but it also had the resilience of a caged tiger. It did not want her to take over its mind, and since she hadn't done this before, she was having a hell of a time doing so.

Trying to halt the attack, it dug its back claws into her ankle. Terris screamed in agony but it couldn't go any further. The control she'd already asserted halted its mobility and she knew if she lost that control she'd lose her life. Anger, rage, and desperation began to fuel her attempts. As they struggled for domination, Terris started to clear its mind, inch-by-inch. She managed to push the consciousness of the wendigo in a corner temporarily and lock it into the back of its mind. After assuring herself that she commanded the creature's movements now, she ordered it to get off of her and stood up.

Staring at the nightmarish vision less than a foot from her, Terris felt her stomach flip. It was just as she remembered, with multiple rows of sharp teeth in its mouth and long, dirty claws on its paws. It stood four feet tall on two legs. Its skin was gray and wrinkled, with loose flesh hanging in odd places. Its eyes were bloodshot and clumps of straggly hair hung from its head.

Feeling its dormant consciousness one more time, she made it turn around.

"Screech!" she commanded it.

For a long moment, the wendigo did nothing. Its mind was empty and it didn't recognize the command, so Terris called up a memory of the terror she'd felt when they'd first heard the creature's call echo in the midnight air. Following her example, it let out a loud, echoing screech at the shadow barrier.

Terris could physically see the shock of the screech hit the barrier of twisting shadow vines. On impact it forced the shadow vines to dissipate.

That's more like it, thought Terris.

"Now," she said directing its mind for another screech, "get that stupid shadow creature."

With no further imagery needed, her wendigo leapt into the air on its powerful hind legs and emitted a long, loud screech echo directly at the shadow man. The shadow put up its hand in defense as if to ward off the screech and disappeared into thin air.

Smiling in relief at Ciardis, who was standing up, Terris ran over to her friend.

"Are you okay?"

"Are you?"

"Hello, ladies," said Barren from the other side of the clearing.

When they looked over at him in irritation for interrupting their reunion, he sighed and said, "Anybody seen the shadow man?"

They looked around, but Barren was right. The man who'd caused all of this…was gone.

Terris let loose a string of curses that her brothers would have been proud of.

And then the cavalry arrived.

Out of the darkness of the trees, Panen warriors materialized. The wendigo melted into the trees with a final screech – Terris's hold gone from its mind. With a little more noise, Lady Vana, Meres Kinsight, and Alexandra also showed up. Surrounding the empty glade, Vana, Meres, and Alexandra were armed to the teeth and looked like avenging angels in the night.

Holding up his hands as if in surrender, Barren said, "I can explain."

From behind him, his mother stepped out of the bushes with a look on her face that promised murder. "You'd better."

Ignoring the tensions between the young people and their guardians, Alexandra's brother Julius stepped forward and declared, "The perimeter is secure. I think we should get a full account of this evening's activities from the youth and *then* you can tear them apart."

When Vana and Barren's mother leveled a glare at him, he quickly amended that to, "Or you can skin them alive now."

Meres Kinsight sighed. "All of you. Everything. Spill it."

Ciardis, Terris, and Barren jumped all over themselves to detail all of the events that had occurred from the time Ciardis and Terris had followed Barren into the forest until the shadow vine barrier had come tumbling down.

"And he never told you his name?" demanded Alexandra while looking at Ciardis.

"Or where he was from?" This query was from Vana.

"No, I tried," said Ciardis, shaking. The night's events were beginning to overwhelm her. The man had tried to kill her. Not that she wasn't used to it, but hell, he didn't even know her!

Terris wrapped a comforting and slimy hand around Ciardis's shoulder and leveled a glare at all of the people upsetting her.

"Well," said Meres, "this is unfortunate. The shadow mage wants to kill Ciardis. I guess the plan to spread outrage and eventually start a human-*kith* war wasn't working. Nothing like an Imperial Companion's death to add fuel to the fire."

"I'm not a Companion," muttered Ciardis half-heartedly.

Vana laughed bitterly. "He's a Shadowwalker; all we need now is for him to manifest necromancy or telekinesis and we'll be right back where we started during the Initiate Wars."

And uneasy look passed across Terris's face as they walked back. Ciardis nudged her to get her to talk, but whatever it was was troubling her too much for her to speak. When she turned to look behind them at Vana and Meres, who were bringing up the rear, the look on her face stopped them in their tracks.

"Something you haven't told us, child?" Meres asked.

Terris stiffened imperceptibly when Meres spoke. Ciardis knew she wasn't afraid of Lord Kinsight. They'd gone toe-to-toe on several occasions while living with the Panen. There was something else going on, but she didn't have time to find out what right now.

"There's one other thing," said Terris, her face a mask of guilt as she looked over at Barren.

Sighing, she continued, "When Barren faced me in the forest just after Ciardis had been taken, his eyes were black...as black as night."

Meres didn't question her, didn't hesitate. "Vana," he shouted. Before Ciardis had managed to turn Terris and herself fully around to face the boy, Vana had his head pulled back at an awkward angle and a silver knife at his throat.

Meres was furious. He moved to stand in front of the two young women while eyeing the boy that Vana held with a knife at his throat. He was furious at himself for letting a threat anywhere near Terris and Ciardis as well as furious at them for not thinking to warn them of this sooner.

Ciardis asked, "What does the darkness in his eyes mean?"

"It means that he could be shadow-touched," said Meres grimly.

"Is that right, Barren? Are you being controlled even now?" Vana crooned in his ear, her blade grazing the skin on his neck, prepared to cut it at any second.

He was scared and crying as he shouted back, "No! No, I was. But I'm not now. He's gone. I swear."

"Why didn't you tell us about this before?" Meres said.

Barren blanched before a sob escaped him. No matter what he said, it wouldn't sound good.

Finally Vana hissed, "Answer him!"

"Because he was controlling me," he finally spluttered.

Meres sighed. "Ciardis, Terris. Go back to camp."

To her surprise, it was Terris who stepped forward to argue with him.

"We're staying." The look he gave them over his shoulder made Ciardis wonder if challenging him was wise.

"This is no place for girls."

"We're not girls." The words were practically snarled by Terris.

"Young women, then," replied Meres with a hint of irritation.

"Whatever is going on we should see," said Terris with a stubborn look on her face.

"It's not a pleasant experience!"

"No one said it would be!" shouted Terris.

Yep, there's definitely something going on between these two, thought Ciardis.

In the meantime, Vana was watching the exchange with something akin to amusement, and Barren just looked baffled.

"Fine, you want to stay," said Meres gruffly. "Does that go for you, too, Ciardis?"

She nodded. Not trusting herself to speak. She wasn't experienced in lot of things, but sometimes it felt like she knew more about the ills and cruelties than Terris, who'd come from a sheltered background in the Western Isles and was bonded at the hip—usually, anyway—to her sponsor. She had a sick feeling that they were both about to get an abrupt training in the tactics used on the battlefield to coerce information out of captives. Meres and Vana were going to get answers out of the boy in any way they could.

Pushing his hair back on his forehead, Meres turned back to Vana and Barren.

"We can't torture you," he said softly. "The treaty between the empire and the people of the forest prevents that. But we need information and we cannot let you just walk around if you know something pertinent, or worse—could be controlled by the shadow man at any moment."

For the first time Barren exhibited some courage. He looked Meres in the eye as he said, "I understand."

"Do you?" Meres asked gently.

Looking down at the knife in his hands, Meres continued, "When I was your age, I thought I understood, but I didn't. I was proud and foolish and thought I could withstand anything."

"Sir," said Barren with strength in his voice, "I understand that I must protect my people. I can't do that like this. I don't know if the Shadow Man is still lurking in my mind waiting to take over, watching my movements. I can't live like that. If you can help, then…then that's what I want."

"Well spoken," said Meres. "The woman holding you at knifepoint has special skills. Skills I won't get into here. But if anyone can break the spell he has on you and decipher the hold, it's she."

Not even bothering to try to move an inch, Barren addressed Vana, "Please, Milady, whatever you can do would help."

"Very well," said Vana. She turned to Terris and Ciardis, who stood silently in the background watching the scene unfold. Her eyes were unreadable, but Terris thought she saw regret in them.

Dropping her knife to the ground with a sudden movement, Vana gripped both sides of Barren's head with steady hands. She swept his legs out from under him with a thrust out foot in the same movement. As he fell, she controlled the fall and they descended to the ground together so she was seated on the ground cross-legged with his head in her lap. Without pausing further, she delved deep into her mage core and proceeded to unlock his mind.

It wasn't pretty to watch on a physical or a magical level.

With a weird mix of fear and anticipation spreading over her body, Ciardis watched as Barren's body began to spasm. His head began to jerk back and forth between Vana's palms soon after that, the shakes extending from his head down his body. Meres rushed over to hold down Barren's torso, but that didn't stop his legs and feet from kicking out. Meres cursed; he was going to hurt himself. The older mage called out to Terris and Ciardis, "Grab a leg and press down."

They hurried over and tried to ride out the spasms. Pain crossed onto Barren's unconscious face sporadically, and Ciardis could see that although Vana was still sitting upright with her legs crossed, she was just as unconscious. Her mind had gone elsewhere—deep into Barren's. Ciardis didn't want to let go of Barren's leg, but she had the instinctive urge to jump into the mind-meld. She didn't know why.

"Don't even think about it," said Meres from where he was pressing down on Barren's chest with all of his strength.

"Your magic and your powers are too untested," he said grimly. "You can—you *will*—do much more harm than good. Stay here."

But Ciardis didn't have a choice. Barren lurched up with one of the most powerful spasms yet and his hand gripped Ciardis's.

Here we go again, she thought wistfully.

And then she was gone, drowning in the sea of twined magic that was Vana and Barren's mage cores. Ciardis, unlike Vana, who had trained enough to lock her body down despite an unconscious mind, fell forward in a slump. Her head fell next to Terris's lap and her body weighing down Barren's legs.

Looking at her friend thoughtfully, Terris said, "Well, that's one way to hold him down."

Meres had some choice curses for that.

CHAPTER THIRTY

Falling into someone else's magic was a curious experience. It wasn't a controlled descent but a fast free-fall along a tunnel of light. She never knew when she would slow down or even if she would. It was exhilarating in that sense. Frightening in many others. This magic was filled with gold—pale and fiery—like the magic a child would want. Ciardis called out for Vana as she looked for the mage in the magic. The answer she got in her mind was very different from the voice she expected.

"Well, little mage," said the Land Wight with satisfaction, "it has been a while since we met."

Ciardis gasped and turned around in surprise. She couldn't see it, but she could feel it.

"Is it really you, Land Wight?" she said. "Your presence is the same but your voice is stronger."

"I have grown," it said.

"Where are you? I can't see you." she said. "What are you doing here?"

"What am I doing here?" it said with gentle amusement. "You're in my presence—in my mind, Ciardis Weathervane."

She stared in awe. "I am? But I was heading for a mage, not for you. And besides, I thought only Sebastian had that ability."

"You were and he does," said the Land Wight. "But you were heading down the wrong path. To the Shadow Mage."

"It was filled with light and—"

"Appearances can always deceive, little mage," the Land Wight said firmly. "You should know this by now," it chided.

"So you're aware of the shadowman?" she said. "The mage?"

"He has taken the Ameles Forest into the darkness where I cannot follow," the Land Wight said.

"How? Why?" she said.

"I cannot answer your second query. But the absence of the Princess Heir has caused pockets to form. Sebastian will fill them in time. I have grown stronger, but I do not yet have the strength to take back all of the land in the Prince Heir's place."

"You sound stronger," she ventured.

"My mind is clearer. I can hear the thoughts of the land and see what must be done."

"Enough to help us here?" she said.

"My ability to exercise my powers is limited, little mage," it said thoughtfully, "I only came this time to protect your mind from harm. I cannot interfere in your battle with the Shadow Mage. I am battling forces in the North that are taking too much of my strength."

"I understand. Can you take me to Vana? I need to help her with Barren's shadow-plagued mind."

There was silence for a minute, and then the Land Wight said, "I will release you into their meld now. Be wary, little mage.

You are reaching for magic that you have not yet learned to control."

And suddenly it was gone and Ciardis felt herself drop. In front of her Vana floated, and she looked Ciardis over with an angry sigh. "I should have known you'd pop in. Ciardis, you really have to learn when it's not good for you to jump into another mage's magic."

"Well—"

"If you're not invited, that's a sign not to interfere."

"Yes, but the Land Wight said—"

"Land Wight?" snapped Vana, "Mother light—*what* Land Wight?"

"The one that was just here." Calling the vibe she got from Lady Vana right then 'irritation' would have been a kindness.

"Child," Lady Vana said kindly, "I can see why half the court wants you gone. You're trouble."

"I didn't call it here," Ciardis replied, "I mean, not intentionally."

She rushed to explain, "The Shadow Mage is aware we're here." Wherever here was.

They stood in front of another barrier…which Ciardis was getting heartily tired of. This once glowed with the golden aura of the tunnel she'd been drawn down but black streaks of lightning broke the continuity – moving in waves across the golden barrier.

Nodding at the barrier Vana said "The Shadow Mage can't hide that his presence has been here – not while we stand so near Barren's mage core."

"So is that barrier Barren's or the Shadow Mage's?"

"It's Barren's magic under the Shadow Mage's will," said Vana, "I suspect the Shadow Mage threw it up when he felt me probing Barren's mind."

Silence fell as they watched the immobile wall.

"We can't get through it," Vana said, raising her hand to push firmly at the wall, "Not in the way that you and Terris did."

"Are you sure? There're no cracks at the seams?"

Vana laughed, "The Shadow Mage learned his lesson once. He won't make the same mistake again."

Her voice dipping low, "Fortunately he wasn't aware I was coming."

Turning to Ciardis she said briskly, "Since you're here you're going to help but don't get in my way. I don't have time to save you or coddle you."

Ciardis nodded and Vana grabbed her hand. With a further word she drove her power at the barrier. When the point of her power reached the barrier Ciardis felt Vana command it to meld. It spread like purple ooze along the barrier wall until it covered it from edge to edge with no gold to be seen.

Through the line of power leading back to Vana she began to pull insistently at the barrier with her magic like the suction of the ocean waves breaking against the beach sand and dragging back into the deep water.

As her pull became greater Lady Vana Cloudbreaker stepped forward and raised her hand. As the power was fading from the barrier, she was *absorbing* it into her body. The barrier began to weaken – buckling under the pressure of her purple seal and its own loss of power.

It began to swirl like water running down a drain and feed into the power line that Vana had conjured. In minutes the barrier had almost cleared and Ciardis heard Vana speak again through labored breaths, "This Shadow Mage is stronger than I thought. But not strong enough to fight me here – not from so far away. I'm going to go *behind* the barrier and clean up this mess. Here's what I need you to do – stabilize the drain with your magic. Can you do that?"

She looked at Ciardis waiting on her answer.

She nodded in return and swiftly reached for the line of power.

"Wait," snapped Vana. She quickly tied off the power feeding into her own core and created a giant withdrawal ball directly in front of her. It looked like the end of a glassmaker's wand right after the tip was pulled from the hot fire – golden and round with a glowing consistency. The black streaks continuously moving through the power only added to its beauty.

"It will continue to feed from the source until the barrier has completely disintegrated," said Vana, "Now you can take the feed."

They transferred it over and Ciardis concentrated on keeping the power flow stable and flowing. It was worrying to watch the black streaks of shadow flowing into the ball but creating a divergent thread wasn't going to happen now that Vana had gone.

Good luck, she thought as she watched the woman tough as nails crawl through the fissures in the now weakened barrier. At first nothing happened and all around Ciardis the pulse of magic continued and then she felt it – a battle of wills on the other side's barrier. What was most disconcerting were the waves of magic occasionally pushing through the broken barrier. They would hit her head on like a high wind after a storm and she would have to brace herself against the on-slaught.

"Vana, hurry please," she said as she watched the walls of the magic began to pulse erratically. Ciardis knew that meant that the battle was affecting Barren. His mage pulse was becoming erratic and his physical pulse was speed up correspondingly. Eventually it would be enough to cause an irregular pulse in a person's heart and if continued could kill Barren from the inside out.

"I don't know how much more of this he can take."

*****

On the other side of the barrier Vana was eyeing a black shadow form with human features and double-edged jagged blades for hands.

"Don't suppose you can talk, can you?" she asked jovially.

The creature stepped forward, raised its bladed left hand and swiped at her.

"Didn't think so," she said as she danced backwards.

It was slow. That was to her advantage. She also didn't think it was more than an automaton – a creature created for the express purpose to serve its master and complete one task. In this case keep Vana, and other mages, away from the pure-black ball of magic behind it. Spherical and hovering a few inches off the ground it had tendrils of shadow leaking from it and attaching themselves like roots to the surrounding walls of Barren's mage core. Vana had no doubt that this was the Shadow Mage's way of exerting control over Barren.

As they continued their dance of swipe and dodge Vana decided it was time to up the ante. The walls of magic around them were pulsing fiercely – a tremor she'd seen in many mages just before they crumbled to the floor with their hearts beating erratically in their chests. Eventually succumbing to heart failure. She didn't want to die.

And she certainly didn't want to be trapped in his mage core if he did.

Jumping back with a leap that pushed her into the air, Vana called up a defense blade of magic. It pulsed with the purple color of her core and acted as an extension of her hand.

With a sadistic grin she said at the creature, "You're not the only one who can grow blades."

And then she struck, again and again and again, in a fiery sequence that said she'd been playing with it all along. Within a few seconds the creature had been decapitated with both of its arms lying by its side and its head a few feet away. She threw out shields on the limbs to keep its body from re-integrating just in case.

Not many mages could do that. But her talents extended beyond breaking into and deciphering complex mage spells – it also lent itself well to keeping those spells broken.

She walked forward and eyed the pulsing black ball that was currently ensnaring the boy.

"Ingenious," she muttered softly to herself, "I haven't seen this level of control outside of the Mind Mages in the North. And it's self-contained."

Taking one last look she changed the blade in her hand into a long whip. With almighty heave she wrapped it around the core and proceeded to squeeze it magically with all the power she had.

Just when she thought it wouldn't break it – it burst with a sudden gale force. The Shadow Mage's power dispersed like a dark cloud in all directions and dissipated in the core.

She heard a startled shout from the other side of the barrier. It hadn't been a warning or a cry of pain, just surprise, so she ignored it for the moment. Sending out feelers she checked to make sure it wouldn't adversely affect the boy, but it looked like his core was merely absorbing everything that was left. She disappeared the whip and made sure none of her own magic was leaking before she left. Walking out to the other side of the barrier she saw the girl flat on her back looking dazed.

Smiling in amusement she reached down to give her a hand. Pulling her up as the girl rubbed her head she said, "That was some burst of the bubble aye?"

Ciardis thought back over the moment before – The barrier had disappeared abruptly and she'd been left drawing on the power and stabilizing *nothing*. Hence the fall.

"You defeated the Shadow Mage," she said with some reproach.

Vana waved a hand, "I defeated the mage's creature. Not the person himself."

"You could have warned me."

"Lesson number two – always be prepared."

"What was lesson number one?"

"How to stabilize another mage's power feed under duress."

"What ever happened to Barren?"

"He's around us. It'll take him a minute or so fully absorb all of the extra magic in his system and reassert himself in his core."

"You mean all of that magic is his now?"

"Every last drop. Kid's going to feel like he's on a high for at least a week."

"Let's get out of here," Ciardis said while rubbing a sore shoulder. Could a shoulder be sore magically? She didn't know but it certainly *felt* like it.

They rose up their forms and prepared to leave Barren's mage core.

When they opened their eyes physically Ciardis groaned and managed to inhale mud. Spluttering she sat up coughing as she tried to dislodge the thick, wet earth from her mouth. With horror she realized that she'd been sitting face first in mud and her body felt like a wildebeest had stomped on it. With one last effort to spit out the dirt from her mouth she glared at Terris, "Why didn't you catch me?"

"Why did you fall?"

"And why in the seven hells do I feel like a horse has run over me?" Ciardis complained while reaching for an aching shoulder.

"Mage wounds," said Vana cheerfully as she sat up.

"Every wound you receive against yourself in a mind mage battle is a wound you feel on your physical self," Vana continued after Ciardis's clueless look.

"Every one?" she asked in disbelief.

"As long as you don't have a proper shielding," Vana said, "Most advanced mages do, which is why younglings like yourself aren't allowed to do the kind of magic you just did."

Ciardis sighed in irritation. She had helped hadn't she? So what was with the censure?

"You look right as rain," Ciardis said sourly, "I guess your shielding worked."

"Didn't have any," Vana said with a smirk, "That Shadow Creature couldn't *touch* me."

At that moment a loud groan can from the boy laying at their feet. He opened his eyes and said groggily, "What happened?

"Long story," Meres said ruefully, "Just know that thanks to Lady Vana and the efforts of Ciardis Weathervane, the Shadow Mage has been removed from your mage core and your conscience."

"Again," chimed Ciardis and Terris at identical moments.

As they began to walk back towards the village Ciardis asked, "Terris what in the world is on your hands?"

"Trust me. You don't want to know."

CHAPTER THIRTY-ONE

The next few days passed slowly as Julius dispatched bands of roving Panen warriors to search the woods around Ameles for the shadow mage. Each returned with no luck. More bodies began to pile up. This time they weren't in the small forest clearing of death. They appeared everywhere, like bloody presents that wouldn't stop coming. One morning Ciardis woke up and stumbled to the baths. Her screams woke up half the village, and half-dressed warriors raced toward the sound of her voice.

She stared at the still water in pain and fury - there was nothing else to do. A griffin—Terris's griffin—lay floating in the water with dozens of cuts lining its side. Blood spurted from its floating body out into the blue water, the red mixing quickly in the underwater currents and turning the pool red.

As she watched the warriors pull the body out with stiff headshakes at the healers who'd come racing in to aid, she felt her heart break. It didn't help that at that moment Helen stumbled in with Terris on her heels. As the sun dawned on a new day, her keening wails broke the still, somber air.

Ciardis felt shame well up in her. Shame that another human would cause such pain to such a kind soul. Shame that a beautiful griffin had lost its life before its kits had even opened their eyes. A fire began to burn inside her. She'd been invested in finding the Shadow Mage before, but now it amounted to more than that. She seen the deaths of many who'd not deserved to leave this life; it had saddened her. But this felt like a knife to the heart, and she couldn't stand it anymore. Pulling apart from the crowd of people surrounding the heartbroken healer, Ciardis walked off determined to do something. What, she didn't know.

She ignored the man following behind her and shrugged on a new pair of clothes. Sheathing her knives and grabbing her glaive, she prepared to move out. If this shadow man thought she'd lose one more friend, one more ally, then he had another thing coming. Stepping out of her guesthouse, she almost rammed Meres Kinsight through with her glaive.

She glared at him for getting in her way and proceeded on. Calling out from behind her he said, "The regiment is in the other direction, Ciardis Weathervane."

"What can they do? They don't know these woods and they aren't mages."

"No," he said in reply. "But the mages with them know where to search."

Halting with her back stiff, Ciardis turned around slowly as she fought not to scream.

"They're here? Now?"

"They're here. Now."

"Vana and Alexandra are already mounted up to ride out to meet them," he said calmly. "We're waiting on you and Terris."

Ciardis eyed him proudly and ignored the slight reprimand in his tone.

"She's probably with the kits," she admitted quietly.

"After you," he said, extending a polite hand toward the healer's center.

She turned, her glaive held in one hand and sheathed knife at her waist. She left the weapons outside the hall, not sure what kind of mood the kits were in. They were blind, but even as young as they were they could sense danger and the presence of weapons. Which made it just that much more confusing as to how the Shadow Mage had managed to sneak up on their mother.

What was she doing out before dawn anyway?

"Feeding her kits," Terris said softly, as if Ciardis had asked the question aloud. "They've started on real meat and needed live prey."

Ciardis grimaced.

Meres said quietly as he knelt by Terris on the ground and gently took one of the litter in his hands. "We'll not let her die in vain. Her kits will prosper. But only after we find that mage."

Terris turned to him. She didn't speak. The sadness in her eyes and in her stance was overwhelming. It was if a ghost of her former self had inhabited her body.

Meres looked at her and back at Ciardis. Terris would be of no use to them, at least not today.

"Let her rest," said Ciardis softly.

"She will not rest here," he said.

"I'm needed here," Terris pointed out.

A loud knock suddenly echoed from the door. They turned to see Barren carrying a bow and a set of arrows at his back with his hands holding the handles of two heavy brown bags.

"I brought the kits some food," he said.

Ciardis eyed the growing bloodstain at the base of the bag and noted he must have hunted all morning for whatever was in those two big bags.

"Very well. Terris will stay here and watch over the kits," said Meres, standing up and putting the kit back in the nest with the rest of the litter.

As he walked out the door and passed Barren, he whispered, "Keep an eye on her. She's not to leave your sight, you hear?"

The boy nodded and Ciardis followed Meres outside to the saddled and waiting horses.

*****

As they rushed in a canter to meet the armed regiment at the edge of the Ameles Forest, Ciardis began to think over what she knew and what she'd seen.

The man had control over shadows—his own and others. He could also inflict pain at a touch and transport his victims from place to place unseen.

He was a mage. That much was clear.

He had said he had a brother—a brother he resented, but no other information had been forthcoming.

Meres hand reached over to slow her horse down before they jumped a short ridge.

"Ciardis," he said, tightening his grip on her reins. "I need you to focus."

"I am focusing," she muttered absentmindedly as she flashed back over the memories.

She bit her lip while trying to remember everything. She was so focused on the past that she didn't startle out of her memories until she tasted blood in her mouth.

Swearing at the pain caused Meres to look over. "Your mouth is bleeding." Ciardis couldn't think of the blood right then.

"It's the brother," she said. "His brother is the key. He's trying to impress him—whomever he is."

Meres raised an eyebrow. "Killing a slew of them doesn't seem to ring true with those goals."

Frustration settled in as Ciardis tried to puzzle over the mystery that was the Shadow Mage.

"War," whispered Ciardis. "He said he wanted war."

At that moment Julius came racing up. "Another village has been attacked. This one at least twenty miles east of here."

"Is there ever any good news?" said Meres.

"There's more," said Julius, looking over at Ciardis. "One person was left untouched. He claims he has information and needs to speak to the Weathervane."

Meres and Vana exchanged a look.

"Did he give his name?" asked Ciardis.

"Ciardis, you've not been this far outside the capitol since your hunt," said Vana. "Do you know anyone there?"

"Not that I know of," she replied.

"Julius, can you have him brought here? We'll speak to him," Meres said cautiously.

"Already done," he replied, pointing to the tree line. "I have my men holding him there."

"Have you left any of your warriors behind?" Vana asked.

"Four, to keep an eye on the perimeter," said Julius.

"Good," she said. "We'll alert the emperor's guard and have them send a detachment to secure the village."

She hesitated before turning back to her horse. "Julius, have your men hold back. Here and in the forest."

Julius's gaze turned steely and cold, but he said nothing.

Quietly she explained, "Humans and *kith* have died. Tempers will flare. We don't want any accidents."

Looking eastward over the approaching regiment, he nodded. Julius said, "I understand. Human and *kith* relations were already hanging by a thread. It would only take one spark to ignite a fire of retaliations."

"Exactly," Vana said.

Staring out at the troops lining the perimeter, Ciardis thought grimly, *That was exactly what the Shadow Mage wanted. A war between human and kith. All of these deaths, all of this terror was merely the kindling before a spark could ignite the region.*

CHAPTER THIRTY-TWO

Prince Heir Sebastian rode at the head of the military formation with the head of the Companions' Council, Regiment Commander Gabriel Somner, Commander Somner's brother, Christian, and Stephanie of the Companions' Guild by their side. His horse shifted under him as he commanded him to halt. They waited for the group of riders detaching themselves from a larger force of Panen warriors to lead their way.

When Sebastian saw that Ciardis was at Meres's side a knot of tension released inside of him that he hadn't known was there.

She was safe.

"Thank the gods," he said under his breath.

Christian, upon hearing him, said in an aside, "Can't imagine the gods had anything to do with it. That girl has the damnedest luck."

A brief grin crossed Prince Heir Sebastian's face.

He looked over at Madame Amber. The woman sat ramrod straight in the saddle with an indecipherable look on her face as she shaded her eyes from the bright sun with her hand. He cleared his throat to catch her attention, but he wasn't sure if he wanted it when those cold eyes turned towards him. Sebastian had the strangest feeling that she didn't like him. He was no stranger to animosity in the courts, though, so he let it go. Some people hated him for being born.

"Prince Heir," she acknowledged with a raised eyebrow, prompting him to speak.

"I think there's more here than meets the eye," he said at last.

"There always is."

As Meres, Vana, Alexandra, and Ciardis rode up to greet their party they dismounted to wait. Ignoring protocol, Sebastian ordered his men to set up camp on the perimeter and to give him the same simple tent and fare that all the soldiers would receive. As they built a fire and sat around, he took in the four who'd spent what felt like months in the forest but had only been a little more than a few weeks.

"My Lord Meres Kinsight, it's a pleasure to see you again," Sebastian said.

"And you, my Prince Heir."

"How have you and your group fared?"

"The Panen people have been excellent and welcoming hosts, but I fear the events I described in my letter have only grown worse. We've lost over a hundred *kith* to the attacks from the shadow creature in the past week alone. It has attacked friends, families, and entire villages, and I fear it will not get any better."

"I've dispatched a group of men to secure the village of Borden," said Prince Heir Sebastian.

"Then I suggest you recall them," said Meres with a sigh. "There's no point."

"We received the bodies of thirty-four men, women, and children at the courts weeks ago," said Sebastian. "But we cannot discount the fact that the rest of the population may be in danger or dying as we speak."

"They're dead," said Julius flatly.

"Who's dead?" queried Sebastian.

"The people of Borden. We went over a week ago to check on the population after seeing signs of smoke rising in the area," Julius explained.

"Every home, every workshop was deserted," he continued. "It wasn't until we got to the village square that we noticed. Bodies piled to the sky. All with the same marks—the slashes on all of the bodies."

"We've seen some of the same at court. Were your bodies burned as well?" questioned Maree Amber. "All of our victims were burned in some way but not with a natural fire. It was as if they were electrocuted."

"Some of the victims in Borden suffered the same," said Meres. "But most, we suspect, died of blood loss."

"Near the base of the pyre, Milord, there was blood," said Vana. "While we'll need spells from your mages to confirm that it was your same group of bodies, at this time it might be safe to assume it was."

"So we have a shadowwalking mage who can control the shadows," said Prince Heir Sebastian slowly. "But as far as we know, he can't raise the dead and has a vendetta against the Ameles Forest and the surrounding communities."

"Correct, Sire," said Kinsight, "I would also add that he has picked his targets well. Killing *kith* in the forest and humans on the border."

"He has also seemed to be sending messages," said Vana thoughtfully. "All of the *kith* were killed in the bloodiest way possible. Not a single one had a merciful killing or an immediate death with their throats slashed."

"We can't tell as much from the bodies in Sandrin," said Maree Amber, "but it does appear that those who weren't burned to ashes received fatal slashes to different parts of their bodies."

"He's trying to start a war," Ciardis said softly.

"Most likely he wants to take over this forest," interjected Vana while twirling a knife.

"Which is not necessarily that far removed from starting a war to wipe out its inhabitants," retorted Ciardis.

"It's certainly a thought," said Prince Heir Sebastian. "But what's more important is who he is and what he's capable of."

"Death," said Meres flatly.

Looking over her shoulder, Vana spied the man that Julius had said he would bring.

"Sire," she said, addressing Prince Heir Sebastian, "another village was recently attacked. All of the occupants died except one man. He has said he wants to speak with the Weathervane, but I suggest we all be present."

Prince Heir Sebastian nodded. "Bring him forward."

As the man slowly approached, hobbling on one foot and uncertain in the face of so many soldiers, the Prince Heir signaled for his healer to come forward.

To the man he said, "Please sit. I'll have a healer attend to you."

To his manservant he said, "Bring some food and water for this man."

After he had been healed and taken some food and water, he quickly said, "Thank you, Milord."

When Maree Amber stepped forward to announce whom he stood before, Sebastian held out a halting hand. He didn't want his title to influence what the man had to say.

"Speak, please," said the Prince Heir in an encouraging manner after the man looked at Maree Amber, clearly frightened.

The man licked his lips.

"I am Askave," he said. "I come from the town of Nine Falls, no more than twenty miles away. My people are—*were*—farmers and herdsmen. Two nights ago, as darkness fell, a man approached town. He gave no name and partook in no ale from the town bar."

"He just stood at the counter for an hour," he said shakily, "and then left. But when he left, I followed him to the street."

Nervously he looked around. "I just wanted to know who he was and if he had heard any news from the capitol – pronouncements from the Imperial court, new trading routes, gossip. That kind of thing."

As Alexandra gave an encouraging murmur, he continued, "He stopped in the street all still-like. Didn't say a word. Then he started asking me questions. About who I was, how long I'd lived here, and what it was like for me. I told him the truth." He said the last word with a shrug.

"Which was?"

"I told him I grew up here my whole life, have no family—was orphaned when I was young you see—and live on the outskirts."

"What happened then?" said Meres.

"He smiled, touched my shoulder, and told me I wouldn't be harmed tonight."

He looked up and touched the shoulder where the mage had touched him.

"I got chills right about then," he said. "I went back inside the bar and never saw him again until the moon rose high in the sky."

Shivering, he looked into Sebastian's eyes with fear in his own. "That's when the killing started. Everybody died. There was blood everywhere. I did haven't any friends here, lived on my own, but there wasn't one person in that town I'd have wished that kind of death on."

The healer touched him again – checking his vitals.

Shaking off the shivers, he said, "I'm fine. I just—the memories…those memories will stay with me for the rest of my life."

"And what did the man ask you to tell the Weathervane?" asked Prince Heir Sebastian softly.

"That's it," he replied honestly. "I'm supposed to tell her exactly what I told him."

Looking around at the gathered group, he asked hopefully, "Is she here? Did I tell her?"

"She's here," confirmed Vana before Ciardis could speak.

Catching on to her warning, Meres said to Sebastian, "Perhaps we should now speak in private, Milord."

Nodding, Sebastian told two surrounding soldiers to take the man to the healer's tent and see that he had what he needed.

Turning back to the others, Alexandra asked, "What could the mage possibly gain from a story like that? What's so important about his life that the Weathervane must know?"

They all turned to look at Ciardis to see if she had caught a message that they had not.

"It's my life. My life before I came to court," she replied.

"What does that have to do with anything?" Maree Amber asked forcefully. "You're not that man and you never will be."

Ciardis thought so, too, but she had to wonder.

Just before a minute had passed, the man came hobbling back, "Milord, there's one other thing. I forgot when the shadow man asked me details. I told him that I had found some family on the other side of the forest. Was planning to move before…you know…"

Ciardis missed the hard looks exchanged within the group around her as she flashed back in her memories to the man she'd met in the bookbinder's shop. The man she thought had been her brother.

I had to have been mistaken, she said to herself.

"Milord," ventured Meres, "we either have a shadowwalker or a necromancer on our hands."

"The only Necromancer in existence is one the Imperial family has complete trust in," Sebastian said with steel in his voice.

"And a Shadowwalker has not walked this Earth since the Initiate Wars hundreds of years ago," said Vana.

"Forgive me, Milady," said Alexandra. "But that doesn't mean they aren't real."

"That is true," conceded Maree Amber. "We must prepare for the worst."

As the group dissipated—or, rather, as Maree, Vana, and Meres went off to talk alone—Ciardis decided to go unpack in a tent. They didn't need her here.

"Hold a minute, Ciardis," called Sebastian.

She turned back patiently as she waited for him to catch up with her.

"What else?"

"What else what?"

"I can tell that something else is bothering you," he said, walking forward and standing face to face with her. "Is there something that you haven't told Lord Kinsight?"

"I've told him everything I know."

She sighed. "But Sebastian, this is personal. I don't think this is an outside group. I think the Shadow Mage is the primary organizer."

Sebastian frowned. "And the Duchess of Carne?"

"Had nothing to do-with this," Ciardis said with an irritated flap of her hand. "This goes deeper. The Shadow Mage has some sort of history with the area."

Sebastian nodded. "That would fit with the story told to us by the survivor."

"The question is who is his brother, and why now?"

"I may have found someone who can tell us how, at the very least," Sebastian said. "The Ashlord has travelled with us. He might be able to give us some answers on the source of the Shadowwalker's powers since their magical disclipines are similar."

"Prince Heir Sebastian," said Maree Amber respectfully from behind him, "we need to have further discussions."

Sebastian nodded at her and looked back at Ciardis hesitantly.

"Would you like to join us?"

Ciardis waved him off. "I've had all I can stand this day. I will follow up with you later."

Turning, she left him and Maree Amber behind as they joined the others. As she walked back, she heard some soldiers chatting. "You heard, right? We're only here because Prince Heir Sebastian had an itch for his main squeeze."

His comrade laughed and snorted. "Not even pretty enough to warrant it."

"What?" his friend teased. "Not good enough for you?"

"Not skinny enough."

Why were those soldiers talking so disparagingly about the Prince Heir, and what squeeze?

"Certainly powerful, though."

"I don't need power in a woman."

It was then that Ciardis caught on that they were talking about her. As she strode forward to confront the lewd louts, she ran straight into another soldier. Stepping back with her hand upraised to ward him off, she scowled.

"Forgive my intrusion, Milady, but those are *my* troops," Somner said firmly. "If anyone shall punish them for their mouths, it shall be me."

Proudly, she said, "See that you do."

She watched him turn to the small area where the soldiers stood and watched as he dressed them down in a way that would make the taciturn washerwomen of Vaneis proud. But she couldn't help but be sad—sad that she wasn't included, that she didn't fit in anywhere. That she didn't belong in the courts like Serena and Sebastian, in the forests like Terris and Meres, in streets like Christian and Stephanie, or, obviously, in on numerous secrets like Vana and Maree Amber.

She needed some alone time to think. Angry at herself for even being sad when she had things she could only dream of back in Vaneis, she stomped off alone in the forest.

CHAPTER THIRTY-THREE

Walking into the woods, which wasn't far from where they set up camp, Ciardis was beginning to regret her fit of anger. But she was tired and the people around her were bringing out the absolute worst in her. Christian caught up to her fleeing form with ease as he hopped onto a fallen tree and proceeded to walk up the steep angle parallel to Ciardis's head.

"You know some people would think you wanted to be killed running away all alone like that," he said.

She had to stifle a laugh when she looked up to see him holding out his hands to balance himself on the trunk of the tree.

"Some people would say I just wanted some quiet time alone," she countered in amusement.

He snorted and flipped off the trunk to somersault in the air and land right in front of her. She stopped in astonishment.

"How'd you do that?" she said in awe.

"Practice."

"Well, Mr. I-Can-Do-Somersaults-in-Mid-Air, how'd you like to be known for a talent that you can barely control?"

"I used to be, you know," he said as he walked backwards in front of her.

As she stared at him she had to admire his beautiful face. But the smirk that was plastered on his mouth was definitely a feature she could do without.

"Really?" she said coyly. "I never heard that."

"I'm a healer," he said with a shrug, "You learn as you go. And at least you didn't kill anybody."

As she watched the shadows play across his face, she realized she didn't know him very well at all.

"What do you mean?" she asked. "Who are you really, Christian of the Somersaults?"

He grinned and opened his mouth to reply, but then the snapping of nearby branches and curses in a familiar voice ended his reply. Out of the bushes emerged Stephanie, covered in bog water and stinking.

"What in the seven hells happened to you?" asked Christian.

Ciardis came over to tentatively touch what looked like slime dripping from Stephanie's shoulders. She hastily pulled her finger back when the woman looked at her with a face that said she'd bite her finger off if it came one more inch closer.

"I fell in a swamp looking for the two of you," she snapped.

"Oh," said Ciardis guilty.

"Told ya," said Christian. "People will worry."

Ciardis sighed and pointed west. "There's a clearing about three minutes' walk west of here. There's a brook nearby where you can clean your clothes."

Stephanie gave her look bordering on crazy. Ciardis could physically see the struggle cross Stephanie face on whether she wanted to be clean or take out the dirtiness on Ciardis.

Apparently her desire to be clean overrode the desire to hurt Ciardis for forcing her out into the woods in the first place. And so they began walking, Ciardis in the lead until they heard the sound of a babbling brook. Stephanie didn't even wait until Christian and Ciardis were on the other side of the running water to start discarding her clothes. She took a bar of soap out of knapsack and dumped the tunic and pants in the water.

Before Ciardis disappeared on the other side of the shrubs into the open glade, she noted a curious tattoo on Stephanie's lower back. Before she could investigate further, she was pulled into the clearing by Christian, who chided, "You really should ask to look at a girl's goods first."

Ciardis gave him a droll look and rolled her eyes.

Walking into the center and trying to forget the attack by the Shadow Mage, she asked him, "So what's the tattoo?"

Christian looked up at her in surprise. "How would I know?"

"I thought you were lovers," Ciardis said with a furious blush as she dipped her head.

He laughed. "No, we'd bicker night and day if we were. Kill each other in a week at most."

She looked at him curiously.

"Don't get me wrong," he assured. "We get along fine. In semi-small doses. We're good at watching each other's backs and under orders."

"Orders from whom?"

"Now that you'd have to ask Stephanie."

"Ask me what?" came the question from behind them. Stephanie stood there redressed in a clean tunic and pants. She must have had a spare in her knapsack.

"Whom do you take your orders from?"

"Whom do you think?"

Ciardis fought not to get angry; it didn't really serve any purpose.

With a sigh, she said, "The Shadow Council?"

Stephanie smirked at her and started brushing her wet hair. "But who runs the Shadow Council?"

Deciding that she could play this game Ciardis walked over to Stephanie, "You said you told the council about me and what happened with the Duchess of Carne. So they have to be in the city?"

She said it as a question and was delighted when she saw a surprise of confirmation flash on Stephanie's face.

Ciardis grinned and held up two fingers. "Secondly, they have to be well connected. Enough to have a torturer on their payroll and spies in the courts."

Stephanie didn't say anything, but she stopped brushing her hair.

"And three, they have to be mages," Ciardis ventured as she looked over at Christian, "because the two of you are. If they have runners with this much power, then the head person needs to surpass you."

Christian crossed his arms and smiled. "Very good, little mage. Now who would you guess?"

"Christian," Stephanie hissed.

"No," said her partner as he waved his hand, contemplating the girl in front of him. "You started this. Let her finish."

But they didn't get the chance. The ground began to rumble and they stumbled backwards as it continued to shake. Ciardis, Stephanie, and Christian hurried to get closer together and figure out what was going on. In front of them the earth began to bulge until a large mound had formed. With one last rumble the mound, at least three feet high, cracked, and out of it poured shadows. Individuals and groups, shapes and objects, dozens came forth out of the darkness. In the center of the moving pit of shadows, a large one began to rise. It smoothed into a human shadow and then a line appeared down the front.

Out of the center stepped a man: the Shadow Mage.

And behind out of the shadows came another man—the one she seen one sunny day in Jovelin's bookshop. The man with the golden Weathervane eyes.

"Hello, Sister," he said politely.

If Stephanie and Christian were startled, they didn't show it.

This didn't look good.

"Who are you?" she demanded.

"I'll be doing the talking for now," said the Shadow Mage with an unpleasant smile.

"You see, my friend here is a Weathervane. One of only two in existence," he said congenially. "By the looks on your friends' faces, they have known about it. By the look on yours, my dear, you didn't."

"Is that why you tried to kill me the other day?" Ciardis asked softly. "So your friend would be the only one?"

The Shadow Mage laughed. "Well, no. That was merely a side bonus." The forest around them and even the brook was silent as the world fell away and all Ciardis could look at was the male Weathervane standing in front of her.

How could there be another? And why is he helping this evil man?

The Shadow Mage glanced between the two and said somewhat sympathetically, as if he had read her very thoughts, "Oh, but you see he has no choice. Show her the bracelet."

The Weathervane stood silent and lifted his arm to pull back his sleeve to reveal the bracelet. His arm trembled with the effort, as if he hadn't wanted to but was forced to reveal the cuff on his arm.

It was a wide silver band. Plain in nature, circling his wrist in a perfect sheet of metal. It was molded to his skin and didn't look like it would come off over his wrist. Not easily.

"That bracelet controls his movements and his powers. It has done so for his entire life."

And then he smiled. "And whoever controls the bracelet controls *him*."

Pain and anger crossed the male Weathervane's face, but he didn't argue with any of the facts.

"If there were another Weathervane I would have known," protested Ciardis. "And they'd never be chained, like you're saying."

The Shadow Mage looked at her with something akin to pity, "I believe you believe that. And that is what's so sad, little Weathervane. Do you know who ordered this?"

"Enough," Christian hissed as he stepped forward. "If you want to kill us, kill us then. No need for this torture."

"This will be through when I say it's through," the Shadow Mage said calmly while looking at Ciardis's shaken face.

Christian interrupted again and suddenly there was a shadow creature behind him that forced him to his knees with its blade at his throat. Stephanie moved to help him and shadows quickly sprouted out of the ground, this time in the form of vines. They pulled her feet out from under her and bound her arms behind her back with thick, dark ropes.

At the Shadow Mage's imperceptible nod, the creatures put thick black layers of shadow over both Christian and Stephanie's mouths.

"Now, little Weathervane, where were we?"

"Ah, yes," he continued in giddy excitement. "The shackle on his wrist, pretty though it is, was ordered by your emperor. But don't think your precious prince didn't know about it. Oh, he knows, and it serves him well."

Ciardis wanted to shout and scream and deny it all.

"You're wrong," she said fiercely.

The Shadow Mage motioned for the gag to be removed from Christian's face.

"Ask your friend over there. Am I wrong?"

Tears running down her face, Ciardis looked Christian in the face. Hoping for a denial. But he said not a word. Just stared at the Shadow Mage with hatred.

"Why?" Ciardis said. But she wasn't directing the question at the Shadow Mage. She was looking at Christian, who was bowed on his knees.

Reluctantly, he turned his eyes to her. "Ciardis," he pleaded, "this is neither the time nor the place."

"Why?" she shouted in his face, tears running down her cheeks as she fell to her knees, "Why have you all been lying to me this whole time? Why is he shackled like a dog by the very man I serve?"

Christian closed his eyes in thought and opened them with bitter anger. "Because your mother didn't just run away from court. She killed the empress when she left the court pregnant."

Ciardis stared at him, uncomprehending.

"They found your mother midway to the North," the Shadow Mage said thoughtfully, "A child—a boy child had just been born. They arrested her for crimes committed against the Imperial family and the death of the empress. And they took her son away from her."

"It wasn't meant to happen like this," Christian said forcefully. "They were going to arrest her but somehow she used her power to control the Weapons Initiates around her. They killed their compatriots while under her control and then killed themselves. They'd already had her son dispatched with a rider back to court. He was supposed to be placed in a new home with a new family."

"But," interjected the Shadow Mage gleefully, "she killed them all, then escaped or died—no one's quite sure which—and her son was forced to pay penance for her deeds."

"Shut up!" shouted Christian at the Shadow Mage. "Ciardis, it wasn't like that—"

Someone was lying, Ciardis knew that without a doubt. She had known her mother. It was true she had very few memories of her but she couldn't forget the memories of the woman with laughing eyes who had raised her as a child. Many times it was the only memory that kept her going when she was found in the village alone with no family and then shuttled from home to inn as an orphan that no one wanted.

But none of the people here knew that. None seemed to know that she had known her mother – not even the man who professed to be her brother. So she put those thoughts of the past away away and focused on the pain of the present.

Standing up with hollow eyes, she said numbly, "It sounds like it was."

Looking at the man behind the Shadow Mage, her brother, she took in a trembling breath and said, "How is this fair?"

"It's the law," said the Shadow Mage.

"I wasn't asking you," she said through clenched teeth. "Why didn't they take me, as well?"

This time her brother spoke. "They didn't realize that she was pregnant with more than one child. Before they arrived the maid had carried you out."

Ciardis took a resolute step forward and the Shadow Mage held up a warning finger.

"Ah, ah, ah, Weathervane," he said warningly.

"What am I going to do?" she said. "I'm not increasing anyone else's powers and I can't do anything alone."

The Shadow Mage watched her curiously. "They haven't taught you much, have they? I guess it's best to keep you ignorant and dependent."

Ciardis was heartily getting tired of everyone disparaging her lessons. Sighing, she said while looking into her brother's eyes, "Take me instead."

"No," was the simultaneous shout from her brother and Christian.

"No," echoed the Shadow Mage with a cruel smile.

"Why?" Ciardis said desperately, spreading her hands, "Female Weathervanes are always, *always*, more powerful than males ones. I know that."

"While that is true," the Shadow Mage said, "you are untrained and untested. More power doesn't mean equal finesse."

"Please," she said, begging.

"No," the Shadow Mage said. "In fact, my job here is done."

As he stepped back into the darkness of the shadows, her brother by his side, she screamed, "Wait! Don't go."

Laughter echoed back at her through the darkness of the shadows. "Ah, little mage. We shall see each other soon."

With that, he disappeared and the shadow creatures dissipated.

Ciardis fell to the ground sobbing.

After a few minutes, Christian approached her. When he dared to put a comforting hand on her shoulder, she lashed out. Pushing to her feet with a strength borne of fury, she began pummeling him with her fists. Hitting him where she could and screaming in anger. He dodged her blows with the ease of years of practice and tried to keep her from hurting herself.

She didn't calm down. She wouldn't calm down. Not until Stephanie finally came forward and tackled her with Christian. As they held her down, she screamed even harder.

"You bastards! I thought you were my friends. Let. Me. Go!"

"No," said Christian. "Not until you calm down." He started to pour his healing power into her to soothe her high-strung emotions, but retracted as soon as he felt her magic swell.

Christian and Stephanie released her quickly and scrambled back.

"Enough," snapped Stephanie. "You may be angry, but you don't want to kill us. Stop raising your power levels and snap out of it!"

Ciardis looked at her from where she crouched on the ground. Sniveling and angry with the world.

"Did you know?" she asked. "Did everyone know?"

Stephanie raised her chin and admitted, "Most of court knew."

Ciardis closed her eyes and choked back a sob. "And they just let me think I had no family?"

"It was an Imperial decree. No one was to talk about the other Weathervane child. Besides, many at court didn't even believe you were a Weathervane," Stephanie said carefully.

Ciardis stood up and turned away.

"Where are you going?" asked Christian.

"Back to camp."

CHAPTER THIRTY-FOUR

She walked calmly into camp, not shouting, not venting, and not screaming. Quietly and with a purpose. But without fail, every single soldier who crossed her path backed away quickly upon seeing her face.

Ciardis headed straight for Sebastian. She had a hunch where he'd be. The Prince Heir was seated on the ground with the same group of individuals she'd left him with earlier. His back was to her so he didn't see her approach. But Meres did. When Meres saw her face he cleared his throat, stood, and stepped forward. Casually he moved through the group, putting his body in front of the Prince Heir's.

When Sebastian stood up to see who had caused the disturbance, he looked at Ciardis quizzically with dark green eyes.

"Ciardis," Meres spoke, his voice quiet. "What's the matter?"

Ciardis looked at him with coldly calculating eyes. For once seeing the world and the people around her for what they were—self-serving and conniving individuals.

Ciardis lifted her hand and offered it, palm up.

"What do you see, Lord Meres?" she said.

He was silent for a moment. "An empty hand."

She nodded. "I thought it was full until a few minutes ago. I thought I had a place to call home and friends to grasp."

"Ciardis," Prince Heir Sebastian said carefully. "You're acting quite strange."

She wanted to believe that this innocent boy becoming a man couldn't have known. That he hadn't deceived her, but she wasn't a fool. Sebastian was the Prince Heir first, a friend second.

"I guess I am," she admitted. "Wouldn't you be if you found out you had a brother that everyone else knew about?"

The entire group of people blanched, and it wasn't because she had practically shouted the words at the end. It was because they knew what she had said was true. She could see it in their faces.

She wished she could say it didn't hurt the most that Sebastian had clearly known, but she couldn't.

Holding out his hand, Sebastian pleaded, "Let's discuss this somewhere more private."

"Why?" snapped Ciardis. "So you can lie some more?"

"I don't think that's a very good idea," said Lady Vana.

"Ciardis, it wasn't like that," Sebastian said. "The Imperial decree was a direct order; no one was to mention even the possibility of another Weathervane to anyone else. For secrecy's sake."

"So what?" said Ciardis slowly. "If he wasn't spoken of, he didn't exist?"

As Meres began to speak, she held up a hand. "Where has my brother been for the last eighteen years? If he wasn't with the family that was assigned to adopt him, where was he?"

"On the northern border," said Sebastian slowly. "At first he was fostered with an old knight family there, and since his powers came in he's been working in the service of the emperor."

"With that control bracelet on his arm the whole time?"

She continued issuing rapid-fire questions. This time to see if the man she had seen in the bookshop in Sandrin was the same person. "Does he have free will? Can he go as he pleases?"

"The bracelet monitors him as a tracking device would," said Lady Vana. "If the minder allows him the freedom, he can go as he wills."

Ciardis nodded. "And who is his minder?"

"That doesn't matter," interjected an advisor to Sebastian. "What we want to know is where you found this information."

"Where I found it?" echoed Ciardis softly, fury overtaking her every limb.

"From my brother," she snarled. "He told me."

"In a dream?" asked Lords Meres quickly.

Ciardis looked at him as if he'd gone nuts. "He's here and he's with the Shadow Mage."

Lady Vana swore and the regiment commander wasted no time in ordering a unit to form up in search of the wayward Weathervane.

Ciardis laughed with bitterness in her tone. "I take it that surprises all of you?"

Prince Sebastian reached out a cautious hand to take hers. She moved out of his reach in seconds, distaste on her face.

"Were you planning on putting me 'in service to the emperor?'"

"No, of course not," were the denials shouted at her from all sides.

But she knew—she knew in her heart that it had been a consideration. But was it still? As she struggled to digest all that she had learned, Ciardis felt the weight of pain enter her heart, that all of her friends had kept something so important from her.

Sighing, Meres said, "Ciardis, it is unfortunate that you found out in this manner, but it was ongoing discussion whether or not you were to be made aware of a living sibling."

"Since you only manifested so recently – within months in fact," ventured Lady Vana, "Lady Serena and I deemed it best, in initial discussions with Damias, to wait until your powers were stable enough for you to meet him."

"Stable enough?" demanded Ciardis.

"Weathervanes can feed off each other in unsettling ways," said Meres Kinsight.

"How did he get here?" questioned Vana.

Ciardis shrugged and said flatly, "I don't know, but I do know that the Shadow Mage controls my brother."

"Which would explain the huge increase in power beyond the abilities of a normal mage, even one with dark gifts like a Shadowwalker," said Lady Vana.

"We will have to make inquiries in the North," stated Prince Heir Sebastian. "This should never have happened. His minder is stationed on the border and needs him to help with the war."

Ciardis noted that she had began to feel ill over the past few minutes. Like her stomach was upset and she wanted to throw up. Maybe it was something she had eaten?

Sharp-eyed, Alexandra asked her, "Is something wrong, Ciardis?"

"No, nothing," she murmured, not wanting to be distracted from the topic at hand.

"If you're unwell you need to tell us," said Maree Amber.

"I did tell you—" protested Ciardis hotly.

"Enough with these secrets," snapped Meres. "The girl should know. Forewarned is forearmed."

Turning to Ciardis, he said, "We mentioned that Weathervanes affect each other in different ways. One of those effects is inducing mild illness—like a stomach ailment—when one Weathervane feels the other conducting magic. If you feel ill it could be because your brother is nearby and is acting as an enhancer or conduit for someone else's power."

Alarm flashed across Alexandra's face.

Ciardis nodded, not wanting to betray the brother she never knew, but knowing that anything he did was being controlled by an outside force. "My stomach is ill."

Maree and Vana cursed and sent out their own magic feelers. They quickly sounded an alarm and soldiers started converging. But whatever they felt also felt them, because it triggered a magic trap.

Without warning they were all transported in the shadows. When they could orientate themselves again, Ciardis saw that they were in a sunny field not far away from the village of Borden. She looked to her friends and counted off who was there: Sebastian, Stephanie, Christian, Vana, Meres, ten of the Prince Heir's guard, Alexandra, Maree, and, Ciardis noted with surprise, someone new—a man with pitch black hair and a tall, gangly body.

"Everyone all right?" called Prince Heir Sebastian. Everyone confirmed with various nods and affirmations.

"Where the hell are we?"

"I think I can answer that," a male voice said. As they all turned to view the speaker whose voice had startled them, many pulled out the weapons that they had. But when they turned to the eastern fields where the voice had come from, there was no one there. As they began to spread out in a tense circle to locate the person, Vana Cloudbreaker held up a closed fist, edging forward into the planted stalks of the gently blowing fields of wheat. She was looking around with both of her sights—magical and mundane.

Ciardis saw something interesting rise up from Vana when she called upon her mage core; it was like an orb with a thunderstorm of purple in it. Misty purple clouds and streaks of purple lightning fought to free themselves from the bubble as it rose in the air. And then it burst, sending the lightning and mist scattered in different directions. When it headed farther east, it struck something curious—a bubble—and like the cling of a sweater after it has been rubbed on polished wood, the purple lightning and mist clung to the new object, spreading like water over its surface.

"Very good," said the voice again as they dropped their complex shield. Its duty completed, Vana's conjured sightstorm of lightning and mist that had clung to the bubble dissipated.

Several individuals stood facing Ciardis's group. None of them looked particularly friendly. Prince Heir Sebastian's guard stepped forward to face the threat.

Ciardis squinted in the bright sun and swore. Was that who she thought it was? What in all the gods' names was the Weather Mage doing here?

The Shadow Mage in the lead smiled a cold smile at Prince Heir Sebastian and the small retinue that stood around him. He had an uncanny resemblance to the strange, stork-like man who stood to their side.

"And who are you?" asked Prince Heir Sebastian with ice in his tone.

"Milord Prince Heir," said the Weather Mage from the man's left with sweat dripping from his brow, "may I present Lord Kastien?"

"Lord Kastien *of*?" said Meres Kinsight in a dangerously soft tone. To strangers he might sound as if he were at just another dinner party, but Ciardis didn't miss the tight grip he had on his dagger and the surge of power she felt coming from him.

"Borden," said the addressed man simply.

At that moment everyone turned to look at the tall, gangly man standing by Alexandra, Meres with more suspicion than all of them.

"What is the meaning of this, Darius?" demanded Prince Heir Sebastian.

"I don't know, Milord," the man called Darius said with more aplomb than Ciardis would thought him capable of. "But I intend to find out."

He strode forward, breaking ranks, ignoring the protests from Vana and Maree. As Ciardis watched him approach the man who could almost be his twin, she looked for her brother among the figures. He wasn't there. Where was he? She didn't want him at the Shadow Mage's side but the alternative meant that he was probably back in the encampment of soldiers.

Why would the Shadow Mage only transport such a select few?

She took in the Weather Mage's form. He looked worse than the day that she and Linda Firelancer had first met him. His form shook where he stood and sweat poured down his face.

Then he turned to look directly at her. Even with the distance between them she could see his eyes. They were black.

"Oh no, oh, for the ever-loving gods, *no*," she said with her voice rising.

Julius turned aside partially, his body still primed for a battle in front of them, and muttered caustically, "What?"

"He's shadow-touched, the Weather Mage is shadow-touched!" she said with a touch of hysteria.

"Are you sure?"

"How can you not see the black depths in his eyes?"

"Brother," said Darius authoritatively, "what are you doing here? Why are you not at watch over the farm in Borden?"

The man in question sneered, "You. I'm here because of you. You never considered me worthy…"

Dread shifted down Ciardis's spine. She'd heard that before.

"You went off to that school of mages and left me to rot in Borden," said the man.

"Timmoris, don't—" said Darius, holding up a placating hand.

"Don't call me that!" shouted Timmoris. "How dare you call me that. Belittling me." Spittle was flying from the incensed man's face and Darius had finally halted, seeing that something was wrong, very wrong with his brother.

"Let's talk about this," Darius said firmly. Waving his hand to encompass the people behind Timmoris, he said, "You've certainly made some powerful friends."

"Them?" said Timmoris with derision.

"The time for talking is over," said Prince Heir Sebastian. "Incapacitate him. Now, Ashlord!"

Ciardis swore, not because she'd just learned that the tall, gangly man was the one and only Ashlord, a necromancer with dark powers, but because dark clouds were gathering on the horizon.

The necromancer paused and turned back to Prince Heir Sebastian with uncharacteristically pleading eyes. "Please, Milord. He's all I have. Let me speak to him. I assure you, he means—"

"Watch out!" shouted Ciardis, pointing frantically at the sky.

Before the necromancer could finish his sentence, a bolt of lightning arced down from the gathering storm. It hit the Ashlord straight on and he slumped to the ground unconscious with grave wounds.

"I guess that's where those burn marks on the bodies came from," said Meres grimly.

Before Vana could lose an arrow into the Weather Mage, Ciardis shouted hoarsely, "Wait, it's not him. It's the Shadow Mage—he's controlling them."

"How?" asked Alexandra. "He's not wearing a control bracelet."

"It's the eyes," Ciardis said. "The shadows are in his eyes just like Barren before Vana released him."

Timmoris sucked his teeth and smiled. "Well, well, such a smart girl."

Then he turned to Prince Heir Sebastian and said, "You are right, Milord. The time for talk is over." Suddenly the gathering clouds became so thick that they blocked out the sun, and the last thing Ciardis heard before a natural darkness descended and the ring of metal against metal began was the maniacal laugh of the Shadow Man.

Prince Heir Sebastian's men had engaged with the Shadow Mage's followers, but with their sight limited to a few feet in front of them, they couldn't extend their defensive perimeter very far.

Maree Amber stepped up with Meres Kinsight to take on a group of the Shadow Mage's followers, including the Weather Mage. They were all shadow-touched and they were all mages by the look of it. They didn't speak; they just fought.

Anxiously, Ciardis looked for her brother. He had to be nearby to enhance the Shadow Mage's powers. But she couldn't see him. Where was he?

Meanwhile Maree Amber grabbed two trees with her mind. She uprooted those, roots and all, and flung them directly at the mages. The trees took out two of the mages. One of the four shadow-touched cohorts lifted his hands and fire flowed from his fingers directly toward them. The Weather Mage called in lightning and they merged their two natural elements to push a deadly mixture of their elemental powers at everyone in their paths.

Maree didn't pause. She threw up a mage shield and kept going.

Behind her, Vana said, "If I can get close enough, I can break their feed to their master."

"How close?" Maree said calmly.

"Touching," Vana said. "And I'll need a minute with each."

"Not going to happen—not now. We don't have enough trained people here to hold off fully-trained mages while you break the holds on their minds."

"Suggestions, then?" Vana called out as the shield went down and they rushed the shadow-touched.

"Knock them out if possible," said Maree Amber with a grunt as she kicked the Fire Mage in the throat swiftly. "Incapacitate them if not."

A different mage had spotted Ciardis and was bearing down on her with the grim intensity of one preparing to kill. She pulled out a knife and glanced around for another weapon. There was nothing in reach, and the glow of the protective barrier from Maree Amber had failed.

Ciardis's opponent called on the plants in the ground to capture her, and suddenly the earth beneath Ciardis's feet was sinking and roots were dragging her hands down.

Scrambling, she pushed up with her hands and feet as much as she could, but her face was already being pulled into the soft soil. *He's going to suffocate me*, she realized. But just as suddenly the plants released her, and she looked up to see Maree Amber's deadly grip on the man's throat.

He was struggling, but she had him at a disadvantage with his face pulled back in her grip and on his knees as he desperately tried to stop her from strangling him. She did stop, but only when he fell unconscious.

Ciardis looked over to thank her while spitting out dirt, but Maree Amber beat her to it.

"Get behind Lady Vana now," she said in disgust. "If you're not going to be useful, at least try not to get in the way."

As Vana dodged opponents, she shouted, "We need a sun mage."

"What do you want to me to do about that?" Ciardis asked as she desperately dodged a sword aimed at her head and came up face to face with the Weather Mage.

Hefting the rock in her hand, she quickly apologized and walloped the Weather Mage on the head. He slumped onto the ground, out cold. The darkened skies immediately opened as clouds disappeared and the sun shone through.

"That'll do!" shouted Lady Vana with a grin.

Ciardis was tempted to say something snarky, and then she saw a long staff weapon discarded by a soldier on the ground. She needed a weapon and that would serve perfectly. Scrambling over with quick feet, she grabbed it off of the ground and turned around to face the person she heard coming up behind her.

Unfortunately it was the Shadow Mage.

He wasted no time having his shadow creatures pin her to the ground and relieve her of her weapon. They began to twist her arms in unnatural directions as she screamed in pain. Suddenly, out of nowhere, Sebastian came from behind him. Wielding a sword, he tried to cut off the Shadow Mage's head. Hearing Sebastian coming up behind him, the Shadow Mage had enough time to duck and knock Sebastian's legs out from under him. The sword swiped the side of his face, but only enough to create a shallow cut through the edge of his nose. A shadow creature turned itself into black vines and wrapped thick ropes around Prince Heir Sebastian's legs, dragging him away.

Lady Vana took his place while Meres Kinsight went after Prince Heir Sebastian.

"What happened?" Ciardis screamed from where she lay pinned on the ground. "What happened to make you like this?"

She looked over at Vana, hoping the unknown mage could come to her rescue, but she was a bit busy battling shadow creatures on all sides.

Looking back at the Shadow Mage, she couldn't help but see a bitter brother, jealous of his sibling and hating what he had become.

All of this. All of the death. All of the misery.

"It has to end," she said.

"Don't worry," he crooned as he reached down to caress her dirty face. "You'll be seeing your maker soon."

"Ciardis," shouted Vana from her battle across the field. "Remember your lessons. What you can stabilize, you can destabilize."

The Shadow Mage turned to Vana with a roar and had a shadow creature lift her up in a dark tunnel of wind and throw her with enough force that she landed with a sickening *crunch* on the other side of the field.

But it was enough. Ciardis knew what she had to do. The Shadow Mage was close enough for her to do what needed to be done.

She reached for Shadow Mage's hand with a pain-filled gasp. Latching on she let loose every drop of power she had in her. She built and built on his power, enhancing beyond his capacity to contain, especially with the male Weathervane's gifts also increasing his.

Satisfied, she pulled and pulled the power to greater heights, unimaginable abilities. And the shadows began to grow, filling the skies with darkness and casting the entire area in black.

When she'd reached the pinnacle and could go no further, she smiled and dropped the power. It swept down with an almighty speed, creating a vortex in its wake. The power was falling at a tremendous speed and pulling its creations with it. It became a vortex of shadows, sucking in all of the power of the Shadow Mage in an ever increasing fury.

Unfortunately the Shadow Mage couldn't absorb all of the shadows at once. They began to push themselves into his mage core, greedy for more power, and when that wasn't enough they penetrated his living body. Ciardis watched in satisfaction as he staggered while shadow after shadow penetrated his back, his neck, his eyes, his hands, his chest, and his head. Each time causing the Shadow Mage to stagger under the impact even more.

"Ciardis, what have you done?" Meres asked with shock written on his face as he scrambled to her side, the Prince Heir limping behind him.

She turned to look at him as she said, "Finished him."

At that moment the Shadow Mage fell to his knees and threw back his head, letting out an almighty scream. For a second the shadows began to emerge from his throat and out of his mouth, and then they couldn't. They were stuck, and the bottleneck only grew with the shadows bulging grotesquely in his throat and cheeks. Until they couldn't expand anymore. He exploded, sending body parts in fragments and shadows screaming everywhere. And everyone within a ten-mile radius was thrown off their feet with the tremendous force of the explosion.

Darkness fell over Ciardis's eyes as she briefly lost consciousness. She lay on her back, watching the skies slowly lighten and the shadows dissipate in the air with a smile on her face.

CHAPTER THIRTY-FIVE

Moments later Ciardis heard someone walking toward her. For the first time in her life her magic was finished. Zero. She didn't have any of it left to fight with. She staggered to her feet for one last battle. Vana, Meres, and Sebastian had been thrown away from her side. She waited and listened for the person approaching.

Out of the dense ground-fog of thick smoke and mist, the Weather Mage emerged. Blood was dripping down his clothes from a heavy shoulder wound and his arm hung limply at his side. But he had a smile on his face that belied the pain he must have been in.Clothes in tatters, he stopped in front of Ciardis and said with a relief borne of freedom from enslavement, "He's dead. I'm free."

Tears were dripping down his face and hers, as well. Smiling in exhaustion at their victory, she felt his joy even in the midst of the destruction and dead bodies they walked around. And then Ciardis saw her—Maree Amber.

The leader of the Companions' Guild and Council was lying at the slope of a small hill. Rushing to her side, Ciardis knelt over her, the woman who Ciardis had thought hated her, but had come at a time when Ciardis had needed her most. Hands trembling, she put her fingers at the woman's throat and felt for a pulse. It was there but weak. A gasping breath issued from Amber's throat and she began coughing. The woman's eyes flew open and she tried to sit up.

"Stop," commanded Ciardis. "You're injured." Turning quickly to the Weather Mage, she shouted, "Go get help."

"Help me sit up," said Maree Amber after another wheezing breath.

Ciardis shook her head. "You look pretty bad." She was eyeing Maree Amber's leg that was distinctly facing the wrong direction; it looked as if it had been twisted inward, and now her kneecap and left foot were facing her other leg. Not to mention the large slab of rock across her chest. Gripping it, Ciardis pushed it off. She couldn't see any ribs sticking out, but that didn't mean there wasn't any internal damage.

Madame Amber coughed again, this time blood trickling out of the side of her mouth. Ciardis pursed her lips and fought not to cry. If help didn't get here soon, the woman was going to die. She might die even if they did get here soon.

Seeing her watery eyes, Madame Amber gave a sharp laugh that ended in a groan of pain.

"Silly girl," she said while gasping for breath, "I told you, you can't cry over every little thing. You have…to…toughen up."

The last words came with distinct pauses, not meant to emphasize but rather because Maree Amber was fighting for every last breath.

Ciardis smiled. Even in severe pain the woman was still chiding her.

Reaching out an unsteady hand, Maree gripped Ciardis's hand in her own. "I was wrong. You *are* insubordinate, headstrong, and silly. And perhaps just the thing the courts need. You must continue to change, girl. Grow strong."

Ciardis nodded, eyes wide.

Another blood-filled cough erupted. "Don't trust the dragon, no matter what she says. And Stephanie and Christian—they can help you. They and all the others on the Shadow Council will help you. You just have to find them."

Ciardis sucked in a surprised breath. "The Shadow Council?"

"You know about them?"

"I *am* them. Or at least I am in Sandrin. There are more—many more. Scattered across the empire."

Before Ciardis could ask anything more, Maree Amber arched her back in an attempt at one final breath and died before Ciardis's eyes.

Silently, Ciardis pushed Maree Amber's eyelids closed as a sign of respect and stood up and looked around. Most people were wandering around and checking on compatriots. Several of the Prince Heir's guard were still alive and had reunited with their charge. He now stood in a sort of moving box of the soldiers, each bristling with weapons.

The threat was over, but they still prepared themselves. She couldn't blame them; that Shadowwalker had a nasty way of turning up in unexpected places. Walking over to the remains of the man who had enslaved her brother and countless others in addition to killing innocent victims, she felt no pity. As she prepared to walk away, she saw something gleaming as it stood upright in dirt. It was a long silver bar with curious inscriptions on it. She pulled it out of the ground. Ciardis barely heard Meres Kinsight shouting at her to put it down before she vanished in the blink of the eye.

Where she had stood, the metal bar clanged to the ground, its sound resonating in the empty field as those left behind looked on in disbelief.

For long moments Ciardis was falling in a void of silence and darkness. And then she felt herself land. The darkness cleared and light and sound filled the void.

Shifting voices echoed in and out of her ears as her eyes tried to adjust to the blinding landscape she'd transported to. As bright sunlight caught her eyes, she threw up her hands in protection and squinted in the harsh sun. The voices grew louder and odd smells penetrated her confused senses. Woodfire and smoke, unwashed bodies and blood.

What was going on?

Her dress was torn to shreds, her hair tangled with roots, her hands were black with dirt, and scratches ran all along her arms. She took tentative steps forward trying to figure out where she was. She was shocked when her bare feet stumbled onto the cold ground hardened by frost, and her breath froze in the air.

Her hair whipped loose around her as she looked around with unease.

Surrounding her in a semi-circle were armed men. They stared at her with shock etched on their faces. Their hands stayed ready at their waists, gripping the pommels of swords. The six men were silently eyeing her up and down, the disheveled girl who had somehow appeared in their midst.

Ciardis tried to speak but her voice broke.

Speaking in a hoarse croak she said, "Where? Where am I?"

The men surrounding her suddenly parted ranks and out of their midst General Banaren appeared. By his side strode Leonidas, General of the Imperial Army.

"Well, by the gods," General Banaren said, astonished. "Ciardis Weathervane, what are you doing here?"

Staring at him with bleary eyes, she asked, "Where is here?"

Grimacing, he whipped off his heavy overcloak and loudly called for fresh water to be brought.

"The frontlines of the war in the North."

Made in the USA
Lexington, KY
22 November 2016